THE LAST RED
SUNSET

ALSO BY JOSE LUIS ALMAZAN

UN GRITO A LA NOSTALGIA
A compilation of one hundred poems in Spanish

THE LAST RED SUNSET

A DRAMA NOVEL BASED ON MYSTERY, ACTION, AND ADVENTURE

JOSE LUIS ALMAZAN

LIBRARY OF CONGRESS CONTROL NUMBER: 2020904318
ISBN: HARDCOVER   978-1-7960-9189-2
             SOFTCOVER   978-1-7960-9190-8
             EBOOK   978-1-7960-9227-1

Book cover image artist/provider Yuriy Kulik/Shutterstock.com

Print information available on the last page.

Rev. date: 03/25/2020

To order additional copies of this book, contact:
Xlibris
1-888-795-4274
www.Xlibris.com
Orders@Xlibris.com
809109

With love.

To Olivo, my dad, somewhere there—somewhere there,
a place that I don't know, a place that I've never been yet.
To Claudia, my mom, and to my sister, brothers, and children—
to all of them somewhere . . . somewhere here.

CONTENTS

INTRODUCTION

This book is a compilation of events that followed in one way or another the fragile steps of some of my ancestors on my father's side, their friends as well as their enemies, their traditions, their own way to survive in the wild, and part of my early years in my grandpa's farm. To this day, my family's story has been unknown, even for my own relatives, who have hardly questioned themselves about their origin. To this day, no one has spoken about it. But I don't blame them; they probably ignore our family's beginnings. My mission in this book is to remember the past, at least a little portion of my dad's family, the Almazán clan, and to recall the experiences that have surrounded my childhood in the farm and my teen years in México City, sharing it with others and making it humbly unforgettable.

CHAPTER ONE

THE MYSTERY IN
THE LAGOON

Instead of my name, I would start this page with my nickname—Hummingbird. My grandma used to call me Hummingbird since I was a little boy. There was a point in my childhood where my nickname made me feel like Speedy Gonzalez, so hyper, until one good day I decided to find out more about it with the typical questions of a little kid. And the answer came quickly; a pleasant atmosphere turned into an enjoyable conversation between my grandma and me.

"Why did you choose this nickname, Grandma?" I asked her with some curiosity. Then I looked straight into her eyes while I charmingly winked with my left eye and smiled.

"Because you are so cute," she rapidly replied while she was smiling from side to side, showing a happy face, and softly scratching the top of my nose with her cold forefinger.

"Grandma!" I simply exclaimed with a spoiled voice and a half-suspicious eye. Then I laughed at the top of my lungs, and we both looked at each other, laughing unstoppably for a few minutes. That happy moment took place at the right side of her patio, and it was part of an unforgettable day. But it was long ago.

Anyways, since that day, I felt like a real hummingbird or like an unknown hero, sometimes both, but definitely something else. I could merely say it. But *cute*? I simply did not know it.

Most importantly, I was there surrounded with countless happy moments and bizarre events that filled my mind little by little and forever, thanks to everyone around me. Yep, I was there, precisely on time, on that strange spot without any plan, even if I still didn't know whether that moment was the wrong one or my lucky hour. One thing was for sure—every single one of those events would change my life forever. I became what I am today right over there, and everything started far away from here. Long, long time ago, when my father was a child in his homeland, that was the moment when everything started for me, for my family, the beginning for us, the moment when, undoubtedly, my fate was born—an immigrant in these lands.

Of course, I believed there were other ways to start this story. But this was the way I remembered it. This was the way I saw it. This was the way I felt it. And this was the way I'd say it.

In this world, everyone has a chance to live with real-life experiences of any type or nature, including strange ways to survive without water or food in the middle of nowhere. Well, you name it. But extraterrestrial abductions or ghostly apparitions of dead people? That sounds crazy and spooky, simply out of the ordinary, don't you think?

We all do; we all have something to tell, no doubt about it. But at the same time, there is a point where you have to be lucky, or you have to be condemned, sentenced to a certain type of punishment, waiting for an unknown relief and understanding to pop out into clear sight. Well, I could say that you have to be, let's say for now, someone special . . . something else.

That day, everything seemed to be normal around the little lagoon that was formed in the wider part of the narrow stream. The blue sky was clear, like one of those paintings from Renaissance times. The sun was totally bright, lighting up all over the place, making even more beautiful the green vegetation and the glittering water that was quietly running in the shallow stream. A few tropical trees grew like giants along the spiral-shaped seasonal stream. And a good number of large leafy bushes surrounded almost half the lagoon, attracting some species of colorful birds, small mammals, and hungry bugs.

Despite all the beauty of the unique passageway, something wasn't normal that day over the water of such a beautiful pond. It was difficult to describe it, but it was something that ran right into me through all these years. For a very long time, I'd been thinking that it might be just a hallucination, a tricky mind game. But, and Fernando?

Fernando was my cousin. He was twelve years old, just five years older than me. He was walking with me through the forest, on our way to my house, when suddenly we both saw something out of this world. No, it wasn't scary at all, simply unexplainable, unusual. There was no danger there that we could sense or feel. In the forest at night, there was sometimes danger because of the dark but not in daylight.

Strange things were occurring over the water's surface of La Poza Airienta (The Haunting Pond), whose name my family used to identify the peculiar spot in the wider part of the stream. It was the strangest thing I had ever experienced in my whole life. I'd never seen anything like it. And I bet it was the same for Fernando. It was the year 1972. These events occurred in the north side of Guerrero State, México.

My name is José Almazán. I was living with my parents, two younger brothers, and a baby sister. My parents' house was small and located in my grandpa's property in El Barrancon, which was a small farm annexed to the Teloloapan municipality, the mole rojo city.

As I'd previously said, it was a clear blue sky, a sunny day somewhere in the month of July. My father used to grow corn in Grandpa's fields. That particular morning, he was in the middle of his work with Uncle Lupe, Fernando's father. They were just working and making a little profit that allowed them to live with the essentials, the basics as human beings, like most of the old-time farmers located away from the city in my town. The routine was the same or similar every day—working, eating, sleeping, and trying to raise large families full of needs—typical for those living in those farms as well as other rural provinces farther away in the map. Working in the cornfields wasn't an easy task. It was hard, an exhausting life with tons of necessities and suffering. Even if my parents worked from dawn to dusk, our life was not different from the others we had known. Food was never too plentiful in those lands, and some of the farmers found the excellent excuse to take advantage of others.

Back in the cornfield, where my father and my uncle Lupe were waiting for Fernando and me, one of those farmers was itching for some kind of problem. Our neighbor in the cornfield was a troubled man who had the tendency to become angry for any reason and always found more than one excuse to argue with anybody. He used any type of small thing to insult or start an argument with people around him. That day, he was claiming that something damaged his corn crop, and he started screaming and yelling to every one of us. But my father, in particular, was accused of causing the damages to his cornfield. Even if my father didn't have anything to do with those damages, he listened to it and remained calm. I didn't say anything. I thought that our cornfield neighbor was crazy.

At first, we had no idea what was happening or what kind of thing our neighbor was saying. My father listened, and then he lifted his hand and removed the hat out of his head. And he slowly ran his fingers through his thick hair two or three times and placed the old hat back over his head. He cleared his throat more than one time and firmly spoke; his voice had the sound of calmness rather than conflict. He used polite words to calm down the anger of the noisy man, but that didn't work even one bit. Then a verbal fight went on.

"Pull out your gun and come closer right now!" the neighbor screamed from a distance.

"You should carefully choose your words before you speak, Mister," my father said with some sense of grievance.

"Whatever," the angry man replied immediately.

"What have I done to you that I don't know, Mister?" my father asked while trying to understand the neighbor's claim.

"Pull out your gun, I said!" the neighbor shouted, louder this time.

"There is no need," my father said softly. And he appeared surprised by his neighbor's request.

"Pull out your gun, or I will kill you right at this moment!" The neighbor continued screaming from loud to louder.

"I don't know what kind of evil entity possessed you this morning, cabrón. But you're totally wrong. You don't even know what you are asking for," my father said.

"Did you hear me?" the neighbor asked, ignoring my father's words.

"I do not have any type of gun with me, Mister," my father answered in a calm way.

"I know you do have a gun. I know that. So pull out your gun and fight with me," the neighbor insisted and paused for a few seconds as he dried his sweaty face with the lower part of his stained old T-shirt. "I'm going to teach someone a lesson!"

"You should know what this is all about. You should. I don't know anything about your problem, Mister. I don't," my father said, trying to be rational and giving the noisy man an unpleasant thin smile.

"Don't laugh at me. I'm not a joke. Do you understand?" the angry neighbor said, questioning my father's thin smile.

"I don't give a peanut. So please don't be stupid and ridiculous. You can stay here and blame people, but keep me out of your mouth. What makes you to think it's me?" my father said with some indignation. Then he turned and looked at me. There was irritation on his face, in his eyes. And for the first time in my life, I saw raw anger on my father's face.

It was important to acknowledge that my father had more than one reason to become angry and to save his integrity and honor. But my point of view in that moment was, of course, different from how it is now. "Mister, I believe . . . you are perfectly wrong in what you've said! I think you're totally cuckoo, crazy!" I shouted, almost screaming to the neighbor.

"All right, hero, I've just heard you! But I'm not talking to you, so don't be disrespectful. I'm not talking to you, little kid!" he screamed from considerable distance.

There was a moment of silence. Soon my father realized that his cornfield neighbor was ready to use a shotgun at any moment. *Anything could happen*, he thought.

That man, blind to his own anger, insisted that my father fight with him face-to-face, gun by gun. There was no other option, no other way to solve the problem. The problem had to be solved in an old-fashioned country's way—shooting—according to our angry cornfield neighbor.

There was no shotgun or pistol in my father's waist belt or in his hands. Then suddenly, my father turned around, facing me; this time, his face was almost red. His eyes were deep brown, nearly black. He looked straight into my wide-open eyes. That angry expression on his face was erased immediately and turned into a lovely smile. Despite the previous war of uncultured words with his neighbor, his voice was still fresh, soft, and friendly when he spoke to me. And with a clear and firm voice, he said, "My son, please go home and tell Mom to send my pistol here." He paused, kept his eyes steadily looking into my eyes for a few seconds, winked with his right eye, and smiled. Then he carefully patted my right shoulder a few times.

A moment later, he asked Uncle Lupe if Fernando would be able to go with me. Uncle Lupe smiled, revealing his perfectly well-spaced teeth, and moved his head up and down as a simple sign of his approval. For him, there was nothing to say; he just had to wait.

"What is it?" Fernando approached the spot where I was and asked me in a low voice, almost whispering.

"That's bullshit," I whispered back close to his ear.

"I don't like this," he said, shrugging.

"Neither do I," I said in a low voice, almost whispering.

"Okay, let's go," he said, lifted his right hand, and rubbed his sweaty face more than once. That day was beautiful, just ruined by our moody neighbor.

On the way home, Fernando and I walked uphill to my little house, where my mom was cooking our meal. Three miles was the distance between the cornfield and my parents' house, located in the other side of the main hill, not visible from its location. Fernando and I rushed to get home as soon as possible; we both crossed the narrow stream that was running through the green forest, almost where the stream spread into a circular pond, almost perfect for its natural shape, breaking the walking trail to the left over the shallow edge of the stream.

The narrow rainy-season stream supplied the pond with fresh water every year between May and October.

The narrow and silent stream running half a mile away from my house was as much a part of the farm as the beautiful pond. It was the perfect place where we, as little boys, took off our clothes and bathed three or four times a week over the shallow edge of the small lagoon but always under my mom's supervision, never by ourselves. On the edge of the pond, at the far side, there was an enormous oak tree standing like an open umbrella whose large branches extended almost halfway across the still water of the lagoon.

Fernando waved away the voracious mosquitoes that buzzed around his ears, jumping on the ground, mocking and cursing them as little creatures arrived from hell. "Breakfast, breakfast! Go away, buzzing bugs!" Fernando exclaimed while waving his right hand around his round face, trying to scare them.

"Come on, come on, go, mosquitoes! Please go get him!" I exclaimed, laughing and trying to wake up the natural sense of humor that was under my playful face.

"Coño carajo . . . no me chingues!" Fernando shouted.

Suddenly, he limped and ran through the water, splashing the precious liquid intentionally toward me. Some flying insects followed him, buzzing like playing with him. The water his feet kicked up splashed on my face while he was laughing and running like a wild beast into the water over the edge of the shallow stream. "What?" I simply screamed and laughed. Then I tried to wipe my face with the palm of the hand. And I thought I should run too to splash the water over him. But the crazy bastard got away and stepped out of the water as soon as he understood my intentions.

He laughed sarcastically. "I knew it," he said and asked immediately while laughing, "Do you want another bath?"

"Damn bastard," I cursed him.

"What could be worse than these bloodsucking bugs?" he asked me while roughly brushing his uncombed and greasy hair with his wet hands.

"Snakes, scorpions, black widows," I answered, and I laughed.

"Umm . . . I almost forgot about those friends," he said and rubbed his eyes softly.

"Yeah, right, chicken. Cua, cua," I said, and I smiled in disbelief.

"Wow!" he exclaimed with a certain relief, and ignoring my words, he paused.

"Look over there, by the tall willow," he said in a low voice, pointing his forefinger toward the trunk of the giant tree.

"A rabbit!" I shouted.

"Shh." He looked at the ground near me.

"What are you doing?" I asked him very slowly in a low tone, almost whispering.

"Give me that rounded stone next to your feet," he said while pointing in the direction of some rocks close to my toes.

"Nope!" I exclaimed and ignored his request.

"What?" he asked, making a face of pure repulsion after I scared the fortunate rabbit.

Then we saw La Poza Airienta just with the right edge of our eyes. We passed the spooky place without any trouble; everything seemed to be normal that day. We had used to hear strange things about that very particular place, strange things like the place was haunted, the place was evil, the place was possessed. Well, please just imagine the other ninety-nine things that we'd previously heard about the mysterious lagoon.

We both walked faster, heading straight uphill. And worried about the cornfield situation, we finally arrived home. Mom was inside her kitchen, preparing the meal for the day. Meanwhile, my little brothers and sister were playing on the kitchen floor under my mom's eyes. "What are you guys doing over here at this time?" she asked with curiosity. "Everything okay?" She looked at our sweaty faces while trying to understand the unexpected arrival that morning.

And with a few words, Fernando and I explained to Mom my father's request. "Mom . . . Mom, it's the truth," I said and smoothed my hair away from my forehead.

She hesitated for a moment, trying to understand what we were told back there in the cornfield. Then she finally agreed. And taking a hanging bag hidden somewhere inside the house, she ended up unwrapping a shiny 1914 Colt Matcher with a silver handle. First, my mother made sure that no bullets were inside the gun. Then she allowed us to touch it. A few minutes later, after removing every single bullet from the gun's cartridge, she wrapped and placed the pistol into a shopping bag. Then she gave us clear instructions how we should carry the dangerous artifact.

Finally, she split the task. Fernando would carry the pistol and the empty cartridges, and I would take the bullets in small separate bags made of polyester clothing. Carefully, she gave us a little training on how to carry such a weapon and told us not to play with it. Her eyelids fluttered, and her mouth muttered something that might have been a prayer to God or to some source of divine entrustment because she said the word *amen*.

Moments later, Fernando and I both left the house and returned by the same route. Anyways, there wasn't another route to my father's corn plantation.

CHAPTER TWO

A STORY TO TELL

O n our way back to the cornfield, Fernando talked about his new life in the farm and how happy he was living in his new house with Gloria and Jorge, Fernando's elder siblings. "José?" Fernando asked.

"Qué pasa, amigo," I answered sarcastically, changing the tone of my voice into a spooky sound and swirling my hands, trying to scare him. But it didn't work.

"Have you ever used a shotgun?" Fernando asked curiously.

"Of course, my slingshot," I quickly answered his question.

"You dummy, I've told you, s-h-o-t-g-u-n. No matamoscas, you dummy," Fernando replied loudly, a little pissed off, and then he paused for two or three seconds.

"Like the pistol," he added.

"Nope. Are you crazy?" I answered to his unexpected question with some kind of concern.

"Nope? What do you mean nope?" he asked and eyed me defiantly.

"Well, I've heard that shotguns are for evil things, for bad stuff," I answered, full of curiosity, and smiled.

"José, I saw my father killing a rabbit with his shotgun," he said, paused, and snapped his fingers. "Just like that." He shook his head and laughed.

"Wow, how extraordinary, ah!" I exclaimed.

"The rabbit jumped out of the grass, and he killed the animal. One shot was enough, right in the head," Fernando said enthusiastically.

"Wow, a single shot right in the head?" I asked doubtfully.

"Well, you'd be surprised," he said.

"Really?" I wondered, incredulous.

"Look, here is the sign of the holy cross, and I swear on it," Fernando said while he formed the cross, bending forward his forefinger and placing his dirty thumb on top of it.

"I see you are proud to say so," I said.

"Yep. I helped him put it on the kitchen's table to remove the skin," Fernando said proudly.

"Fantastic," I muttered and gave him a thin smile.

That conversation changed my mood in part because I never like shotguns. Also, the day was getting hot and humid, even if it was scarcely before noon. The rays of the sun seemed to glow around us, reflecting our silhouettes on the ground and penetrating the fragile top of the dense vegetation like a sharp blade on butter. Soon the warm touch of the sun embraced the green valley, and the heat was almost unbearable that day. So I cleared my throat and told him that I knew a story about our family. "What I am about to tell you, it's something that I really know about our family's past," I said in a low voice with a little sense of mystery.

"Ha ha! You don't scare me, Hummingbird. But I'm all ears," Fernando said defiantly. Soon my words became the center of his attention and curiosity while we both walked on foot freely through those valleys without any type of concern or restriction.

One day in the summer of 1955, a fourteen-year-old kid was watching his elder brothers Narcizo and Guzman working in their cornfield. That kid was Olivo, my father years later, always a generous human being. In some people's eyes, my father's elder brothers were criminals. Grandpa used to welcome everyone in his home or his farm's properties. Sometimes the newcomers were strangers looking for a short stay or shelter against the weather in the rainy season or sometimes friends with a bad reputation. But Grandpa always lent a sincere hand to all of them.

It was a Saturday afternoon. Grandpa comforted himself with his family in the picnic area located just outside the corral around the large patio but not too far from the patio's entrance. A few members of his family were sitting on wooden benches and some standing around the rusted barbecue grill. A bundle of wildflowers mixed with a few red and pink roses was Grandma's artwork that day. She put fresh water into a large chipped ceramic container for the flowers and placed the floral display on top of the picnic table. A long piece of homemade butter and small chunks of Mexican parmesan cheese lay over a circular plastic tray located next to the white bread that Grandpa had baked earlier in his mud brick oven built on the right side of his patio. Plenty fillets of wild catfish lay flat over large leaves of plantain on the right side of the barbecue grill, as well as a dozen fresh tilapias stuffed with curly parsley, epazote, garlic, onion, and slices of fresh tomatoes into the belly, tied with a thin stainless steel wire to retain the herbs and vegetables stuffing.

The family was about to barbecue the first set of fish fillets when three men emerged out of the blue from the forest. The intruders were approaching the house, riding good blood horses quietly. At first glance, the newcomers were between thirty and thirty-five years old, but they looked older for their appearance. They arrived from beyond the mountains to Grandpa's farm, and all belonged to the village of Pueblo Nuevo.

Grandpa noticed the older of the strangers first. He couldn't be wrong about them judging from their age and particular looks. *Epifanio and his brothers*, he thought. That was right, the outsiders were brothers; their names were very well known in the north side of the state. The three brothers looked strong as they had too much life in front of them. The young life that was rushing out in every breath day by day gave the brothers the tough look of an announced death.

The newcomers simultaneously placed their eyes on Grandpa, who was sitting on his chair next to Grandma, waiting for them to introduce themselves. Even if he had a clear idea who these people were, he waited for them to speak first. Meanwhile, Grandpa's family remained in silence in the same spot; some of them were seated on wooden benches located under the biggest tree in the picnic area. My father, Guzman, and few others were standing next to the barbecue grill with some cooking utensils in their hands.

"You're not doing them any favor. You have your own family to worry about," Grandma said to Grandpa in a low voice, almost whispering, while her eyes scanned the newcomers from toes to head. Even the sleepy Xoloscuintle got up quickly, seemingly quite disgusted with the outsiders' arrival, and started barking crazily.

Grandpa lowered his eyes without any word. Then he lifted his face and turned his attention to the visitors. Suddenly, he screamed out to calm down the noisy dog. "Hey! You relax! Come over here!" he exclaimed and petted the nervous dog.

"That's a beautiful dog, a great specimen. And it's brown, like El Mecco, my dog," the youngest of the outsiders said from a short distance in a low voice to the man who seemed to be the leader.

"Yeah, this dog seems a fine specimen," he answered coldly.

"Good day, everybody," the newcomers said simultaneously after they tightened the horses' reins on top of the barbed-wire corral that surrounded the uneven patio.

"Good day," Grandpa's family responded.

Minutes later, after they dismounted and secured the horses, one by one, they walked toward the picnic spot. They approached Grandpa, who still sat on his chair, observing them quietly. "This is my dog, Xoloscuintle, who is a seven-year-old Labrador mix," Grandpa said gently, running his fingers through the dog's head hair.

"Wow, this dog seems an intelligent animal," the youngest of the brothers said enthusiastically.

"Mr. Odilon, my name is Epifanio Cuevash. These two ugly guys here are the luckiest men in the world. They are my brothers, Francisco and Chon," Epifanio said politely, introducing himself and his two younger brothers with considerable kindness, affection, and good sense of humor shining around him.

"Nice to meet you, sir," Francisco and Chon said to Grandpa almost simultaneously, holding respectfully their straw hats against their chest, and bowed briefly toward him.

"The pleasure is mine," Grandpa said kindly. "This is my family—my wife, sons, and daughters, eleven altogether, some of them living here, some of them out of the farm. My little Mary died long ago at the age of two." Grandma, who was sitting next to Grandpa's chair, noticed that the buttons of Epifanio's shirt were in the wrong holes, making visible from a short distance the pistol under his shirt, well attached to his belt on the right side of his waist.

After the strangers introduced themselves politely to Grandpa and to every one of his family, they began to converse without any suspicion of bothering or bringing tragedy into Grandpa's family. That was how Epifanio and his two brothers, Francisco and Chon, arrived and stayed for a while, almost four weeks, in Grandpa's farm. "Blessings and good wishes from our father," Epifanio said.

"And, Mr. Odilon, thanks for your understanding," Francisco completed the sentence in a generous and humble way, like he really meant it.

"Indeed. I know your father. And it's been twenty years since the last time I've seen him. But he knows where my farm is located . . . or not?" Grandpa paused briefly. "Next time, I'll send him a map so he can find my house, don't you think?" he added as a slight reproach. That had just come up like a cold-water bucket to every one of the brothers.

"What does that mean?" Epifanio quickly asked.

"Well, it's no burden, not at all, to have you guys here in my land. But it seems out of the blue. I've heard many people gossip about your activities, and it worries me. That's what it means, Epifanio," Grandpa said while his dog softly barked and licked his right hand, warming part of his skin.

"Everyone keeps questioning our activities. That's nothing new for us," Chon said, looking at everybody around, and then he smiled and paused. "We can't cover our past with a single blanket or the sun's light with a single hand. Right, Epifanio?" Chon waited for his elder brother's support.

"You are right, we can't cover the sun with the palm of our hand," Epifanio answered. Then he started laughing right away, spreading his good sense of humor to everybody. Epifanio was tall with a large chest, a friendly man with an enthusiastic smile. His physical appearance inspired a lot of confidence at first sight. He had a round face with a flat nose and a thin mustache with dark brown hair. Indeed, he was the leader of a successful gang with various members under his command.

Meanwhile in Grandpa's mind, something warned him about the danger threatening the safety of his own family's future. But he didn't understand the unexpected warning. Indeed, he had made some progress in agriculture than any other farmer around. Grandpa, whose property included a huge barn as well as farming fields, was the best in the region during his time. The stables built over the vast land were always with a considerable number of horses, goats, and cattle.

"See, the small difference between a loyal friend and a loyal criminal friend is almost nothing, Mr. Odilon," Epifanio said and smiled.

"I can't say the same for you. But if you say so, I can't complain either," Grandpa responded.

"I'll always remember this, a hand of a good friend. It's always remarkable and unforgettable. And I really mean it," Epifanio said respectfully.

"Great!" Grandpa exclaimed, laughed, clapped his hands, and immediately accepted them. He welcomed them with open arms.

Grandma simply lifted her face and turned away without a word; her expression with a voluntary gesture of rejection said everything. "Wrong people," she simply muttered to herself.

"No worries, Mr. Odilon. We won't cross the line. You are doing a lot more than what you realize. Thanks for your hospitality," Chon said gratefully.

"Most important is you guys are safe here. Just remember this: Never cross the line because then you will lose trust. And you'll be out of this place immediately. Don't steal. There is nothing honorable about being a thief," Grandpa advised his well-known friend's sons.

"You just said so. And I agree with it," Chon said and slowly clapped his hands.

"When you steal, you harm someone's pocket. When killing, there is no word for it. You'll be in complete debt with the Almighty, a huge and unpayable debt," Grandpa said and slowly moved his head up and down.

"There is nothing to be afraid of, nothing. We have it very clear that, one day, we'll pay for everything at once. I know. It's harder to pay the full amount in one shot than to pay for it little by little. We'll pay for it either way. We'll do it. We'll pay for it one day. We'll certainly pay for it," Francisco said, looking at Grandpa's eyes ironically.

There was a moment of silence after Francisco's words. Then Grandpa opened his arms and, with a sincere gesture, invited his guests to eat. "Well, gentlemen, please serve yourself. Today will be the day that you guys eat at my house. There is plenty of food. Coffee or cinnamon tea?" Grandpa told them.

"Thanks. I sincerely think that we'll feel better with full bellies," Epifanio said, smiling. Then he walked toward the picnic table, picked a glossy plate, and placed a well-cooked fish fillet on it, giving a huge bite to the tender meat.

Francisco took the last fish fillet for himself and passed the last baked potato to Chon, his younger brother. "Órale ese," he said enthusiastically. Soon they all raised some tacos to their watery mouth, eating slowly and chatting.

"Delicious, your cooking is totally delicious," Epifanio said to Grandma.

She stared at him briefly. "I don't know," she said and paused. "Hunger, thirst, and necessity never give someone enough time to select, not even to think which food or drink might be better." Grandma rapidly said it with some flame of dislike for the intruders.

"Wise words," Epifanio said and smiled.

As a tradition in the family, Grandma served them a cup of warm lemon tea, hojitas de limón as she called the citrus drink. Then she walked to her kitchen and showed up with a tray of homemade sweet bread and a large jar of fresh lemonade.

"How's your father?" Grandpa asked and placed his eyes on Francisco.

"The old man is fine. He's still riding horses at his age," Francisco answered instantly.

"I'm glad to hear it. He's been always a horse lover," Grandpa said while pouring cinnamon tea into his clay cup.

"This is a very interesting place to live in," Epifanio said, looking at the forest all around the farm.

"First time that I see blue flowers," Chon said curiously and paused while eating. "Wow, I can't believe it. I didn't even dream about blue flowers."

"It is a beautiful place. The ponds have some fish and the valleys an immense variety of fauna and plants," Grandpa said.

"Wonderful land," Epifanio said.

"These hills are a great source of peace and comfort," Grandpa said.

"I totally see it with my own eyes," Epifanio said.

Just before sunset, the excitement of the family's picnic was over. Washing up the grill and the barbecue utensils and taking away leftovers of grilled food into the kitchen was a task for everybody. And for the rest of the day, the brothers divided themselves between Grandpa and his family, sitting here, sitting there, talking here, talking there, laughing and saying funny jokes, turning the afternoon into a remarkable, good time. The conversation followed its course, and each of them toasted for the great time that afternoon except Grandma, who was straggling and redoubling her effort to push away all her thoughts against the newcomers.

Later in the evening, the three brothers were allowed to sleep in the kitchen floor. It was the only space available inside the house. The farm had large stables for the horses and some cattle. But the cozy house was small.

"I left some stuff for you guys. Everything you need is inside the kitchen. Please help yourself, get comfortable, and rest," Grandpa said to Epifanio and his younger brothers.

"Rest?" Chon asked and paused. "Bad guys never rest, Mr. Odilon." He was full of enthusiasm and crazily laughed.

"Well, you guys rest. I'm going to watch these things closely, and I promise it," Grandpa said, showing good care for them.

"Please, Mr. Odilon," Epifanio said, quietly laughing, as he kindly thanked the man.

"Have a good night, and don't forget your prayers, if you know any," Grandpa happily said, walking away slowly to his room.

"Thanks. I'll include you in my evening's prayer," Epifanio answered kindly in a half-joking mood.

"Please do it!" Grandpa exclaimed softly and briefly paused. "I'll appreciate it."

Epifanio and his two brothers were ready to sleep on the kitchen floor shortly after they got into the house. They spread on the kitchen floor a rug made of palm, which they called petate, and one of the three blankets, along with some pillows, that Grandpa had placed on top of a chair. "Time to sleep. It's time for a good nap, champs!" Epifanio exclaimed in a relaxing mood to his brothers.

"I won't argue with you," Francisco said, yawning. "I'm totally wrecked after riding these hills." He was half-sleeping and yawning.

"I guess we're all set. Please don't fart, especially you, Chon," Epifanio said and laughed.

"As Your Grace wishes, big brother," Chon said slowly.

"I'll sleep like a rock tonight. Please don't wake me up with your farts, Chon," Epifanio said, and then they both laughed.

"Please be quiet," Francisco demanded with a soft voice. His words dissolved in the air into another yawn as he hadn't enough energy to talk; he yawned again. Later that night, wrapped in a couple of thick and soft blankets, the infamous brothers fell asleep.

The following morning, as soon as they woke up, Epifanio set the fire in the kitchen's fogón and placed a pot of water to boil with ground coffee; minutes later, they joined Grandpa outside on the porch. "Good morning!" the three brothers exclaimed almost simultaneously.

"Mind if we join you?" Epifanio asked respectfully.

"No, not at all. I don't sleep too much these days," Grandpa replied and paused. "But I woke up late this morning." He smiled. Grandpa was wearing a fur costume called gabán. He shook his guests' hands and gestured for them to sit down. They all had a cup of coffee, and Epifanio offered his to Grandpa, which he refused with a simple no.

"How did you guys sleep?" Grandpa asked politely.

"Well, I sincerely don't remember the last time I slept so much," Epifanio answered and smiled.

"That's fantastic. These last thirty-seven years have been the healthiest years of my life," Grandpa said, expressing his enthusiasm for his good sleeping.

"Not too bad for a farmer," Epifanio said, throwing back the weight of his body on the chair.

"I'm a farmer, a farm's man, and this is where you're going to find me dead," Grandpa told Epifanio and smiled.

Indeed, Grandpa was a man of natural talent for the wild. He was good at whatever he did around the farm. The rainy season was his favorite time of the year. *When the paradise is green and the grace of the sunset turns red in the sky*, he once said.

"What can you tell me back in the 1920s?" Epifanio asked.

"The 1920s, hmm," Grandpa replied and paused, trying to adjust his mind into the past. "Like I said, it was something else, something merely different. I was twenty when I got married. I left the house, my father's house. Immediately after, I bought these lands. My mother died when I was a kid. So I grew up under my father's care. Years later, I met my wife and came here. Since then, we've been living in this place. My sons and daughters were born here. This is the only home they all know," Grandpa said slowly. Then he softly coughed two or three times and held his hand close to his mouth.

"That's amazing!" Epifanio exclaimed and paused while looking at the rich green grass carpeting the vast land over those valleys. "And everything through hard work, ah?"

"Yes, sir. Big part of this land has been saved as feed grass for my cattle and horses," Grandpa said with a certain air of delight while stretching his right arm, pointing with his forefinger at the grassy green valley in front of them.

"That's a phenomenal idea. See, as I've said, you're a genuine farmer," Epifanio told him courteously.

"Thanks. I like the smell of dirt and vegetation when the rain wets the ground. It's the natural scent and beauty of Mother Nature," Grandpa said and softly rubbed his face.

"You got to have some good blood in you, Mr. Odilon," Chon suddenly interrupted, talking slowly as if he was sleepy or tired.

"That . . . probably," Grandpa said and paused, shaking his head slowly up and down while softly biting his lower lip. "And here we are as good as anybody else. Within natural terms, we live simply well."

"That's awesome!" Chon exclaimed.

"First time we came here—I mean, the first year, we used to eat potatoes and carrots mostly," Grandpa said.

"What about sickness? I mean, bad times?" Chon asked curiously.

"Ah!" Grandpa exclaimed, interrupting Chon's question.

"Good morning, everyone," Grandma suddenly said while coming out of the kitchen, bringing a tray with four or five clay cups filled with some aromatic, sweetened, thick liquid.

"Good morning," the outsiders replied courteously and almost simultaneously.

"Everybody got up early, ah," Grandma said and passed a cup of hot chocolate to everyone.

"Chocolate!" Chon exclaimed and paused. "It's been a long time since I tasted hot chocolate."

"Thank you, darling," Grandpa said to Grandma.

"Sweet bread is coming, pan dulce," she said while walking toward the kitchen.

"Thank you so much. Thank you so much," Epifanio and his two brothers said to Grandma gently.

"Sorry, Chon, you asked about sick days," Grandpa said, paused, and tasted his hot chocolate. "As I said, health is important. No one is exempt from illness. We all have our bad days. But we all learned how to deal with it somewhere here. And with the Almighty's help, we have everything we need."

"See, as my brother just said, Mr. Odilon, there is good blood in you," Epifanio said and smiled.

"We do not sicken here, as people do in the cities, with contagious and incurable diseases. Here in the woods, we live to grow very old, poor but old, or we die from something else," Grandpa said.

The breakfast was tasty and splendid, and the conversation revolved entirely around the topic of the farming land and health issues. The first morning and the following days for Epifanio and his brothers were the same. Every morning had a similar routine in the house. Everybody got up early, and Grandpa gave them the usual greeting: "God bless you all." And a little chat with the three brothers was useful. From time to time, Grandpa's sons joined in the morning talking as well. The breakfast was a large meal, always served in the regular dining table. The atole was made of ground corn, ripe pumpkins, amaranto seeds, or roasted pinto beans mixed with milk and cinnamon sticks.

In truth, Epifanio and his two brothers were not killers. They gained their well-known title of criminals because they had stolen cattle mainly in the south region of Guerrero State, Mexico. Their illegal activities reached the ears of the authorities since 1953. That was when they became outlaws running away from justice and hiding themselves from place to place, adding to their shoulders an increasing list of enemies on top of the local police and soldiers from the southern state's government. The result of their robbing activities affected the brothers immediately. From that moment, their life was hanging by a thread, and they knew it clearly. There was a point where they were trying to hide themselves in different places to avoid getting killed. And one of those places was Grandpa's farm.

For the three brothers, the idea of facing the law and paying for their crimes was far away from their minds. It was unusual for bandits to do it that way; to pay in prison for their wrong acts was a scary thing. And for them, confronting the law was out of the question, out of their mind.

The community's law enforcement authorities organized a formal agreement between local civilians and nonlocal individuals, including a large group of victims, and a federal soldiers' squad to stop the three infamous brothers and catch them dead or alive. The semi-organized group put a tempting cash prize for each of their heads; $20,000 was the reward for each of them. Undoubtedly, Epifanio and his two younger brothers were at the very top of their enemies' list. Among the brothers' enemies, the Patiño clan was the one closest to them. The family ties with some of Epifanio's friends made the Patiños the most dangerous rivals for them.

Living in Grandpa's ranch, there was not much time for them to think about wrong stuff. There were lots of work to be done. They had worked every day from sun up to sundown, three weeks in a row, on the cornfield without any sign of trouble. There was not any problem, no problema, zero complaint.

For a while, Grandpa thought that the brothers would change for the better, that they probably were looking for an opportunity in his remote farm. He guessed that the brothers must have been fighting among surrendering, remaining free, and running away from the law. He even encouraged them to stop and to start taking responsibility for their wrongdoings. But all those thoughts were only in vain, just thoughts, just an illusion.

Indeed, according to his own belief, Grandpa was a man of certain knowledge, a peaceful man with a vivid sense of humor and abundant respect for the life of others, a man of integrity who, in the silence of the tropical nights in his remote ranch, had conversed with Grandma and his sons about the principles of being good and helpful to others. As he wisely said, intelligently or not, he chose to live in the farm. He owned something—a land with some mountains, green valleys, and unexplored ravines with small streams of water flowing silently through the dense forest, everything full of life. But most importantly, his family was fine with it.

One day, late after work, just before sunset, Grandpa and Grandma walked and sat outside on the open porch. Epifanio was sitting there with his brothers. "This place is amazing," Epifanio said.

"This is the landscape that always surrounds my house through the whole year with a shallow stream passing through the left side of my farm. This is what I see in my mind . . . wherever I go," Grandpa said with great delight.

"Fantastic," Epifanio said.

"This is the kind of life I had always dreamed of," Grandpa said, turning back his attention to Grandma, and gave her a fresh smile.

"Like the old days, pure and simple," Epifanio said.

"I've heard about the city, about Mexico City," Grandpa said to Epifanio.

"Wow, that's a large city. I've been twice in Mexico City. Many people live in nice apartments. Some of them have good jobs in restaurants or in bars. Some owned profitable businesses, like grocery stores, transportation, fast food on the street—you name it," Epifanio said.

"But living in the city, it would probably bore me," Grandpa said and paused briefly. "Perhaps I love livestock—you know, some horses, cows, farm stuff—around me." He held a glass of drinking water with his right hand, sitting next to Grandma.

"Maybe one day I'll buy a house in the city," Epifanio said, giving a thin smile to Grandpa and Grandma.

"No, not the city. Definitely, the city is not the place for me. I could probably get lost in a matter of minutes, ending in the other side of the world," Grandpa said, paused, and looked at Epifanio a couple of times. Then he smoothed his gray mustache and beard as he continued expressing his point of view about the city. "Perhaps in the city, owning a property is difficult and sometimes a dazzled illusion. You might think you own it, but you don't. What's the real amount to be paid from your pocket? Two or three times the real value of the property. As you can see, the appearance of profit is a shone unreality," Grandpa said, expressing his own very peculiar opinion.

"Hmm, it makes sense," Epifanio said, thinking and shaking his head slowly up and down, giving the honors to Grandpa to continue with his perspective.

"Then your property is finally paid. Awesome, you did it. But your debt is not over yet," he said and paused to drink some water out of his glass. "You have to keep paying money over the property for the rest of your life, even if you are retired from work or not. There is no exception to it. You're still paying it." He paused again while taking a deep breath and exhaled. "Here in the farm, the opportunities are few. You don't have much, especially when it comes to cash. You stimulate your living with some other strategies and using your own imagination, which means always a lot more freedom from acquired responsibilities."

"I've never thought about it," Epifanio said, paused, moistened his lips, swallowed his saliva, and softening his words repeated in a low voice, "I've never thought about it."

"I could visit the big city, but leaving the wild for the city? Never, my friend. Here in the ranch, I don't have unnecessary bills to pay. I don't ask permission or pay for any type of permit to cut a tree or to dig a hole on the ground into my own property. Here, you can have all goods, except ice cream," Grandpa said, sharing his point of view about the city and the farm.

"Generally speaking, I think it is totally effective your point of view. Yes, sir," Epifanio told him, considering Grandpa's words.

"My farm is a land of few opportunities but far away from imposed rules. It provides me enough to live and to achieve part of the remaining goals in peace," Grandpa said with natural enlightenment of meaning for his ranch.

Since young age, Grandpa always had the tendency to develop his own independent life as best as he could, always responsible to shape his future and prosperity with his own hands based on his hard work, personal interest, and taste. Besides rising cattle, pigs, and horses, corn was the natural crop year after year, spreading over the valleys like rain, favoring him as a good farmer. Corn, pumpkins, and beans ruled the green valleys from side to side from June to mid-October.

"A small paradise in the middle of nowhere," that was how he defined his farm. His ranch was his baby, his everything; he was living and dreaming on the top of the mountain with some kind of prestige and uninterrupted peace in his little world. Even if he was just a regular humble farmer, not much for too many people, for him, that was the maximum, simply the best.

Epifanio and his two brothers seemed to have great respect for Grandpa. They listened in silence when Grandpa was talking to them for their own good.

20

But for the three brothers, to work in the cornfield wasn't what they'd liked to do for a living. And helping my uncles Narcizo and Guzman wasn't what they'd really enjoyed.

The outlaws certainly knew it very clear. There was a big reward, a nice prize, for their skin, for their head, to anyone able to provide information to stop them or to kill them in cold blood, which was highly recommended for most of their enemies. But they always trusted and never doubted Grandpa's family. They felt safe in Grandpa's farm. For its location in the forest, no one could dare trespass its boundaries or walk on foot the old trail in the middle of the woods. *No one*, they thought.

My father was barely ten years old when he started placing foot on those trails, walking on it on the way to the cornfield with his elder brothers, Narcizo and Guzman, and then a time later by himself. His first assignment was to take the food and drinking water to feed his brothers and some workers in the corn plantation. But once he reached the age of twelve, he worked half day in the plantation, returning home at around sunset with them.

The work in the cornfield was carried between eight in the morning and five or five thirty but before sundown. Chon frequently stopped labor activities to smoke a cigarette and chat for a few minutes to stretch his arms and straighten his back. That was the daily routine on the cornfield for most of them.

Evidently, for Epifanio and his two brothers, everything seemed normal. But that particular day, the brothers started shooting hints—hints about what they should do to put cash in their pockets. They discussed the next strike—how and where they would stay, how long they should wait to strike again, and how they organized themselves years ago when they started the cattle business. "You know what?" Chon asked all of them and paused. "We celebrate every time, anywhere. Hell yeah!" He moved his head proudly. "With fine liquor, delicious food, expensive clothing, and the best—beautiful women. Love surrounds you, my friends." Chon tried to spark motivation and curiosity for the rest of the men listening to his words.

"And then we moved out again with all the good stuff—money, all paper cash—my friends," Francisco said, complementing his brother's disturbing words.

"Okay, we had enough of that sort of thing, Big Wallet," Guzman said cautiously.

"Ha, I like the name Big Wallet. It goes well with you, Francisco," Epifanio said, laughed, and turned his eyes straight to his brother, who was in a serious mood and without words, with eyes and face lowered to the ground.

Meanwhile, Chon was laughing from loud to louder, while the rest of the men remained in silence, just watching him with steady eyes but without any word.

Chon was the youngest of the outlaws with very few signs of morality, almost nothing. He was tall and skinny with a natural pale color in his face. Since his first day in the cornfield, he liked to work without a shirt. He first took off his light-brown cotton shirt before he started the day in the plantation. One hour later, he was soaked in sweat. He always looked sticky as a boiling pot with some mixture of wax, glue, and candy in it.

That day, an unusual conversation went on between my uncles and their supposed friends. My father used to remember that. "What's your age, Narcizo?" Francisco asked.

"I'm seventeen," Narcizo muttered. Even if he appeared surprised by the question, he answered quickly and kindly but in a very low voice.

"No good. He is too young," Epifanio said to Francisco.

"Hmm, never mind, never mind," Francisco responded to his elder brother.

"What are you guys talking about?" Narcizo asked in a mix of kind and angry tone but with a soft voice.

"No worries, no, no. Francisco just wants to know your age, my friend," Epifanio said, looking straight into Narcizo's eyes.

"Uh, yeah . . . sure," Narcizo said.

"Anyways, you're much too young to even know of these things," Francisco said to Narcizo.

"Well, speak it out, or shut your mouth forever," Narcizo said with some anger.

"Never mind, kid," Epifanio said.

"If it's something that you guys want to talk, please do not hesitate because of my age. By the way, I know how to keep secrets," Narcizo said with polite gesture, "probably better than you do. Otherwise, you guys wouldn't be here." He said it sarcastically with half-suspicious eyes over the outlaws.

"Well, well, we can talk man to man now," Chon said, smiling. He put his hand into his pocket and brought out a pouch of tobacco. As everybody watched him, he began the task of making his own cigarettes by rolling and teasing out a small portion of dry leaves of the popular plant with the help of his fingers and wrapping it firmly into a smooth piece of corn husk with both hands. Chon kindly brought the cigarette to his mouth, licked one side to moisten the nonfiltered roll, struck a match, and held the flame to light his piece of art. He sucked the cigarette while his cheeks went in and out like a certain type of reptile. Then he softly exhaled a tiny spiral of smog, and a grayish smoke rise from his nose and mouth and vanished immediately in the air. He coughed softly two or three times, moving his head proudly up and down; *distinctive* was merely a characteristic to describe part of his personality.

"My ears are wide open, dear friend," Guzman said, watching Chon smoking his cigarette.

"My deal is to expand, to have a bigger group and move up our activities to Hidalgo State. I insist that you guys should come with us. This is a onetime invitation. Don't waste it," Chon said calmly.

"My brother is a man with good eyes for this business. Undoubtedly, he is a visionary man. Hidalgo State would be first and then Chiapas State," Francisco said with remarkable enthusiasm.

"Well, could be lots of money for you, my good friends. Come with us," Epifanio insisted, giving a touch of emphasis to his brothers' invitation.

There was a silent moment. Hundreds, thousands of thoughts were running through everyone's mind and sharpening the most hidden corners of their brain. For the outlaws, the idea was clear—involving Narcizo and Guzman in their robbing activities would give them more chances to continue being on the run and have a safe place to stay.

Finally, Guzman interrupted the silence. He slowly walked a few steps, stood up in front of the man, cleared his throat, and asked, "Are you out of your mind?" he asked, nearly shouting, placing his eyes steady over Epifanio's face.

"You don't know what the hell you're saying!" Narcizo screamed softly from a short distance.

Epifanio, visibly surprised, looked back at them one by one and then a second time. And carefully, he walked slowly a few steps away, keeping his eyes wide open on Guzman. But his expression showed that he understood none of it. And he simply muttered a few bad words and swallowed his pride intelligently.

"This is not what my parents will expect from me and from my younger brothers. And it isn't what we want for them," Guzman said firmly.

"Please don't ever mention it again," Narcizo said, placing his eyes straight on Chon.

"It's fine. Don't take it so seriously," Epifanio interrupted.

"Don't take it so seriously?" Guzman asked Epifanio, mocking him in a loud tone.

"Okay . . . okay," Francisco intervened.

"So you guys are stuck here in these valleys," Chon said.

He paused, smoked his cigarette, and with some coughing asked, "What happens with you, people? I mean, your pockets, your dreams, or you've just forgotten about it? Umm, I mean, what do you want from here?"

"That's something that shouldn't be your concern," Guzman answered quickly.

"Look at your daily routine. And for a moment, just forget everything about this eternal misery. Every day your necessity is taking your life out of your hands and waste it over these lands. How much enjoyment do you have out here? Because there isn't enjoyment living with tightened hands or empty pockets, even if you guys think that this land is a paradise. So please let me help you to plant the seeds, and your decisions will be the fields, the fertile soil to germinate thousands of seeds to grow your goals, your dreams, and to share the most prominent harvest with many others like you," Francisco said, ending with a deep sense of inspiration, trying to convince the small group around him.

"Do you know what this is?" Guzman asked, looking at Chon and Francisco simultaneously.

"I don't know. What's wrong with these batos?" Chon asked his brothers, and then he paused. "It's a brilliant idea. But they don't give a damn about it." He smoked his cigarette.

"Well, you guys don't seem to understand. There will be enough money for you. So you don't have to work these lands anymore," Francisco said, trying to persuade Guzman and Narcizo.

"You don't get it. You don't get it because you don't work these lands," Guzman said.

"Look, when we grew up, we had nothing. And if we had something, it was always very little, very reduced, always small portions of everything, even our parents' love. And the worst was we have seen our parents live in extreme poverty, bitter misery, without any type of distinction or some respect from others. Years ago, we've heard people gossip behind our backs, that we own nothing in the village. The reason for us doing this is simple—we are able, in one way or another, to provide our families what they never have had—money, food, and respect. Yeah, they have respect, believe it or not. We don't," Epifanio said ironically.

"See, would you do the same for your family? Would you sacrifice yourself for them?" Francisco asked directly to Guzman, and then he spoke louder. "Of course, you'll think twice because to do this, you need a crazy mind or large cojones, yeah. You really need some guts."

"Well, well, I see the devil has disguised himself as a good friend to come to these lands," Guzman said with a soft tone but sarcastically while turning his attention to Francisco's words.

"I feel so sad for you all," Francisco said.

"How can you say that?" Guzman asked to Francisco, looking straight in his eyes. "You are evil, man." He added this with a certain deception.

"Ha! For you, I might be evil. But for my family, I might be a hero. You, for your family, might be good. But for others, you might be a fool. As you can see, it's one or two. But always balancing good and evil, that's what I am," Francisco said, approaching Guzman angrily.

"Enough! Knock it off!" Narcizo yelled, trying to smoothen the rough argument between his brother and Francisco.

"Hey! Don't give me these rotten looks!" Francisco exclaimed immediately to Narcizo.

"And?" Narcizo said and walked toward Francisco.

"Hey! Knock it off, Francisco, and you too, Narcizo!" Epifanio screamed.

"It looks like you guys had a shitty childhood," Guzman said.

"Childhood? Life in general, my dear friend, it's not always joyful for everyone. But for too many, it is fair enough. I definitely can see how it began for you, my friends, here in this farm," Epifanio said.

"What in the world are you guys doing here?" Guzman asked after he finally caught a deep breath.

"When are you guys planning to leave my father's farm?" Narcizo asked, interrupting Guzman's question to the brothers.

"Your father needs to ask because we don't know," Chon said.

"No. Now you guys better start thinking to leave. The sooner, the better," Guzman said firmly.

"I just told you, your father needs to ask," Chon said.

"Seriously?" Narcizo asked and walked toward Chon.

"Hey, hey, don't take it so seriously. I was simply expressing myself," Chon said.

"Why did you come here?" Narcizo asked Epifanio and paused. "You guys don't belong here. I have to ask you to leave." He looked at every one of them.

"Everything that you guys have just said sounded like an insult to us. My old man did not set out in these lands to raise bandits like you," Guzman said.

"An insult? How?" Chon asked.

"I certainly think you'd better get off my property. You must leave this place, go home, and start packing," Narcizo said and pointed toward the house with his hand.

"Yeah, we will leave as soon as we figure out where to stay," Epifanio said.

"And we don't want more problems with the sorchis or polis around here. Did you hear me, Narcizo?" Chon asked, paused, and followed the young man with a sarcastic look. "I can help get you a girlfriend."

"No, thanks. I don't need help about it. Things are clear. I see how far you could go. You guys leave these lands, and I'll keep my mouth shut," Narcizo said seriously but with some suspicious meaning.

"Please leave us alone. We like to work these lands. We like to live decently," Guzman said.

"We are decent farmers, hardworking people," Narcizo said.

"Wow! This is totally right. You're right!" Francisco exclaimed.

"I will ask you guys to leave and stay somewhere else. We don't want future problems," Guzman said.

"Listen, guys, that's it. There is nothing else to be said. You guys leave us alone," Narcizo said, expressing displeasure for that conversation.

"Okay, then we will go," Epifanio agreed.

"I think it is extremely unlikely that you guys didn't understand our point. However, we won't waste our time or your time." Francisco said calmly, clearing his throat softly and spitting on the ground.

"Everyone has one life to live, and we should respect it, right?" Guzman concluded, scanning deeply with his eyes every one of the outlaws but especially Epifanio.

"Okay," Epifanio said softly, looking over the ground. "No grudges to hold, right?" He looked back into Guzman's eyes, giving him a thin smile before Guzman turned back and continued with his work activities.

"Don't worry, no hard feelings, but you have to leave soon," Guzman said from a certain distance while a flock of small gray birds flew scared overhead.

"Saltaparedes. Come on, let's go home!" Guzman shouted and paused while looking at the sky. "The birds . . . a storm would reach these cornfields. Come, hurry up. Let's go home."

That afternoon, a turbulent blast of angry wind blowing around them and a loud rumbling of thunder sounding far away helped calm down the unpleasant argument in the cornfield. "Five twenty" showed on Francisco's watch, time to go home. It was the hour when they usually left the cornfield every day.

That afternoon, the outlaws redoubled their footsteps in an effort to reach Grandpa's house first before anybody else. It was around seven in the evening when they finally arrived home. The first person they heard immediately was Grandpa. "Enough for today, ah?" Grandpa said, standing on the edge of the open porch. He looked at each of them with curious little glances and a few doubts in his mind.

"Yes, sir," Francisco answered simply, unsmiling.

The curiosity for the brothers' strange mood inclined Grandpa to walk downstairs on the open porch of his house, and he suddenly missed a step. He fell and dropped the empty plastic bucket and a basket with some bread while his heavy body tumbled down the unpainted wooden porch a few times. The brothers ran quickly toward Grandpa. Epifanio bent over and helped himself to get up. "Are you okay?" he asked, totally concerned.

"Yes, don't worry. I just can't deal with these shaky legs anymore. Caramba coño," Grandpa said while brushing with his right hand some pieces of dry leaves out of his old shirt. "Thank god I'm still in one piece." He added this with a sense of humor.

"Lucky for him, no broken bones, just some bruises and minor scratches in his arms and elbows," Grandma said to my uncles, who were approaching the house's patio precisely at the moment when she was helping Grandpa clean up his clothes after the unexpected fall. It was Grandpa's diagnostic that afternoon. Besides the scratches and some bruises on his body, he was fine.

A strong wind and the intermittent thunder's rumbling near to the house were enough for them to get inside the kitchen. The oil lamp was on, but most of them were in silence while Grandma was placing the food on the dining table.

The next day, Epifanio and his two brothers didn't go to work in the cornfield. It seemed all they wanted to do was talk with Grandpa, sitting on the big patio, drinking coffee with him and Grandma. The morning after that just before noon, Epifanio asked Grandpa, "Is it true that you and my father met when you guys were kids?"

"Yes, Epifanio. I loved your father like a brother. We grew up together. When we were teenagers, he was a great kid. He learned a lot about hunting, which was his passion," Grandpa said.

"Well, my old man's still a great hunter!" Epifanio exclaimed and smiled.

"He shot and killed a running deer when he was just fifteen years old. Since then, he gained self-confidence shooting with his rifle, and he became a great hunter," Grandpa said.

"We know that. He also told us what a great person you are," Epifanio said while looking at Grandpa.

"I clearly remember that boy, the young kid from those years, a longtime friend," Grandpa said slowly.

"My old man told us once that you were good at whatever you did as a child," Epifanio said.

"Well, we spent lots of time together when we were young boys. Then later, he married your mom, and I married my wife. And we saw each other just a few times after that. Last time that I saw him was twenty years ago, when I found him traveling in the bus to Arcelia. That time, I told him the location of my farm, but he never visited me. And look at me now. Here I am talking with my friend's sons. One time I told your father that his memory was better than mine," Grandpa said while still sitting on his chair and sipping his coffee intermittently.

"Well, he told me that your creativity is awesome, that you would be capable of making anything out of God knows what," Epifanio said, smiled with a certain grace, and shrugged while looking without distraction at Grandpa's face.

"Nonsense. No, no, of course not," Grandpa responded and smiled.

"Well, with all due respect, you've got something. No doubt, no doubt about it," Epifanio said. He found himself in an excellent position to have an open conversation about what really had happened back in the cornfield. And at the end, they were determined to leave, and he was ready to talk to Grandpa about the truth.

He slowly picked up his coffee cup and seemed to spend a long time swirling the black liquid inside the glossy cup with the metallic spoon in his right hand. Then he slightly sipped two or three times the aromatic coffee and spoke, trying to keep the strength of his voice firmly. "Mr. Odilon, we can't live here anymore. We are leaving today," Epifanio respectfully said.

"But it's late. You guys can do it tomorrow," Grandpa suggested.

"You're right, daytime is better," Epifanio said.

That day, the three brothers postponed their leaving until the following morning. They thanked Grandpa for having them in his farm. And Epifanio told him that they were going to be close by and coming up back the following year, bringing their father with them to rekindle their friendship.

"Can I ask you something, Epifanio?" Grandpa asked.

"Absolutely. You are a good and honorable man. I'll answer anything you ask," Epifanio said without signs of hesitation.

"Did something happen between you guys and my sons?" Grandpa asked.

"Sort of. See, we are bandits. We are going the wrong way. Your sons are good, decent boys," Epifanio said, looking right at Grandpa's eyes.

"Sure, they are. They believe in hard work," Grandpa said.

"That's what I understand as honor, just doing what is right." Epifanio said and winked with his right eye at Grandpa.

"There's nothing wrong with being a good person, living a decent life. But I've also told my boys not to go around with the wrong stuff or waste time on people who can't even have the word *gratitude* in their vocabulary because, let me tell you, every person born in these woods knows the difference between gratitude and being ungrateful," Grandpa said literally.

"See, we took the other way, the bad side of the road, people might say the easy way. But it's not. I will say we took the hardest way. We took the unpredictable. While little, we grew up with almost nothing. When I was a little kid, I wanted to be a jinete. Being a bull rider in my village, just imagine . . . who wouldn't be happy and proud of me? Chon, my younger brother, wanted to be a bus driver. Sadly, we failed and became thieves at an early age. We got everything we wanted . . . except freedom. We ruined our freedom," Epifanio said bitterly and paused for three or five seconds. "Yeah, we believed that we were worthless. And by this time, we don't believe that. Now it's a fact—we are worthless for what we are, for what we do, but not our families. They certainly have what we don't."

"Look, no one deserves to be on the run. You guys are tough enough to put an end to this and confront trouble the right way," Grandpa said, straightening himself the best he could over his wooden chair and fixing his toes on the ground with some discomfort.

"Things have been a mess for many years. We can be excused for one or two for some . . . but not for what I've done through all these years," Epifanio said.

"You are a hard worker as well, a decent and clever man as I can see with my own eyes," Francisco said, admitting a significant reverence toward Grandpa while attempting to change the subject.

"Thank you," Grandpa said and appreciated the gesture.

"Sometimes life is not fair for some of us," Epifanio said in a low voice, almost whispering.

"But life is life. And it's from this world no matter what. I want you to see it. This activity of yours is going nowhere. And I really mean it," Grandpa said, looking straight into Epifanio's eyes.

"Day by day, we certainly walk over the edge," Epifanio said.

"One person's actions can impact others' lives forever," Grandpa said clearly.

"I wish I hadn't started that conversation with your sons in the cornfield," Epifanio said with some regret.

"That thing just doesn't seem right to me, and you should know it, Epifanio," Grandpa said. He finally understood the silence between his sons and the three outlaws for the last two days in the farm.

"This is a fertile land with tropical weather. In the rainy season, these valleys are saturated with moisture and water, making the fertile land grow corn, beans, pumpkins, and vegetables and raise a large number of cattle. As you can see, I encouraged my sons to work these lands and respect someone else's property," Grandpa said.

"Some people succeed in working the land. Some others don't. And I feel glad for you and your sons. We will be in the next town for a while looking for a place to start a new life. We will be in touch, trust me," Epifanio said.

"Awesome!" Grandpa exclaimed.

Next morning, Epifanio and his two brothers approached Grandpa and Grandma to say goodbye. "Well, good luck then," Grandpa significantly said.

"Please forgive me for what we have said to your sons. I know it is unpleasant for you," Epifanio said in a tone suggesting he might actually mean what he said.

"Well, what you guys have said to my boys is not acceptable here or somewhere else, especially when among friends. Of course, it is bad. But learning something about regret, appreciation, and the desire to patch mistakes, it's always a wonderful thing that should be compelling and turn into a tradition to be passed from one generation to another in the same way. And I will beg you as a friend of your father, who is a good man, to forget all about it as we will forget the bad and remember the good," Grandpa courteously said while he showed a sincere gesture and a thin smile to Epifanio and his brothers.

"Thank you, Mr. Odilon," Epifanio said.

"Look, I'll be honest with you, guys. I'm telling you this because I have my sons, my boys. And when I'm looking or talking to you and your brothers, I feel like I'm looking and talking to my own sons, my own family. And like I said, we all can change if we have the desire for it," Grandpa said sincerely with a certain hope to be heard.

But at the end, Grandpa knew so clearly who these people were; and allowing them to stay in his property, even if it was for a short time, was a big mistake, a foolish decision. He knew how wrong it was. But in his little world, he was far away to imagine what was coming for him. You never put lions and lambs in the same cage or bugs and reptiles in the same box. No matter if you have to load Noah's ark, you simply don't do it.

But now that the outlaws were leaving his farm, it was a time for celebration, he thought, a blessed time, especially for one person—my grandma. She seemed to be happy; a big burden had been removed out of her house with the bandits' departure. Grandma looked at Grandpa intently and smiled as a simple sign that everything was all right once again. Even if she never liked the outlaws' arrival, there was a visible smile that day on her face.

She walked a couple of steps and stood next to Grandpa's right side, smiling involuntarily. She felt that something was connected back in her soul, something that was removed since the first day that Epifanio and his two brothers set foot in her house. As Grandma said to Grandpa, "Tell me who your friends are, and I will tell you who you are."

"I really thank you for your kindness and hospitality, Mr. Odilon and Mrs. Fausta," Epifanio said while Francisco and Chon were walking the horses out of the wooden stable, getting themselves ready to leave Grandpa's farm. And once again, they'd find another place to stay, marking their own trail for a possible return to the cozy farm.

"That's not a problem," Grandma happily said without any hesitation over the outlaws' departure.

"What do I owe you for all this favor?" Epifanio asked.

"Nothing," Grandpa rapidly responded.

"Well, thanks. Sorry to have disturbed you, and we'll be in touch soon," Epifanio said while leaving the farm.

"Goodbye and God bless you all," Grandpa said.

"Hey, maybe I'll come back soon and sit down with you on your patio all day long, watching the red sunset over your land, drinking coffee over and over again," Epifanio said from a considerable distance. While riding his horse, he looked over his right shoulder to Grandpa's face with a look that seemed to say, *We'll meet again.* Indeed, Epifanio turned into a real sentimental man when it came to goodbyes and stuff like that.

"Okay, Epifanio, please go to Mass and recite the holy creed. I know you can do it!" Grandpa said loudly, waving his hand as an act of goodbye.

"Trust me, I will. God bless you too. Wishing you and your family prosperity on this magnificent land!" Epifanio said loudly.

That was the last time that Grandpa and Grandma saw those bandits, those outlaws who just brought tragedy to Grandpa's family.

CHAPTER THREE

THE TRAGEDY

It was horrible what happened to my father's elder brothers just two days after the outlaws left the farm. It was around one o'clock. The sun was setting in the hot afternoon over those hills, warming the wide green valleys around. Some flocks of scared birds came out of the forest and flew low across the sky.

Earlier that morning, five men had worked in silence until one of them, named Nacho, put the large azadon on his side. And he showed them how fast he could work, twelve or more times faster without pause, and all the things he could do better than them. "Amuse yourself, little Nacho," Guzman said, smiled, and showed a thumbs-up.

The rest of them happily clapped. "Olé, matador!" they all exclaimed at once. Nacho smiled, opened his arms, and slowly bowed toward them like he was in the middle of a bullfighting arena in front of a one-thousand-pound fighting bull with sharp, pointed horns.

"Olé, matador. Amuse yourself!" Guzman exclaimed once again while he was laughing loudly.

"Not too bright, brother, come on. Sunny sun!" Omar cheered happily.

"Graccias. Thanks to all my fans. Oleeé, vale puéss!" Nacho exclaimed gratefully, mocking the Europeans' Spanish, while he bowed his head toward the men, pressing his chest with the palm of his right hand.

Those words and movements made the men want to laugh out loud not because they found Nacho comical but simply because they were in a good mood. And they gave him a loud cheer immediately. "Ha, la, laá. Piece of art! Ha, la, laá. Olé, vale. Olé matador!" They did not imagine that their future was not in the cornfield anymore, not even in their own hands. And of course, they didn't know that the funny moment would be the last for them.

Local police and several soldiers emerged from the forest; some civilians followed them. They all had shotguns, rifles, and revolvers. The intruders surrounded the area from east to west, coming from the south side of the cornfield.

Down there, Narcizo and Guzman were working with other three men. They were laughing about Nacho's jokes. No one of them noticed someone else's presence there; no one sensed the evil that afternoon until it was too late.

A few minutes of noise and bullets were enough to destroy the life of five good men, the life of others as well—their families. The intruders began to shoot without any type of warning. They overtook the place violently, popping out from the south side of the forest, all of them with weapons in their hands, ready to kill. They attacked without mercy. "Kill them all!" a man shouted from a distance.

"Kill them!" one of the civilians exclaimed.

That was when the shooting turned unstoppable. The rain of bullets impacting the ground was lifting a cloud of dust, and small pieces of green corn plants were pushed into the air savagely. "Come on, come on! There, over there!" some of the attackers were shouting from loud to louder, running down the hill, and squeezing the trigger of their guns.

A fourteen-year-old boy, who eleven years later would become my father, was just about to set foot in the plantation. Suddenly, the boy heard the first wave of fire and the shouting of the attackers. Immediately, his happy smile vanished out of his face, and his eyes seemed to grow bigger in every blink, watching in silence the grotesque and foolish scene.

"There, over there! I got it!" someone yelled.

Confused about the unexpected attack, Guzman stood on his feet, trying to understand. He never realized that he was a clear target for several soldiers. "Get the one there!" a man who seemed to have a certain military rank or some kind of leadership in the group, like a sergeant, ordered ruthlessly the small group of soldiers, stimulating their destructive killing instinct.

My father hesitated; he didn't know whether to run or not. He was totally confused for a moment. That cruel scene was something unexpected for him. Should he keep walking, or should he just run? But something inside his mind warned him about the risk that afternoon. He must hide himself quickly into the flowering jarilla bushes. The short vegetation there was the only chance for him to survive.

The group of soldiers was a considerable number; many of them had two rifles hanging from their shoulders. Some soldiers were running, others cautiously walking. But all of them fiercely came into the cornfield, breaking the occasional silence with a burst of bullets shot from their fire weapons toward the defenseless men. Several bullets struck them down mercilessly until not a standing man was to be seen.

There was never a response to the fire of the villains. They massacred those five men violently, without mercy, without any valid justification. They were blind, erroneously shining for their ignorance, without having the right information about those poor men.

My father, who witnessed everything, couldn't do nothing else but to hide himself and stay still in the jarilla bushes along the cornfield. He didn't know where to go or where to run. And like I said, he was just fourteen. It was hard for him to take that as truth. But that horrible scene in front of his eyes allowed him to understand the danger around him. But how could he respond to those miserable bastards' aggression? He only had an old slingshot hanging down over his chest from his neck and nothing more than one dozen small stones rounded like marbles in one of his worn pants' pockets.

Nothing . . . nothing better but to stay hidden and alive, waiting for the perfect moment to escape those gutless cowards. He continued watching from his hidden place while sounds of bullets were whistling and buzzing near him. And some swirls of fine dust danced through the beams of sunlight that came through the scarcely green leaves of the jarilla bushes.

He remained quietly hidden in those bushes a short distance from the dead bodies. He had no alternative, no choice, but to stay and remain in silence. From time to time, he closed his eyes while sheltering himself under the flowering bushes, imagining and wishing that everything was just a bad dream while bullets and more bullets flew constantly, scraping the ground around him, reminding him that everything was real and far away from being a nightmare. Resigned to what destiny might bring him, he remained calm, well camouflaged under the bushes, holding his sadness and squeezing his eyes to hold his tears.

After they killed the helpless men, all the shooting and shouting stopped for a few minutes while the cornfield seemed to be empty, lifeless, and silent for a little while. Then again, intermittent shooting continued in the other side of the hill; that was Uncle Mingo, one of the eldest of my grandpa's sons. Mingo and his wife were trying to defend his brothers. But it was already too late. They were dead.

Meanwhile, uphill at some point of the forested mountain, next to a cave sculpted naturally into the ground by Mother Nature was a young man cutting some logs for firewood with his ax. That man raised his head slightly, finding incomprehensible the sound of shooting coming from the cornfield. And holding a rifle with his hands, he looked and intended to locate the unusual shooting somewhere down the hill. From his position, the vision was poor and only extended to the edge of the plantation, which was surrounded with a thick cloud of dust and smoke. And the brave brother silently came down from the mountain, guided by his instinct to protect his brothers with his own life. That man was my grandparents' eldest son, Uncle Antonio. He took several deep breaths, and after a little while, he engaged himself in combat.

Uncle Antonio couldn't find the way to have the enemy close. But he managed to shoot and scare them, forcing them back in the forest. From his position, he was only able to hear some hollow voices echoing in a constant flow of sound from the cliffs along the mountain and confusing him, making him unable to locate the enemy into the woods. After several minutes of shooting, his good luck changed quickly.

The soldiers, in their excessive anxiety to hit the shooter, discharged a flurry of bullets fiercely into the forest. Then—zas!—Antonio was struck by a bullet right over his left thigh. He pulled the bullet out of his leg and applied wild arnica salve as a disinfectant. Then he tightened the injury carefully. And as soon the panic had passed slowly through his brain, he painfully intended to leave the hot spot, going downhill to find a safe path to escape through the forest with the help of a wood stick under his armpit.

Suddenly, he stopped despite the strong pain on his injured leg. He flattened his belly and chest against the ground. Three soldiers were there, hidden, waiting for him to be a clear target. Fortunately for him, the soldiers were facing the opposite side, and then he noticed more of them close by. He stayed and held his breath continuously until they left.

For about one hour, that particular spot in the cornfield had been covered with a cloud of dust formed by the bullets' impact on the ground. Little by little, the thick cloud of dust was dissolving away, leaving the air full of a burnt gunpowder smell and smoky, thin dust, making visible again the nearest part of the forest for my father, where his thoughts, eyes, and surviving instincts were pointed for him to escape. In the meantime, the other side of the cornfield was full of activity. It wasn't hard to hear voices and distant shooting for a little while coming from the south side of the valley. He was just about two hundred feet from the cornfield's north entrance.

"Hurry up! All of you, hurry up!" soldiers shouted from a distance.

Distant shouting, distant shooting, distant voices followed the scary scene. Four dead bodies lay down on the bloody ground. Six soldiers and two civilians were approaching the massacre's spot with rifles on their hands. My father recognized the civilians at once—the Morales brothers, members of the only family who used to have grudges against them. They were obviously involved in the killing. He slowly put his fingers to his lips and nodded.

36

The soldiers turned up two dead bodies, those who died facing the ground. And they cleaned the fallen men's faces using corn leaves to remove the dirt and blood from their face. Two soldiers lined up the dead. Then they all looked at them one by one carefully. "Which of these batos is Epifanio?" Soldier No. 1, who seemed to be the sergeant, asked the eldest of the Moraleses.

"None of these dead bodies belonged to Epifanio or his brothers, Francisco or Chon," Morales answered.

"But the outlaws were here working on the cornfield. I saw them just before yesterday," Soldier No. 2 said.

The sergeant pressed his lips in disapproval; he barely knew anything about the fallen men. He looked up straight to every one of the men around him, and he nodded toward them silently. Then he took a deep breath. "Life was never meant to be without mistakes. But this—" he said when someone interrupted him.

"It doesn't make a lot of sense to me. These guys are part of Epifanio's robbing gang. So we are fine, my sergeant," the eldest of the Moraleses said.

"No, we're not. I just don't understand what exactly is going on over here," the sergeant said, coughed, and cleared his throat.

Soon after that conversation, my father's horror increased when the attackers realized that a man was missing. "Sergeant, my sergeant, they were five of them." A third soldier spoke in a low voice to his superior.

"Well, in this case, we'll have one little task to solve. Then it will be done," the sergeant said. After those words, searching for the other man was a priority for them.

The blood was everywhere as empty bullet shells coated the massacre's perimeter. They'd followed the bloody trace on the ground, going through the jarilla bushes. The life of an injured man was pulling away from the thin string of his good luck, challenging his unpredictable destiny that horrible afternoon in a remote cornfield.

Suddenly, someone started screaming loud. "Here! Over here, I've found him!" the youngest of the Moraleses shouted.

"Got it all?" the sergeant asked while approaching the scene.

"Yes, sir, I think so."

"Good boy!" he exclaimed and wiped his bloody hand on the flowering vegetation.

"Damn, what is that awful smell?" one of the soldier sarcastically asked while approaching the injured man. "I knew it. It's a dead man's smell." He laughed with exaggerated sarcasm.

"Look, Officer, he was born poor and scared." Juan, who was the youngest of the Moraleses, said, laughing loud.

"Poor, yes, but scared? I doubt it. I got nothing to hide," that unfortunate man told Juan Morales and stopped the crazy laughing almost immediately.

"That's a big lie!" Juan Morales exclaimed, placing his narrow eyes into the injured man.

"Shh," Soldier No. 2 said slowly, turned his head, and looked at Juan for a few seconds.

"Don't you think I know . . . what you are?" Juan asked the injured man from a close distance.

"No. You are lying. You don't even know me at all," the injured man said.

In fact, Juan Morales found a young man badly injured, trying to escape. That man was Narcizo. They all circled the dying man after they found him. He was sitting sadly on the ground near a guaje tree. There was blood all around him, and fresh mud was all over his chest after crawling. His pale face revealed pain and agony at the same time.

A tall soldier fixed his eyes intently on him for a minute or two and then sententiously remarked, "You are dead, boy. But I'd like to hear your name first." He approached the young man, who remained sitting on the ground with his eyes lost somewhere in the distance.

"Tell me your name, young boy," Soldier No. 3 demanded firmly.

"Narcizo. It's my name," he said, looking at the soldier and everyone around.

"Good boy. But your name won't help you. I personally will kill you," same soldier said slowly, standing in front of him.

"Then . . . what are you waiting for?" Narcizo said slowly and looked up in the sky instead of the soldier.

"Stand up. Come on, get up," Soldier No. 2 ordered.

"I can't," Narcizo said.

"What? You can't?" that soldier asked with some air of frustration.

"I can't get up. My leg is broken," Narcizo said.

"Aha, I can see. That's why you're stranded here!" Soldier No. 2 exclaimed and slightly softened his expression toward the defenseless man.

"I can't stand up," Narcizo replied.

Then a tall soldier standing behind him aimed his rifle straight to Narcizo's head. And immediately, a cocking noise sounded in the back of his head. "This should help you, boy," Soldier No. 3 said, laughing out loud while aiming his rifle over Narcizo's back.

"Oh, God, you know it. We are good men," Narcizo said, moving his head up and down and pressing back his wounded abdomen with his right hand slowly.

"Let's see what you have, boy," Soldier No. 3 said, still standing behind Narcizo and pressing harder the long tube of his loaded rifle against the head of the unfortunate man.

"We are decent farmers, hardworking men," Narcizo said firmly.

"Not sure about it. But you are afraid to die," the same soldier said in a very low voice, almost whispering at the back of Narcizo's right ear. "Am I wrong, boy?"

"Please, if you have to shoot, just shoot, like a man," Narcizo said.

"Pardon?" Soldier No. 3 asked surprisingly and paused. "Beg for your insignificant life. Beg to me, boy. And I'll shoot you!"

"You are a despicable coward with a gun in your hands. Without your gun, you'll walk head down in front of me," Narcizo said, trying to turn his head to the right side to look at the soldier's eyes. But he couldn't.

A moment later, the same soldier took a few steps back, raised his rifle from Narcizo's head, and walked away from the injured man. Then he joined the group silently with a confused expression on his face. Meanwhile, the rest of the savages remained in silence, just watching the dying man.

A second soldier walked forward and analyzed Narcizo from toes to head. "Tell me something that I don't know. Where is Epifanio?" he asked Narcizo as he nervously rubbed his thumb and forefinger together.

"I don't know," Narcizo answered honestly.

"Where is Epifanio?" the same soldier repeated the question louder this time, approaching Narcizo almost face-to-face in absolute authority.

"I just told you. I don't know," Narcizo answered.

"I'll ask you one more time," Soldier No. 2 said and paused. "Where are those outlaws?"

"Somewhere out there but not here," Narcizo said and weakly pointed some place behind the mountain.

"Atta boy, eh?" the sergeant said, looking at Soldier No. 2, and smiled briefly.

"My brother Guzman died, and I am dying all because of Epifanio and his brothers, but I don't know where they are now. They left the farm two days ago, and I don't have any idea where they might be by this time," Narcizo said in humble way.

"Here is another chance. And we will let you go home. Where is all the stolen cattle that you guys robbed, and who else is involved? I want to hear names. Tell me about it," Soldier No. 2 continued asking him.

"You are wrong. You've just killed the wrong people. We're simple farmers. We work these lands to feed our family. We don't steal cattle," Narcizo said clearly.

"Well, it's your life boy, isn't it?" Soldier No. 2 insisted.

39

"I should pull out my pistol to kill you, bandit," Juan Morales said to Narcizo, accusing him directly.

Questions kept coming from the soldiers, and Narcizo's answers did not satisfy them. There was a plan B for the soldiers. It would be no problem to obtain the answers for all those questions. "Torture him," they agreed.

The Morales brothers and one of the soldiers tied up Narcizo's ankles roughly with a nylon rope. They pushed him on the ground over his back. His femur was broken, and bloody flesh was visible out of his torn clothes. They pulled the man and dragged him through the weeds.

"You are already halfway, boy, to being a dead man," Soldier No. 2 said in a sarcastic way while dragging the man over the ground.

Juan Morales was pulling Narcizo's legs using the nylon rope around Narcizo's ankles, taking him through the jarilla bushes, only a few meters away from my father's hidden spot. Lying down on the ground over his back, Narcizo saw the metallic knife coming toward him. Then he felt the sharp blade cutting into his flesh. One of the soldiers stabbed him in his right arm and a few seconds later gave him a severe stab in his right leg using the same knife while the older of the Moraleses was cutting half of Narcizo's middle finger from his left hand.

"Ah! Ah! Ah!" he screamed repetitively from extreme pain. His bloody body was shivering, shaking, twisting disproportionately over the ground. The meaning of pain had never been so complete, so excessive as it was for him that day. And the worst was there was no way he could make it clear to them what they were not even able to understand.

"Got enough?" Juan Morales asked, almost screaming to Narcizo.

"I'm sorry, boy, but this is the way that you choose your death," the sergeant said, giving the order to Soldier No. 2 to kill Narcizo.

"Dear God, just give me the strength that I need today," Narcizo whispered and exhaled deeply.

"You've got your choice, boy," Juan Morales muttered.

"I will kill you slowly and painfully, my friend," Soldier No. 2 said, paused, and looked at him straight in his eyes, cocking his rifle and touching Narcizo's face with the tip of his weapon.

"I've just heard you talking and talking. You should know that everybody dies. It's getting late. You should finish what you've already started. There is no way back," Narcizo said in a low voice with a kind of resignation.

"Great, not a problem," Soldier No. 2 said and blew his weapon a kiss.

"Dear God, please let me approach your kingdom. I really beg you for mercy. Bless my soul and guide my way, if it's possible," Narcizo said and looked at the sky.

40

"Did you hear it?" Soldier No. 2 asked, looking into Juan Morales's eyes.

"Dear Lord, with your infinite gratitude, protect me, blessing this day in which you've decided to take my life. Please take me where I belong. Take me home" were Narcizo's last words.

"Enough! That's enough! I had heard enough of it!" the sergeant yelled, placing his eyes full of meaning on Soldier No. 2.

Narcizo opened his mouth as if he wanted to speak; when no words came out, he closed it tightly. He really tried to say something, but this time, his mouth was completely dry. Narcizo had trouble moving his tongue and forced himself to lick his lips and swallow some saliva. Then he softly coughed and weakly spat bloody saliva out of his mouth. Despite a tiny tremble in his body and the horrible pain, he got up in front of them, standing up on one foot and exposing his dying body to them. His heart had begun to beat from fast to faster in matter of seconds. One of the soldiers, more terrified than the dying man, walked briefly and looked behind him, afraid of something or looking for something but holding a rifle with his hands nervously.

My father lost sight of Narcizo. He remained lying down on the ground against his belly, holding his breath. He flattened a few small bushes and corn leaves to witness the suffering scene from a short distance. Then he lost sight of his dying brother. But he was able to hear his last words. And that was the last thing that my father remembered from his brother.

There was no pain in the world worse than that, to witness with your own eyes your loved ones' suffering. He wanted to stand up, fight, and defend his brothers. But a kid alone with empty hands got undoubtedly zero chance. *Wait, remain quiet, don't move, don't expose yourself. They will kill you. There is no point in dying like this.* These were some of his thoughts while my father was hidden in the cornfield. He wasn't afraid to die, but he needed to survive to denounce these brutal murders. He softly sobbed and rubbed his wet eyes. At this point, it seemed to be the best idea.

The screaming stopped; a brief silence was replaced by a heavy breathing sound coming out of the nearby bushes. Then a single shot trembled the ground, and few seconds later, Narcizo was dead. They shot him right in the center of his chest. His body shook from the impact of the bullet, and then he collapsed and fell on the ground while he struggled in vain to survive.

The executer soldier jumped quickly over his feet after his bullet went through the injured man's chest, breaking some bones and driving out blood with small pieces of flesh from the man's back. A few seconds later, the spectators cheered Soldier No. 2. Their plan was completed, filled with blood . . . with innocent blood. "Perfect target!" Soldier No. 3 exclaimed cheerfully.

Then Soldier No. 2 took down his rifle and walked away back to his sergeant, who was watching the scene from a certain distance with the rest of them. "Clean shot. You didn't get any blood on your uniform, did you?" the sergeant asked his subordinate after complimenting the clear shot.

"Blood? Only on my hands but not on my clothes, my sergeant," Soldier No. 2 answered his superior.

"A piece of candy for you," Juan Morales said, walking and tapping the soldier's right shoulder with the palm of his right hand.

"Yeah, if you say so," Soldier No. 2 responded coldly.

"Hey, Sergeant!" Juan Morales exclaimed while approaching the uniformed man. Then he paused. "Sergeant, you guys did good . . . really good. My respects." Then he looked and stayed for few seconds in front of the surprised sergeant and gave him a military salute.

"So what would you like to do now?" the sergeant asked, looking straight into Juan Morales's eyes.

"We don't want to waste time or risk anything. Let's get out of here, if you agree with me," Juan Morales said.

"I still don't understand why we're going through all this," the sergeant said to the Morales brothers. Then they left the plantation and vanished into the woods.

Carefully and crawling over his flat belly, my father approached the spot where Narcizo was earlier painfully screaming before everything turned silent. When he looked, Narcizo's body was lifeless on the ground. He was dead; he was gone forever. He was done, no more. The young kid sat next to him, sobbed, and cried almost in silence. Then he closed his dead brother's eyes forever and hysterically yelled to the infinite, "No, no, no! Please, no, no, no!"

As for Guzman, he died instantly. They got him really bad. The impact of three bullets found the left side of his chest, destroying his left armpit and his heart, while another bullet had gone clear through his left shoulder from side to side.

Calixto was shot right over his throat. A single bullet crossed his windpipe. He drowned in his own blood.

Nacho was simply unrecognizable. Most of the impacts hit the upper side of his body. And Omar's skull showed at least four impacts, one in his forehead.

Unjustly, five good men were murdered because of ignorance and little information from the local and state authorities. They were manipulated for the Moraleses' own interests to get those lands in one way or another, no matter what. It was something that never happened in years.

CHAPTER FOUR

GRANDMA

A few miles away in the opposite side of the main hill, Grandma and Grandpa were talking in the cozy patio around their house. The patio was adorned with colorful patches of multicolored roses and carnations. Some geraniums potted in large clay pots surrounded the delightful place. Small plastic containers with red and white flowers were hanging from the lower branches of the zapote tree next to the entrance of Grandma's vegetable garden, enhancing her enjoyment of the plants. She grew vegetables and herbs like chocolate mint, named this way for its dark-colored leaves; *Majorana*; epazote; thyme; cilantro; parsley; and few bushes of muicle, as well as oregano. Typical herbs that she used for tea or for the final touch of flavor and aroma in her daily cooking.

A crooked row of totolonche bushes with ripe berries lined the other side of the garden. The moisture in the ground allowed to grow throughout the year all kinds of plants and vegetables, like carrots, tomatoes, tomatillos, piquin peppers, collard greens, onions, radishes, celery, beans, and huauzontles, the hairy amaranth according to the Nahuatl. The farm had some mango, plum, and plenty of guava trees just outside the patio. A large guamúchil tree was between the forest and the house's calmíl, not far from the barn.

The small house with a picturesque patio was at the edge of the forest. It seemed to be built in the middle of nowhere. A large paradise in the wild—it was how Grandpa used to remember that place. "A unique place in an unknown world," I would hear years later in Grandma's own words.

Grandpa sat and leaned back against his wooden chair's headrest, stretching his arms all the way to the back of his sore neck. "Ahh." A relieved sound popped out of his throat through his mouth for four or five seconds while bringing the weight of his body to the front. His eyes were looking to the shadows of the hills over his vast land.

Outside the patio was a patch of dark green grass where the main picnic area was situated. Three large tables and some wooden benches were hardly visible through the morning haze in the rainy season from Grandpa's porch. The view from the picnic site was fantastic in a sunny day, almost perfect. There was a narrow strip of tulips with red flowers not far from the barbecue area. "The tallest tulips that ever existed," as Grandma said. And of course, her ancestors' flowers, yellow cempazúchitl, the Aztecs' symbolic marigold, were transplanted with her own hands four or five feet away from the tulips.

It was a peaceful and relaxing view with a few pointed mountains, a vast landscape around, and a quiet narrow river passing through the hills. A lonely florifundo flourished next to the left side of the river. There was a short line of higueras also visible from the picnic spot on a clear day. Years later, they would find out that florifundo and higuera belonged to the group of poisonous plants for high levels of toxins.

Certainly, as my Grandpa said, that place was a little paradise in the middle of nowhere with lots of beauty and tons of danger. Those lands were the perfect habitat for coral and rattlesnakes, scorpions, black widows, patas de res, and a peculiar half-tailed lizard wrongly named escurpion. Well, even mountain wildcats had been seen in the forest close to the farm. My father and his brother Antonio, when they were little, witnessed some of the villagers killing a mature lion while attacking a donkey nearby. That was just a onetime matter. But certainly, who really knew what was hidden in the forest? Anyway, Grandpa was a strong believer and more than once said, "Wild animals belong here. We're taking their habitat. They belong to Mother Nature, just like you or me. And every one of us should learn through time to get along with the wild, with the unknown, and to benefit from it without destroy it." No doubt, that place was a place of wonderful things, as well as of danger.

The first time that Grandpa and Grandma saw the amazing place was early in the spring of 1918. They were a young couple in those days and quickly fell in love with those lands. Grandpa had to count all his coins, including every single cent inside his pockets, for him to complete the required amount to buy that beautiful land. The property included a small house built over the main valley surrounded with a large dirt patio, where they stayed in the beginning.

Besides their love, their enthusiasm for farming brought them together. The marriage between the two was a true and unbreakable partnership. One was there for the other and vice versa, simple as that. Just one year after their marriage, another member joined the young couple, Antonio, their first son. And through the years, they raised a small army in the farm, having the last child in 1947.

Through the years, Grandpa would turn all his property into a very nice farm. He enlarged the house, not that much but some. He added two more rooms and built large stables for his horses, donkeys, and some hybrids. The living space inside the house was divided into five rooms, the kitchen being the longest room, where Grandma undoubtedly spent good times during the day.

There were tiny windows in the house except the one in the kitchen, which was double in size. The doors were closed most of the time. So the strong rays of the burning sun were totally excluded from inside the house in the hot days, keeping all the rooms cool and fresh as a natural cave. The kitchen, being the biggest room in the house, had a very particular window right next to the cooking area, where the smoke came out and vanished magically into thin air.

The drinking water was put into a large clay pot that they called tinaja, located over the homemade mud bricks in the right corner of the kitchen. Certainly, it wasn't ice water at home. But the clay pot kept the water fresh always, even in the extreme heat of the hottest day in the summer.

Cattle, corn, and Cincho cheese were the main source of income in the farm besides horses, poultry, pigs, and pumpkin seeds, which supported them as well. Grandpa used to run his farm with some of his sons, and Grandma was always at his side. And from time to time, Calixto, Nacho, and Omar joined them, coming on foot from El Salitre.

Grandpa, at his middle age, was profoundly happy. It was the first time in his life that he owned something—something that he really enjoyed. But life had something else to offer, something that he never even thought or imagined in the remotest corner of his brain. Tragedy was near him, and soon would come knock on his door in a very unpleasant way.

"Woman, I really appreciate everything that you have done for us," he said to Grandma.

She smiled with gratitude, took Grandpa's right hand, and squeezed it softly without saying a word. She just remained in silence, sitting next to him. Both of them were far away in their thoughts to imagine the horrible tragedy in the cornfield.

Minutes later, Grandma got up from her chair. She pulled her long hair through the circle of a rubber band. And her dark brown hair mixed with lots of gray shone against the bright rays of the sun while she walked into the kitchen. She was looking through the spices that she carefully kept into the old cabinets that Grandpa rebuilt when they first arrived to the farm. She wanted to find something that would give a tasty flavor to the tender pork chops.

Inside the kitchen, there was a pretíl, a rectangle platform made out of homemade mud bricks flattened and smoothed with yellowish clay in which she placed a three-legged carved, porous stone with a large rod made out of the same material. She and her daughters ground the nixtamál there, kneeling behind the metate to grind the tender corn kernels with the meclapítl against the curved, flattened stone to prepare the dough for fresh tortillas and memelas. Those were the perfect utensils for Grandma to grind the boiled corn kernels or nixtamál for fresh, homemade tortillas. Her comál, a rectangular griddle, was over the fogón, the cooking pit inside the kitchen. It was located on the right end of the pretíl, in which she burned the firewood to cook her family's meals.

The kitchen's interior was adorned with some jarritos, little clay pots, and a few frying pans hanging from the walls. A plastic tray pan with some clean cups on it was placed almost on the center of her pretíl with ceramic dishes next to it. Most of her old dishes were already chipped around the upper side after long use. Everything inside the kitchen seemed exaggeratedly organized, like an antique museum or something similar.

Eight wooden chairs surrounded the large dining table, where she always kept a lit candle right on the center. Next to the candle but on the right side was a large coffeepot. And a cinnamon tea jar followed a basket of baked corn bread that surrounded the three-legged molcajete in which she ground roasted green tomatillos, serrano peppers, garlic, onion, and half a dozen fresh jumiles to prepare Grandpa's favorite salsa.

And when it came to jumiles, "Yuck, disgusting," the majority would easily say. "How can you eat that? How can you eat those insects?" Good question. Jumiles were popular in the northern side of Guerrero, southern side of Morelos, and some other parts of Mexico. It was an old tradition mainly among the farmers. Their traditional meals in the farm consisted of boiled or refried beans, poultry, rice, eggs, pork, and dairy products, mainly Cincho cheese, some butter, and sour cream. And one or two times every year, they would enjoy some red meat.

Grandma's kitchen was organized but always half lit. Its lonely window was not enough for the sun's rays to reach the well-covered space. She increased the light inside the kitchen by lighting a small kerosene lamp, which she called candíl.

The house's roof was made of silver-gray asbestos, more shiny than colorful, reflecting the light as a glass from a long distance during a sunny day. The grayish roof had a single gutter in the right corner, where Grandma used to fill some buckets of water during rainy days to wash everyone's clothes at home. There was no running water through the pipes or anything like that in the house, which meant they had to fill the house's tank or pileta every day. They had no choice but to make several trips to the water well with two buckets per person to bring the precious liquid and to keep la pileta in good shape.

She chewed a handful of pecans that Grandpa had mixed with roasted sunflower seeds and salty peanuts from the kitchen table. "Umm, fried pork chops and bean soup for dinner," she said to herself in a loud voice.

Grandpa was still sitting outside, eating red-colored prickly pears. He'd heard Grandma talking inside the kitchen. "Hey, honey, are you calling me?" he asked while expulsing out of his mouth some seeds from the tasty fruit.

"Nope, I was just talking to myself," Grandma said while humming a tune.

"Well, I have no worries if you talk to yourself, but it worries me when you answer yourself." He was teasing her, laughing in a gentle and loving way.

"Oh please, for the love of Coatlicue!" Grandma exclaimed while recalling the Aztec goddess who protected females back then. Coatlicue was the mother of Huitzilopochtli, the god who advised the Aztecs to leave Aztlán in search of the Promised Land according to the Nahuatlan mythology in the Mexicas' beginnings.

"You should try las tunas rojas. The red prickly pears are the sweetest fruits these days," Grandpa said and paused for a brief moment before he continued talking. "I picked the ones that seemed best to me." He cleaned his mouth and mustache with the side of his right hand.

"I can see you still remember the prickly pear thing, ah?" Grandma said and smiled.

"Of course, sweetheart. I still remember those years. When the prickly pear time arrived, we first met each other, and then . . . we found ourselves frequently at the same spot, always with the same sweetened excuse—red prickly pears again," Grandpa said in a lovely voice.

"Oh, my darling!" Grandma exclaimed and exhaled.

"There are different kinds of prickly pears, some very good. But to me, they all tasted alike. They all tasted like red prickly pears. You should try some," Grandpa said and insisted more than once.

"I'm eating pecans. By the way, you've removed the nutshell very well. You really know how to use the nutcracker, I would say," Grandma said as a compliment.

"Thank you, honey. Some people didn't know how to do that," Grandpa said.

"You're welcome, my man," Grandma said.

"Woman, I gave myself out . . . I gave myself out since I first met you. I guess my soul is the only thing that belongs to me," Grandpa said, teasing her.

Then Grandma came out of the kitchen; she stood by the door. With hands over her hips, she gave him a serious look. And walking slowly toward him, she placed a kiss on his cheek, and then she returned quickly to the kitchen.

"Weren't you in the middle of something?" he asked and gave her a happy face.

"Nope, my man," she answered from the kitchen. Then they both laughed out loud from a certain distance.

Grandma was in her mid-fifties. She was a courteous woman with light brown skin, long straight dark brown hair with grays on it, a friendly smile, and narrow black eyes. She was a happy person highly proud of her family and her ancestors' culture. Always content of her native features, she was a direct descendant of a small group of natives who once walked down from the mountainous area out of the jungle, where her ancestors lived in seclusion for centuries. The Spaniards never conquered them. Small groups of natives escaped and set foot in La Sierra Madre del Sur; entered deep in the jungle, unexplored land in those days; and never returned to their ancestors' flourishing plazas. They remained non-mixed many years after La Conquista in 1500s. As a child, Grandma spoke Nahuatl, her ancestors' dialect, which she always called Mexicano because of the Mexica or Aztecs. It was after she met and married Grandpa in 1918 that she improved and dominated her Spanish.

At the age of nine, her happiness was tarnished for first time in her life. She became an orphan; the yellow fever swept half their community, including her mother, father, a sister, and three elder brothers. She, an elder sister, and her younger brother, who was five, were the only survivors from her house. That house that once was full of happiness was empty and hopeless for them. Soon after the impromptu and rapid burial, they moved into Simon's house, their uncle. They grew up under his care, and Simon became Papa Simon for them.

There was a time of raw struggle for everyone. Money and food were the typical problem. Grandma, her elder sister, and the younger brother turned out solid and strong. Even if there wasn't a single penny in their pockets, they worked hard to help Papa Simon raise his own family. Those were hard times. And undoubtedly, those difficult days built the solid character within them, not to mention Papa Simon's hard hand on it.

Simon frequently worked at any place and made his little money here and there. But he was always close at home to keep an eye on his family. He knew how to farm corn and some other seeds besides making mud bricks and handling wild horses. Several offers had been made to him to work in the silver mines of Taxco, but he always refused to take it in part because of the language. He spoke Nahuatl and very little Spanish, insufficient to handle a conversation.

"Your daughter is very beautiful," Grandpa said to Papa Simon when Grandpa first met Grandma's family.

"What did he say?" Papa Simon asked Grandma with concern when he couldn't understand Grandpa's language. Then Grandma half-translated it in Nahuatl. Papa Simon remained in complete silence, no words.

Moments later, he took a more serious posture, changed his attitude, and stood almost by the house's door. He told Grandma, "Please ask him to leave."

"But, Papa," Grandma complained quickly and nervously.

"Please ask him to leave. But he can come back in two months, and then we will talk about it . . . my child," Papa Simon said with soft words while looking into the young girl's eyes.

"Okay, Papa," Grandma responded with some relief and smiled toward Grandpa.

"Well, not to admire the attributes and the whole beauty of a woman is to be blind or to be a fool or both," Grandpa said politely, complimenting Grandma after he failed to exchange some words with Papa Simon. And of course, Grandma didn't translate those last words to him.

"There is always good luck and happiness somewhere. Most important is to be honest to each other. And there will be good luck somewhere for each of you." Grandma remembered Papa Simon's words when she left his house and married Grandpa. And those words were Papa Simon's blessing for the newly married young couple.

My grandma at eighty-five

From left to right: Aunt
Clarita, Uncle Antonio, Aunt
Rafaela, and Grandma

My dad at fourteen   My dad in 1973

My mom   Me at the age of six

CHAPTER FIVE

TIME TO GO HOME

Disoriented and scared after being hidden for a time that seemed an eternity for him, my father grabbed his bag with his left hand. He got up slowly after the scene had passed from his eyes and processed in his mind. And he started running away from the cornfield, trying to escape through the forest as quick as he could, leaving behind the sound and the moisture of his heavy breathing after facing the horror of his brothers' killing.

"There is no pain in the world worse than the one that you or someone else might have inside the soul," he said to me many years later.

At that point, he couldn't imagine his life without Narcizo and Guzman anymore. Restless, he moved through the dense forest, ignoring the strange noises from cicadas, crickets, woodpeckers, and all living creatures. That flying and running environment welcomed him under the large branches of tall trees. It was hard to walk and absurdly difficult to run over the narrow passage of the trail, where some tree branches hung almost to the ground. Countless holes and bumps were perfectly covered by thick layers of semi-decomposed organic matter, like dry leaves and crumbled remains of fallen branches, making it even harder to escape the odyssey without noise.

He obviously went to some trouble slipping away from the cornfield and running through the woods. He stopped to catch his breath in the middle of the lonely forest; hundreds of mosquitoes buzzing around him were voracious for his blood. The humidity in the fresh air was mixed with a strong smell of skunk urine. But inside his head, the sound of a clock was ticking from fast to faster. There was no time to lose. He needed to get home as soon as he could, he thought. And he ran again.

Back in the cornfield, the group of assassins never knew that someone was watching them, much less that the witness miraculously escaped alive. Unfortunately for them, my father recognized the Morales brothers. They set up the ambush, supplying information to the authorities to kill Epifanio and his two brothers.

At the other edge of the forest, my father finally found himself approaching the flowering bushes around the calmíl. The blazing sun was shining intensely over the asbestos panels on top of the house, reflecting its bright light almost like glass. A dog was barking unceasingly when he arrived to the surroundings of the little house. That dog was Xoloscuintle, mistakenly named for its species since the animal had a mix of Labrador breed. It had nothing to do with the other species and surprisingly the only dog in the farm.

Immediately, Grandpa became aware that something wasn't right. He got up from his chair and walked, turning his attention toward the edge of the calmíl, standing almost by the entrance of the patio. Grandma, who was inside her kitchen frying some pork chops and boiling beans into a large clay pot, worried for the dog's unusual barking, turned off the cooking fire and jumped outside the kitchen, surveying the place carefully with her eyes. Suddenly, they realized that their young son was coming to the house, running scared and sobbing with his clothes soaked in sweat. They both ran to bring the young man into the patio. Grandpa looked on him several times while Grandma was cleaning his face and neck soaked in sweat from the running using the lower part of her cooking apron.

My father bent forward to calm down Xoloscuintle and petted the loyal brown animal with his trembling right hand until the energetic dog silenced its cry. Something in the young man's expression told them there was something wrong there. "For god's sake, what happened?" Grandpa asked desperately. It was painfully clear that something was wrong; something wasn't right.

"What happened to you? Did someone hurt you?" Grandma asked lovingly, trying to comfort her young son.

"My . . . my brothers were killed," my father said with a sad and broken voice.

Although they clearly heard his answer, they asked him again. "What . . . what happened to your brothers?" Grandma asked desperately.

"Dad . . . Mom, Narcizo and Guzman are dead in the cornfield," my father answered disconsolately.

Grandma looked into his eyes, and she understood that her young son really meant it. As soon as those words reached Grandma's ears, tears ran over her cheeks. A strange feeling ran through her whole body, her face became inflamed, and a sob drowned her voice for a moment. Then she screamed to the infinite, crying from the death of her sons.

My father lifted his face; his sad eyes were brimming with tears. He was just a scared young boy, but he straightened up the best he could to explain what he saw in the cornfield. "Oh dear god! That's not possible!" Grandma yelled, crossing her fingers and looking up as if she was waiting for a divine answer from the sky.

"My good son . . . my little boy, you are fine," Grandpa said, comforting his young son while tears flowed down over his cheeks.

"What are we going to do, Papa?" my father asked, sobbing, almost crying.

"It's going to be all right, son," Grandma said, and she broke off and cried, holding Grandpa's right hand with her left hand and hugging her young son with her right arm at the same time. She could hear the strong whizzing of her son's breath coming out from the nostrils and mouth of the scared young boy.

"I'm sorry, Mom. I'm so sorry," my father said while his heart was pumping faster than ever that afternoon.

"Don't worry, my son, that's not your fault. I won't let anything bad happen to you. I promise it," Grandpa said.

Soon after those words, Grandpa's face turned pale, and he couldn't breathe. Grandma immediately ran to help him by bringing a plastic bowl full of water and a small bottle of alcohol from her kitchen while my father was trying to sit Grandpa on the chair that was next to them. She lifted the bowl full of cold water over Grandpa's head and poured the fresh liquid over his face and around his neck, holding an alcohol-soaked cloth near Grandpa's nostrils.

The panic lasted only a few minutes. And shortly after, he recovered in silence while trying hard to clear and focus his thoughts. He washed his face in cold water out of a plastic bucket and walked firmly, giving them the support of a husband and a father. He was fine; he was safe. He was breathing normally again.

"We can go now, darling," Grandpa said softly.

She hesitated for a few seconds, and then she moved her head slowly from side to side. There was something in his eyes that caught Grandma's attention. He was crying in silence, and he showed his sobs for the first time while his heart was pounding. "No . . . not yet. I want you to stay here, Odilon," Grandma said, concerned for his high blood pressure.

Grandpa listened and walked a few steps to move an old chair that was in front of his patio. He sat with some tears in his eyes, placing down his sad face on his hands, and gently cleaned his eyes using his fingertips. He was devastated. "I'm okay. I am ready. We'll need to pick up the bodies. Tomorrow in the morning, we'll find a messenger in El Salitre that can help us bring my other children from Apaxtla. For now, let's take five horses to the plantation," Grandpa said, referring to the rest of his children, who temporarily were residing in the outskirts of Apaxtla, a municipality located at the opposite side of his farm.

Grandma took a deep breath and shook her head slowly from side to side. Knowing Grandpa for thirty-seven years, there wasn't much to say. "Then let's go if you are fine. Please get on the horse," she said while keeping her eyes on the forest.

They all jumped on top of their horses and started riding to the cornfield with huge consternation. They left the house so quiet. Even Xoloscuintle was watching them in silence while sitting on his butt on the house's porch, where Grandma tied the dog's leash. Nobody could see them. Nobody could help them. They were on their own. There was no other people close by. The nearest village was El Salitre, located miles away. *After all, everyone deals with any kind of thing in their best understanding or in the best way, don't they?* they thought.

The vast green forest infested with all kinds of insects was the only way to the cornfield. Riding the horses under the immense canopy formed by the hanging branches of tall trees was not an easy task. Every few minutes, a dark cloud of flying insects swarmed around their faces, leaving behind an itchy discomfort around their nostrils and ears.

Just before sunset, they reached the cornfield. All the hopes to find someone alive were delusive. Afterward, they saw a dozen of bald-headed vultures spreading their large wings, flying around the area, watching down over the cornfield, keeping the eyes steady over the dead men. Then an ugly bloody scene ripped the bottom of Grandpa's heart. It was notorious the way so much blood had been spilled over that remote land, where justice was far beyond the law in the 1950s.

My father remained silent under the red sunset over the cornfield, where his two elder brothers lay dead, along with the other three men. Little by little, his mind returned quickly to what he'd seen earlier that fateful afternoon. "Dad . . . did you see?" my father asked.

"Please be quiet. No talking, please, my good boy," Grandma said in a low voice.

"Did you see what they've done?" my father asked, almost whispering.

Visible from a certain distance, four lifeless bodies lined up over the bloody ground. The cold silence gave no evidence that someone might be alive. Grandpa jumped out of his horse's back and helped Grandma do the same. Then he placed an aggressive look toward a curious coyote who was sneaking along the bloody surface in the cornfield. "Get out from here!" he shouted and threw stones at the animal, which ran into the wild. My father tied the horses' ropes to some large bushes around them.

For a moment, they just stayed there, comforting themselves quietly, almost in silence, thinking, shading their wet eyes to look at the sunset, which seemed grotesquely red instead of yellowish. Tragically, Grandpa used to say "red sunset" in the middle of the summer sky. But it was difficult to imagine that in a place like there one; with a rare and picturesque red sunset full of beauty, there was too much pain and heartbreak for them.

"They are right there," Grandpa finally spoke, holding Grandma by her shoulders and walking forward, approaching the bloody scene quietly and slowly. They all stood silently for a moment as they adjusted their eyes and mind to the lifeless scene. And they contented themselves with watching them from a close distance while my father was holding Grandma's right hand as a son's support.

Grandma's expressive eyes searched her husband's face and looked compassionately at him. Then she turned her eyes over the dead bodies again. What she saw made her blood run cold from toes to head. Her eyes looked over the bloody mess. There was blood all over the ground.

Grandpa looked in vain for any sign of life in those unfortunate men, who were quietly on the ground. Some of the dead bodies had wet dirt inside the mouth; their eyes were wide open and cloudy with fine dust. Everyone's face was covered with dirt, and their hair was hard and stiffened by old sweat, dirt, and dry blood. Grandpa swallowed a sob; his eyes became wet. And his voice was about to break.

"No one is alive," he sadly confirmed.

"For god's sake, that's not possible," Grandma said, sobbing and cleaning her eyes with her left hand. A cold wind blew through the plantation, shaking and constantly dropping down over her forehead the too large worn palm hat that was firmly attached to her head. The bloody scene made her restless. How horrible it was. How awful and painful it was to be there, watching everything that was important and full of meaning for her family. Now everything was turned into a broken reality, a broken dream upside down, just right there in front of them.

"I still don't understand all this," Grandpa said sadly while he partly combed the dead men's hair with his fingers and closed their eyes forever.

"Dad . . . I saw at least a dozen of soldiers and some civilians with them. The man in the green T-shirt was Juan Morales, and the one with the baseball cap was Chico Morales, his elder brother. I clearly recognized them, and both of them were talking with the soldiers," my father said.

"The Morales brothers . . . are you sure?" Grandpa asked surprisingly.

"Yes, Dad. I recognized them, no doubt about it," my father said firmly.

Grandpa didn't say anything for a few minutes; he was organizing his thoughts. Then he spoke in a low voice to his young son. "You must not, under any circumstances, talk about the Moraleses to Antonio or Mingo. I'll do it, my little son."

Grandma pulled out of her bag some white sheets and covered all the bodies one by one, wrapping them from head to toe. Then after a brief moment of silence, she had made the sign of the cross over them and commended them to heaven, to God.

It was painfully clear that life had been tough on both of them. But it wasn't finished with them yet. That awful day was just the beginning of their suffering.

"Oh god, this pain is huge for my soul today," she sadly said.

Guzman's body was second from left to right and then Calixto and Nacho. Omar was first. "Where is Narcizo?" Grandpa asked my father.

"Dad, my brother Narcizo is down the hill," my father answered.

"Where?" Grandpa asked.

"Dad . . . look straight at those trees down below. That's the spot where he is."

"Well, we'll go down there, son," Grandpa said. Narcizo was killed three hundred feet away from the north entrance to the cornfield.

"Little son, please bring the white horse with you and follow me. Let's pick up your brother," Grandpa said, looking carefully at his young son.

"Okay, Dad, I'll follow you." My father immediately obeyed.

"Honey, let's bring Narcizo over here," Grandpa said to Grandma cordially, trying to find some comfort from his wife.

"Oh god, darling," she said with a disoriented look in her eyes. From the appearance of Narcizo's body, Grandpa instantly knew that his son was tortured big time before he was killed. He always was a remarkable boy as Grandma said. She felt a painful sadness for him. The young Narcizo was lifeless, alone, helpless, just him downhill. He was dead in the middle of the jarilla bushes. The flowering spot was where the assassins left him lying down on the ground on his back, facing the sky.

Grandpa and Grandma spent a few minutes praying for the soul of their dead son. Shortly after, they both lifted Narcizo's body and placed the young man on top of the horse's saddle. "Please, darling, wrap the fabric sheet around his body and pull the rope tighter," Grandma said softly.

"Can we wait until morning, Papa?" my father asked, concerned. "It's already late to take them home."

"No, son, we'll have to do this tonight. We won't go home. We'll take them to El Salitre for the burial," Grandpa said and paused briefly. "I'm sorry, little son."

"I'm really scared," Grandma said while pointing at the forest.

"What are you scared of?" Grandpa asked.

"I don't know. It's just a bad feeling," Grandma answered and paused. "I'm scared of whatever is up there or down the hill." She paused again, this time scanning with her eyes the dense forest around them. "Walking through the forest at night . . . I don't know. I just don't know."

"There is no other way. We must do it tonight," Grandpa insisted.

My father hissed.

"What is it?" Grandma asked in a low voice.

"Nothing, probably an animal," Grandpa replied while looking at the bushes nearby.

"There. Over there, Dad . . . a roadrunner!" my father exclaimed.

"See, I told you, nothing to be afraid. It was just a bird," Grandpa said calmly.

Then they headed straight uphill to pick up the rest of the bodies and Grandpa's horses. There was so much to do, and it was getting late. Suddenly, a few flocks of small birds came out of the bushes, flying near above them, crossing the reddish color of the sunset through the sky, disappearing slowly into the vast canopy of the forest.

CHAPTER SIX

LIFELESS CARGO

Because of the hot weather, Grandpa suggested that the bodies be taken immediately to the burial place. And once in the small village, he would find someone to take the bad news to Calixto's, Nacho's, and Omar's families. Grandpa couldn't hide his pain. His heart was totally broken. He walked slowly and faced his wife, placing his arms on Grandma's shoulders and kindly kissing her forehead. "One day we'll be all together again!" he exclaimed, comforting her. Grandma opened her mouth to say something, but she couldn't. She didn't know what to say, and she just took a deep breath, squeezing her eyes not to cry.

"We have to take the bodies out of the cornfield tonight. I will come in a few days to pick the working tools," he said softly.

"You're fine. I guess I could agree with you," Grandma told him.

"Well." Grandpa paused, trying to figure out how he would explain this to his friends' families. "Well, they are dead. And I need to take them. There is no time right now to bring their families here," Grandpa said to Grandma.

"It sounds awful, but it's the best way," Grandma said. She took a deeper breath this time. And Grandpa was still trying to figure out how this horrible thing happened and why while his horse was farting and snorting at his side.

The three dead men—Nacho, Calixto, and Omar—weren't related to one another. But they were friends who used to come to work in Grandpa's farm every year. They all belonged to the nearest village of El Salitre, a small pueblo just fifteen minutes away from the cemetery and no more than twelve miles from Grandpa's cornfield.

"They probably were still out there running away," Grandpa said, pointing to the hills in the south side of the plantation, referring to the assassins.

"Just when everything seemed to be going better," Grandma said.

"Yes . . . when everything seemed to be fine," Grandpa agreed.

"These poor men didn't deserve to die like this," Grandma said and paused. "But now . . . they're angels of heaven."

Grandpa cleared his throat a few times before he removed the wide hat out of his head. And rising his right hand slowly over his head, he ran his fingertips through his smooth hair and brushed his grays three or four times. The sun went down, and part of the cornfield was reflecting the reddish and semi-golden color of the sunset among the corn leaves. He wouldn't know where to begin. There were a lot of ideas in his mind but not one specific to put into practice. *They got a little behind. That's right*, he thought and stopped hesitating.

"Please, darling, come help me," he said to Grandma cordially.

"Hey!" Grandma yelled while trying to scare something out of her head. A bumblebee buzzed in front of her face. Grandma blew the humming insect away far out of her sight.

"Are you okay?" Grandpa asked her.

"Yes, I'm fine," she answered and paused. "It's just the hum of insects in the cornfield."

"I need your help," Grandpa said.

"Olivo, please come hold the horse for your father," Grandma said to her young son.

"Okay, Mom," he said.

They examined the condition of the dead men and managed to turn the bodies upside down one by one on top of each horse. The arms and head hung over the left side of each equine; the legs were hanging on the opposite direction while their bellies were holding the entire weight of their own dead body. They tightened the lifeless men firmly against the horses' saddles with some nylon cords.

Sadly, the main slope of those valleys was marked with one wooden cross in memory of the fallen men. Grandpa and my father dug a shallow hole in the ground and placed the improvised cross into it. A lonely cross with a small pile of stones around it was left on the cornfield like a memorial monument, a mourning gesture, or simply an announcement to possible passersby that some people died there.

Suddenly, strong waves of wind blew through the cornfield, lifting the large leaves of corn glamorously into the air like obeying a certain magic and undulating happily under some source of dancing music from another dimension. Little by little, daylight was vanishing over the cornfield. But the sky didn't get dark until late. For that time, the sky wasn't dark yet; actually, it was more red than dark.

But the sky was nearly dark. Soon the moon and stars would witness Grandpa's journey through the forest.

With some difficulties and against the wind, they started walking forward to reach a narrow trail uphill. The old trail was rebuilt a few generations ago to drag logs since that forest grew trees with a gigantic height. But in the ancient times, the original trail was once the main trading route for the natives. But that was long ago. Usually, in the rainy season, the forest hid an immense part of the trail under its vast canopy, as well as a large number of fauna and flora—animals that we didn't even know anything about in part because many of those creatures were nocturnal and plants that we didn't know yet.

Despite all the disadvantages around them, they walked along the edge of the woods, exploring and searching the historical trail that was practically hidden in the forest. They kept walking until they came to a spot that they liked. They stopped for a couple of minutes and looked at one another with a silent look that meant everything. Then they started to reach the edges of their mind; the dark side of the forest was already within them.

That was a little more than a rough dirt trail into the forested woods of a wonderful and mysterious nature. That was more like an entrance to an unknown world, a place whose look at night none of them could have imagined. They knew about the existence of certain poisonous creatures that flourished and grew from small to an unknown size, such as fatal spiders and scorpions almost the size of a peanut having the ability to kill a human being, countless types of poisonous snakes capable of inflicting painful wounds by injecting deadly venom. Undoubtedly, that place was the boundary between the real and the unknown, where the emerald green of the forest turned dark at night.

The forest was infested with thousands of insatiable mosquitoes, biting here, biting there, and disturbing the horses. They were provoking the equines to react violently from time to time. Nothing seemed to stop those flying bugs or exterminate them. It looked like all the flying insects were swarming toward them. Wherever they went, the hungry bugs were there, following them with an insatiable appetite for fresh blood.

In ancient times, the old-timers had traveled that trail through the woods to reach El Salitre coming from Puerta Grande Farm but only in daylight. Many years later, the same trail would be in front of my grandpa and his family at night, like a completely unknown world for all of them. Nobody liked it. That place made them vulnerable and exposed to any type of danger inside the woods.

The dark of the night ruled under the large canopy of giant trees, and the stars were lighting the immense sky. They disappeared into the forest, wearing leather sandals that they called huaraches, passing through the rough terrain, and walking forward through the night. Naturally, peculiar things abound in the woods day and night. A big part of the wildlife in the forest was nocturnal, and if you had an imaginary mind—let's say a fascination for the perverse, vague, and evil and undoubtedly a vivid eye for the unknown—then, my friend, the forest would be a perfect scenario to experience the real horror of the night. Nocturnal creatures may fascinate a good number of people but may scare a large number of others. It might differ depending on the case, but nocturnal animals had a scary reaction to escape from human presence.

Flirting with the grotesque and conquering the unpredictable, anyone would see strange things in the woods at night. There was no doubt about it. You would see whatever your mind wanted you to see—crooked tree branches that resembled people hanging from the neck, weird tree shadows that looked like people watching you, small bushes that looked like multilegged creatures or giant tarantulas, accompanied by sounds like someone's footsteps were behind you. And it would creep through the night; no matter how macho you can be, goosebumps would raise your fears. It would increase your blood pressure, turning your nerves into a knot under your chin, suffocating your chest, and making even worse the thoughts of your sharp mind to the point that you didn't want to be walking last on the line, not even first because you could never know what was ahead or behind you. Certainly, a big number of wild creatures lived in the natural environment of the forest, some nesting on the ground, some in the hollows of trees; but either way, they were skillfully feeding their offspring with insects, seeds, and berries and taking care of them with the best defensive instinct.

The perception of what they were seeing in the dark, the strange sounds of nocturnal animals, the cracking sounds of the trees, the alien shapes of certain plants at night, and being far from home, taking five dead bodies to the burial site—that could have been glancing the edge of the underworld. "Watch your step," Grandpa repeatedly said to Grandma.

"Don't worry, I'm fine," she said. Even if she was in pain, these words were common in her vocabulary.

"Son, watch your mom and yourself," Grandpa said.

"Okay, Dad," my father responded most of the time.

The horses were moving slowly over the right passage that followed the course of the narrow trail into the natural darkness of the forest. The only thing hanging from Grandpa's right hand was a single oil lamp partly lighting the hidden trail. Grandma and my father followed him, lighting the rest of the path with a small flashlight on my father's hands.

Though the moon was bright, it seemed brighter than ever. There wasn't much light under the forest canopy that continually changed its aspect because of the thick moisture in the air while the darkness ruled the night serenely. Everywhere they looked, a haze of darkness covered both sides of the trail through the forest.

The air was so full of mist that the view of close objects on the ground was merely poor. The humidity in the air as a result of haze and moisture made the night considerably colder. They found themselves alone, silently walking through the dark forest with their own resources and skills. They had a single oil lamp, a little flashlight, and five horses carrying dead bodies.

There was a rough spot on the trail where they skipped several bumps and rotten tree branches over the ground. That particular part into the forest seemed a spooky picture of hell. They walked through it awfully quiet, which allowed them to hear clearly the strange animal noises coming from the back of those trees and bushes growing on the edge of the cliff. But every one of them seemed to ignore the sounds of the night into the woods. Noisy cicadas and crickets chirping somewhere in the trees seemed to have a concert night, followed by the lights of huge lightning bugs flying under the forest canopy. Strange buzzing sounds of nocturnal animals and insects were coming from everywhere as if repelling the human presence around or something similar. There was an intermittent crashing and tapping sound coming farther down the cliff as if someone was hammering wood or some solid object. But it wasn't possible in the darkness to figure out what it was.

They walked three miles desperately under the gigantic dark umbrella of the dense tropical forest. All around them was obscurity; just the light from the oil lantern was visible from a certain distance. Strange winged insects were attracted by the light's glow, flying around and roasting themselves with the lamp's heat. *Even if the forest is a dangerous place at night, wild beasts more destructive than humans don't exist among those valleys and mountains*, Grandpa thought.

Finally, after forty or fifty minutes had passed, they were out of the forest. A few hours of slowly walking brought them to the edge of a vast plain. Everything was quiet in front of them. The moon was shining, lightning far away, distant in the sky. There was enough moon out there in the sky, enough light to reflect the large silhouettes of the horses and the lifeless load on top of their mounts. They walked along the tree line, reaching the lower side of the hill along the course of the almost dry stream, crossing over the grainy sand of the riverbank in which fresh water had disappeared long ago precisely in that part of the quiet stream. Minutes later, they approached the high plains above.

A plain terrain in front of their naked eyes was in sight. That land was even, well flattened by Mother Nature, nearly seven miles wide, and they needed four or five hours to cross it. When they finally stepped on flat ground, the horses sped up slightly and galloped faster, forcing them to hold the horses' reins to decrease the galloping. Obviously, making them walk faster would get them tired sooner. The well-trimmed trail in front of them seemed as if it would never end. But besides the adversity and his own struggle, Grandpa tried to be optimistic, spreading some motivation to his wife and son. "We are almost there!" Grandpa exclaimed, pointing toward the lonely hill by the end of the large plain.

"Wow!" my father exclaimed and paused. "It seems far away." He showed slight signs of tiredness.

"Come on, I need you. You're my hero son. We'll need to support each other. You guys are all I have," Grandpa said while trying to reach Grandma's attention.

"And so do I," Grandma responded.

They disturbed the sleeping birds nesting in the bushes as they walked along the well-formed passage on the trail, which the people from surrounding villages used to maintain, trimming or removing large plants out of the dense vegetation that clothed the plain terrain and leaving the walking trail visible from a considerable distance, even in the night under a full moon. There were a freshwater reserve surrounded by limestone and an old willow next to it on the right side of the wider part of the trail. They stopped there for almost one hour to rest and refresh themselves, allowing the horses to drink water.

They sat in the cooling quiet place as the stars seemed to move slowly out from the mantle of dark sky. Cicadas and crickets sang repeatedly the same annoying tune through the dark of night as if those creatures followed them with their endless concert once again. Looking up, they could see a full moon shining under the immense sky. "Dad, look up. Look up. Look up to the sky," my father said hurriedly.

"It's a falling star, my son!" Grandpa exclaimed, watching the sky and tracking a flying light crossing part of the sky.

"Certainly, I think that might be the soul of my brothers around us," my father said with high hopes in heaven.

"Yes, they will always stay around us, my little son," Grandma said, comforting her young son.

"Mom, what happens to a dead man's spirit when the body dies?" my father asked, full of curiosity.

"Well, we could say . . . umm, if the person was good in life, the person will go with Christ. The person could walk with our Lord," Grandma responded and gave her son a hug.

Minutes later, they would be moving again. The horses began to follow Grandpa slowly, who was trying to reach the desired end of the trail through his unexpected journey. The horses were tired evidently with a heavy load on their backs. All of them were close to reaching the village, Grandpa thought.

Grandma's feet were swollen significantly. She was exhausted, but her shattered heart remained in one piece.

After a little while, Grandpa broke the silence as usually it was. "Do you see that?" he asked Grandma, pointing straight ahead with his right hand.

"Yes, we are getting close to El Salitre," she said and shivered a little.

"Thank god. Mercy to ourselves and our horses!" Grandpa exclaimed.

"God's mercy, it's the most precious gift," Grandma said.

"Well, we had gotten far out our home, where there was no one near to help us. What could we have done without God's help?" Grandpa said and looked up the immensity above them.

"You are a brave man, Dad," my father said and paused. "Me too. I'm brave."

"Sure, we all are that, my son," Grandpa said.

"And for those bad men that killed my brothers, I will give them what they deserve . . . one day . . . one day," my father said with some signs of revenge.

"God will punish them. Let me tell you, dear son, violence will make problems bigger. We don't have to get our hands dirty with someone else's blood. Justice will come from God at any time," Grandpa said while he seemed to look for something beyond the eyes of his young son.

"But they killed my brothers. We can't stay like this. We'll have to avenge their death. We have to be even, square, with those bastards," my father said with a thin voice angrily, about to break into a silent cry.

"Indeed, your father is right, my little boy. I know . . . I know the way you feel. But God sees everything with his eyes, my good son. I want you to be a good man, not an evil man," Grandma said to her young son, embracing him with the sweetest gesture of a mother.

"Mom, we can't wait for it. Whatever belongs to heaven, it's for heaven. Whatever happens around here, it's from here," my father said and paused for a few seconds. "Is there any justice in it?"

"Tell you what, it scares me to think about revenge. That's not what we want, son. Justice will come from heaven as we all believe in it," Grandpa said, comforting his son.

"Justice? How can there be justice in it, Dad?" my father asked while they all kept walking. "They were innocent people."

"Our destiny comes to us from heaven. It has been written far away, from beyond the stars. Dear son, you've been through a lot, but it's God's will. Please have faith. Wait, be patient, be a calm man, don't ever hurry," Grandpa said, firmly convinced of his faith in God.

"Indeed, divine justice will come out at the end. It always does," Grandma said and paused briefly. "Son, let me tell you, this life is like a restaurant. No one goes out without paying. Got it?"

"Okay," my father agreed quietly.

"Your mother is correct. I had pictured in my mind the same idea many times. Even if it's hard, we'll leave things in God's hands," Grandpa said.

"We had always depended on God for everything, my good son. And we will continue in the same way," Grandma said.

My father didn't say anything. He just listened to his parents silently. For he was like living in a different world surrounded by a cloud of darkness.

Meanwhile, at the far end of the sky where daylight began, a dense radiance like a shooting star broke through the sky dome. And once again, a new day was born. Then the morning's sunshine bathed the small town. The morning finally came to El Salitre, and they were just next to it.

There was a great plain near the village with a dense and extensive forest at one side, almost by the edge of the small village, where the trail broke and opened into a crooked, dusty street to the left, simplifying the village's main entrance. Typical houses of sun-dried adobe partly lined both sides of the main street. A white chapel was visible far out, almost by the end of the street.

They finally arrived to El Salitre, and soon their proximity to the village created curiosity. Even some angry dogs barked toward them. A clean-shaven young man in his thirties, with some hint of beard under the skin as was common to most people in the region, and his pregnant woman were the first people who intended to help them. She whispered something in her husband's ear. Then they both walked toward the newcomers, unconditionally demonstrating their support.

As the local young man moved forward to lend a hand to Grandpa, a vague flash of memory came to him in his son Guzman's voice. *Dad!* That was the wisp in his mind for a second or two, his dead son's voice.

"When meeting new people, it is polite to speak out your name," Grandpa said self-consciously.

There was a square plaza right in the middle of the large street intentionally built to establish the village's center. It was shaded with some tamarind trees and tall pomegranate bushes planted right on the center of the wide street. A wooden gazebo was a silent witness to many conversations under its shade. Some grocery stores adorned the square place with hand-carved doors and iron-barred windows in considerable intervals. La Pantera Barbershop, with its typical white-blue striped pole steady over the entrance, was open daily from Monday to Saturday but not on Sundays. It was the last business open at the end of every day.

Soon their unexpected arrival would be the center of attraction, arousing the curiosity of the people in El Salitre, with a crowd dismayed by the situation. "Last time that I was here, the village seemed smaller," Grandpa said in a low voice to an old man while walking and approaching the village plaza.

"We have some more people this year. Neighbors from surrounding areas established here," that old man responded.

"Umm, that's great! The village is getting bigger!" Grandpa exclaimed with a nice expression.

"Yes, sir," the same old man agreed.

As soon they began to cross the square, more people started appearing outside their homes, some out of curiosity, some for unconditional help. But in the end, everybody had the same thought, expressing their condolences and giving their support, like the old man who was outside the barbershop; he ran to his house and brought clean clothes to replace Grandpa's, Grandma's, and their young son's dirty clothes, stained with dry blood from lifting the dead bodies. "Here, here, try this. Change your clothes," that old man said while he proceeded distributing the clothes among them.

They remained in silence without speaking a word until Grandpa thanked the old man. "Good Samaritan, God bless you!" he exclaimed.

And rapidly, more and more people crowded the place. Some of the supporters lowered their heads as a sign of respect for the fallen men. Indeed, people who had never seen them before demonstrated a cordial affection and favorable support. And all of them professed goodwill toward their unfortunate neighbors.

As the crowd gathered on the main street, some teenagers went from door to door, spreading the bad news and asking people for some help. Some families waited inside their houses, watching them from hidden lookouts. Instinctively, everyone knew what to do and what was needed to help others in most cases.

So bad news ran quick into town. Calixto, Nacho, and Omar were natives from El Salitre. And now they were truly dead.

As it grew late in the morning, the horses fell into a desperate mood after walking the entire cold and bitter night. Lucky for them, they didn't fall in a ditch or in some cliff the night before. They all walked through the village. At the moment, it was difficult to hear the cracking rhythm of the horses' hoofbeats. More people joined them to the cemetery while walking through the rough terrain on the street.

The three dead men from El Salitre were passing for the last time into the main street. Every member of their families struggled to understand what had happened to them. The kiss of the sun began to warm all hearts while five dead men were taken to the cemetery.

A lonely voice came from somewhere, from the left side of the street. "Anyone of you would like to have a cup of coffee?" an old lady asked while watching them from her house's front porch.

"Did you say coffee?" Grandpa asked.

"Right. Would you like some coffee?" the old lady asked from the same spot where she was standing.

"Coffee? Yes. Please give me some. Coffee would be great!" Grandpa exclaimed.

"Coffee for you and hot milk chocolate for your family," she said while bringing the warm drinks in large plastic cups.

"Thank you. God bless you," Grandma said, being the first to thank the old lady, who showed respect for their loss. The tears came softly, and Grandma began to cry again before she even tasted her hot cocoa.

Minutes later, they approached the well-cared-for cemetery's entrance in the company of a good number of people. It was a magnificent cemetery without a name, fenced with stones piled up about shoulder high. There was a small altar inside the little white chapel built over the cemetery's entrance. And the image of Jesus Christ, crucified over the wooden cross on top of its roof, was truly remarkable.

A lady in her fifties with a puritan appearance and wrapped with a black veil around her head was reading passages of comfort from the Bible. She walked toward the cemetery and opened the entrance's gate, blessing all the dead men one by one, before they proceeded into the cemetery. Some people marveled at seeing the altar and the image of our Lord attached to the wooden cross and listened attentively to the Bible readings.

Soon they addressed themselves in a wide-open space in one of the empty corners inside the cemetery. A short time later, people cut the ropes around the dead bodies and carefully placed them on the ground, laying them next to one another over the brown blanket that Calixto's mother had spread on the grass. At the moment, the bodies were pale and stiff with visible dark spots over the skin. The mourners had laid them on the ground as they were, unwashed and dirty. Grandma folded their arms over their chest and covered everyone's face with a large cloth.

Meanwhile, the horses were turned loose to feed in the spiky leaves of tender vegetation, hanging their heads and eating fresh grass that was reflecting the morning's glittering dewdrops over the stems and spikes under the shiny sun. According to the inherited traditional beliefs, the relatives were supposed to keep awake for the dead men, giving them a more appropriate funeral ceremony. But in this case, it would be an exception. The mourners would be just praying for the unfortunate men's soul and bury them before the corpses fell into a decomposed stage from the heat of the weather.

Three men using a sharp, pointed stone marked and cut the unbroken carpet of fresh green grass over the burial soil and lined up five rectangles on the ground. "I'm going to dig the graves," Grandpa said while approaching them.

"No, sir. Don't worry, we'll do all the digging," one of them said.

"Thank you. We really appreciate all your help and support," Grandpa said softly.

Then they started digging by hand, using crowbars and shovels to remove the fresh dirt under the grass. A tall and skinny guy from the crowd organized the working men in small groups of five or six to dig each of the last resting place for the fallen men while the rest of the mourners were praying and comforting themselves. There were no coffins; the dead men would be buried in the same clothes they died the day before, all bloody and dirty. People stood on their feet, praying the Lord's Prayer all together around the unfortunate men, whose dead bodies lay silent on the ground.

A small group of four or five attractive young women hardly reaching their twenties curiously walked toward my father, who was next to his parents. "Where is he?" the one who seemed to be the youngest of them kindly asked my father.

Her name was Pilar—Pilli as my father used to call her. She was one of the prettiest women from that village. Besides all her beautiful mestizo attributes, she seemed to have a wonderful smile complemented by a black birthmark as a natural tattoo just above the right side of her mouth, decorating the smooth tanned skin of her face and matching the beauty of her long combed hair that fell in waves down her back.

"He is over there, the second from right to left," my father said while walking them toward the dead bodies.

Somehow Pilar managed to remove from her neck the worn scapular with the image of the Virgin of Guadalupe stamped on one side of the Catholic relic. And she begged to God for the eternal rest of Narcizo's soul. She remained for a few minutes prostrated on the ground as she was asking God to hear her supplication. Powerless with some tears in her eyes, she finally stood up, and then she bent forward and placed the blessed scapular into Narcizo's hands. She walked away in complete silence, holding her tears back in her eyes.

Meanwhile, my father returned to his parents' side. "Who is she, son?" Grandma asked my father curiously.

"She is Pilli, a good girl, decent and very kind," my father answered.

"Pilli? But Pilli who?" Grandma asked and insisted to know more about the young woman who approached Narcizo's grave in such a loving way.

"Mom, she is Pilar . . . Pilar Tecocuahtzi, Narcizo's girlfriend," my father responded.

"Umm, we didn't know that," Grandma said.

"Mom, he was in love with her."

"Let the rain of our prayers wet our lands, our hearts, with God's blessing this time," an old woman said from the crowd, interrupting my father's brief conversation with his curious mom.

And then everyone prayed, praising God in a loud voice. "Our Father, which art in heaven! Hallowed be thy name! Thy kingdom come! Thy will be done on earth as it is in heaven. Peace today, tomorrow, and forever!" People kept praying over and over.

There was a moment of silence. The bodies were lowered down slowly into the empty graves using nylon ropes and some kind of wide rubber bands. There was an intense smell of fresh blood around the lifeless bodies that even an unexpected uniformed visitor arrived to the burial site. Authorities in the village were almost useless as they were in some other towns. Just the big-mustached sheriff and one of his few deputies showed up to the cemetery just to witness the sad event. "Kind of hot, eh?" the sheriff said while approaching them.

Someone hummed very low from the crowd.

"My deepest condolences to all of you, and if there is something that we can do for you, people, you know where to find me," the sheriff said and quickly left the scene riding his horse with one of his assistants by his side. "And if there is something that we can do for you . . ." That was everything he said, pretty much the same thing, nothing remarkable, just the typical "So sorry. We are with you. We will keep you updated. We will find out who did it." And blah, blah, blah. Nothing helpful because none of those deaths were investigated properly by the authorities.

Life there in the 1950s was unlike anywhere else in the country's farming regions. Justice was far away beyond the law. Many men were killed there back in time. Some single women were forcedly taken for marriages against their own will. And at the end, the local authorities didn't even have files for those crimes.

Justice—as far as I can tell, very little—seemed to have changed in those remote farms. The political system in these days hardly set a strong foot through its representatives in those lands. So people still living almost in the same way as their ancestors lived sixty or seventy years ago in those lands forgotten by time. Suddenly, the words of my father came to me when he asked Grandpa to avenge his brothers' death: "Justice, that might be in heaven or somewhere else. In the cities, most of the time, the offenders are punished by the law but not in those remote farms where we came from."

In an organized manner, people around the graves ritualized the burial of those five men traditionally, praying constantly for the eternal rest of the dead. Some mourners prayed loudly on their knees, others facing the ground and praying in a low voice. It was a silent moment once again. Grandpa was assigned to be the first person to pour a shovel of fresh dirt over the dead bodies that lay flat at the bottom of each grave.

It was around noon when Grandpa put the first shovel of fresh dirt into one of the graves. He started with Guzman, his hardworking son, his hardworking kid, and then his remarkable boy Narcizo. Calixto, Nacho, and Omar followed them as his unforgettable young friends. "God bless all of you!" Grandpa exclaimed, loud enough to be heard. And silently, he retraced his footsteps to bring his family to the edge of the graves.

Grandma tried to hold back her tears by closing her eyes and squeezing it for a short time. But she couldn't. Little by little, the bodies were out of sight from their families and friends, who sadly were standing right over the edge around the graves. A few more guys were using wide shovels to fill the graves with dirt, placing fresh colorful flowers on top.

When the burial ceremony ended, the priest sprinkled holy water on top of the new graves and blessed it in the name of the Almighty. Then he walked back to the church, thanking some of the people for the big support and comfort. "Thank you, all of you, for coming. God will increase your prosperity as he wishes," that religious man said and walked away with some of the mourners.

Guzman was twenty-five and Narcizo barely seventeen. Guzman left a young widow with his two children, girl and boy, Roselia, who was barely two years old, and baby Juan, who was just two months old. Narcizo left a beautiful girlfriend, Pilar or Pilli.

At the grave site, the mourners recited a Padre Nuestro and a Santa Maria. Some of them had tears in their eyes. They were crying.

Grandma walked toward the graves of her fallen sons. She knelt next to the right side of the rectangular grave filled with Guzman's body and prayed for the soul of her dead sons. "You will be living in my heart for the rest of my days," Grandma sadly said. An old woman came from the other side of the grave and wiped Grandma's tears with a white cloth.

"Excellent!" a woman said loudly from a short distance and paused. "That's very, very interesting. Wow . . . wow . . . wow!" The people turned their attention to the sweet female voice. A strange woman in her thirties was hardly walking, approaching the new graves. She was beautiful. She had long brown hair and light brown eyes. But she should have been out of her mind to appear laughing in the cemetery. She came to say who she was undoubtedly.

"I . . . am . . . I . . . am . . . I am Lucy, a very well-defined demonstration of beauty around here . . . and everywhere, my dear friends. Quite the specimen, don't you think, guys?" that strange woman asked while moving her hands sexily over the well-formed structure of her body. There was a brief silence, and then her beautiful eyes surveyed the crowd coolly. "I was at home, yes, at home." She paused while showing a brief attack of hiccups. "Yes, I was at home when the bad news reached and tested the most important part of my ears, my tympanum. Wow . . . wow! I can't believe this at all. Me? A widow twice without even being married once. Oops! How absurd it is." She laughed unpleasantly, covering her mouth intermittently with the palm of her right hand while she was stumbling around between drunk and sober but more of the former and acting like a smart and fool girl at the same time.

Lucy was evidently drunk with a huge resentment in her heart. She wore a gold pendant, a unique piece of old jewelry that had belonged to her mom when her mother was young, and Lucy had inherited it upon her mother's demise long ago. The beautiful lady tripped over her feet. Kindly, one of the villagers grabbed her arm and help her sit on the ground next to Omar's grave. "Gracias . . . osito!" Lucy exclaimed while the supposed teddy bear walked away, ignoring the flirting of the lady.

Minutes later, the woman who showed up laughing was sobbing and crying. In fact, Lucy was Omar's longtime girlfriend. She owned the only cantina in El Salitre. With her gaze lost in the distance, she remained sitting on the ground next to her boyfriend's grave.

"I . . . I asked you to marry me. Anyways, I'm too poor to buy my own bread." She paused and sobbed. "But . . . but . . . I'm light and dark at the same time," she said without sense. Lucy paused again and, this time, cried louder. "But you told me that I didn't live a decent life. Omar . . . you knew my life. I own the cantina, but it doesn't make me a bad woman. That's only part of my job inside here." She paused, longer this time, pointing and tapping the upper left side of her chest. "Inside here, I have feelings like you, like anybody else. Hell yeah. You said that I wasn't good enough for you to marry me," Lucy said sadly. "Lovely bastard." Some ladies were trying to comfort the sad woman. She kept talking about some anecdotes between her and Omar.

Among the men in the crowd was one called Temo, a distinguished and quiet guy with a simple but notorious appearance. He was a man with considerable height and vivid eyes nailing into the distance like looking for something and nothing at the same time. According to some villagers, he was the most interesting dude in El Salitre. And they fondly nicknamed him "the Judge." "Dangerous man," an old lady from the crowd whispered close to Grandpa's ears, pointing her bony and shaky forefinger with some discrepancy toward Temo, who was approaching Grandpa.

The mysterious man was holding a toothpick with the right side of his mouth and, from time to time, playing with it, moving it between the upper side of his tongue and against the interior of his chubby cheek. He examined Grandpa with frank interest while approaching him. Then he spat out the toothpick, cleared his throat a few times, and coughed softly as he spoke. The Judge, he liked to be called when it came to nicknames. However, he introduced himself to Grandpa with a few spoken words but surprisingly with very well-educated manners. He carefully wiped the sweaty palm of his hand over the soft fabric of his shirt and kindly extended it toward Grandpa.

The stranger shook Grandpa's hand and held it for a little bit. Every single gesture in the man's face was engraved on Grandpa's mind. His approach was full of grace and tranquility, as well as confidence and self-control. Then with some significant discretion, he placed in Grandpa's hand a piece of white paper with a few written words on it. "Here, there is a written message for you," Temo said while looking straight into Grandpa's eyes.

Grandpa, with trembling hands, folded the paper and put it in his right pocket. He seemed highly nervous and confused as though he had expected more words that had not been said from the curious man. "Okay," he said with a soft voice.

"We must get all of them—I mean, all those rats," Temo said in a low tone, almost whispering to Grandpa. But his voice trembled with anger when he saw all the pain surrounding the victims' family.

Grandpa looked at him and made an effort to stop or avoid that conversation. But it was badly comforting; it gave him an illusion of help to put the pieces together in the puzzle and to get even with his loss. It was a splendid idea to equalize things, a great hope of revenge in the inner part of his mind, in the deepest corner of his broken heart. There was a possible satisfaction of revenge in front of him, a dark relief—but still a relief. And he seemed not at all uncomfortable with the natural reaction that Temo's words produced in his brain. That was something similar to *I like it, but it scares me.*

Anyways, what could be more catastrophic for him in this life? he asked himself. Even if Grandpa had made his choice since the first moment he faced the death of his two sons, inside his mind, the written note that the stranger gave him was a nice package of possibilities.

Temo, "the Judge" as he was vulgarly known, was a very good hunter. And he chose to make a living by hunting others, by hunting bad guys. *But more deaths, they wouldn't solve anything. Nothing would bring his dead sons back to life again,* Grandpa thought.

After recovering from the surprise, Grandpa analyzed quickly what he had heard from Temo while blowing and wiping his nose. Soon they began to speak in a low voice. "Mister, right or wrong, I have done no more than what I got paid for, a tooth for a tooth, an eye for an eye," Temo said.

"Well, we all have different ways of thinking about others, even about ourselves. But everyone knows how to fix things in their own way," Grandpa said.

"There is nothing we have not seen before without pain," Temo said in a very low voice to Grandpa.

Grandpa looked in silence and gave him a wink and a thin smile, trying to place his own thoughts away from any manipulation. "Well, I guess you have everything you need in this place," Grandpa said and paused. "I mean, to make living."

"I am so sorry for your loss. If you want, we can arrange a chat in the future. Lucy's bar is where you can find me most," Temo said.

"Uh-huh." Grandpa slightly nodded.

"Anyways, what's left from them?" Temo asked and paused.

Then he slowly looked Grandpa right into his eyes, emphasizing the answer to his own question. "You!" he exclaimed softly.

Temo knew very well how to persuade people when they were weak. *That's the right moment*, he always thought.

That weary afternoon dragged away minute after minute, hour after hour, so slowly. The sun began to burn so rapidly that people shook their hands fervently as a sign of unconditional support as they started to vanish little by little after the burial ceremony. In the middle of fraternal hugs, some tears fell down. Grandpa and Grandma both stared at the sky as they stared at the new future. And little by little, their pain would dissolve into the endless procession of difficult slow days and nights, they thought.

CHAPTER SEVEN

BACK TO THE FARM

E xhausted and tired from the excessive heat and the necessity to return to the farm, Grandpa and Grandma started to saddle up the horses with their young son's help. By this time, the crowd around them had dispersed and left them almost alone. Grateful to everyone, friends and supporters, and with great effort, the family made their way back home. Grandpa invited them to his house for a chat and a cup of coffee, but only some accepted the invitation for the next few days.

In the return trip to Puerta Grande, the name that Grandpa chose for his farm, Grandma accepted a basket of fresh bread from a woman who was standing outside her humble house and waiting for them to pass. She thanked the local woman for the baked bread and kindness. Then they left El Salitre, leaving behind buried deep in the ground the bodies of their young sons somewhere in the village's old cemetery.

On the way home, they headed up for the same trail that had brought them to El Salitre. They rode in silence for a while until Grandma burst out crying; there were anger, fear, sadness—everything at once. Every breath she took was a painful reminder of her misfortune. And countless questions were devouring her mind. *Why my sons? Why their friends? Look at them*, she thought. She always kept them in line, in their best behavior since they were little kids. And then what? Indeed, getting or bringing a stone from somewhere else's property was a serious thing for Grandma and Grandpa. They both encouraged their children to respect someone else's property. That was what they both called raising a family in an old-fashioned, rigid, disciplined way. And they did it.

And in the end, how can life be so unfair to end up like this? That was not fair, she thought, and a bit of sadness pushed tears out her eyes again.

With not much to do, they walked home with empty hands and broken hearts, tired, and defeated. How could they smile, relax, or sleep? There was no way for any of those things, at least for the moment. Grandma was no longer the same person; even the fresh breeze was harder to breathe. This time, she felt the moisture in the air becoming hotter and thinner than ever before.

Finally, they arrived to the farm just before it was dark. Her first night without her sons started with some trouble sleeping. Grandpa waited until Grandma profoundly fell asleep, and then he covered himself with a blanket just before midnight. "God, help me," Grandpa muttered and watched the moon through his room's little window while the princess turned heavenly in the dark sky, spectacular like a fine work of art made of magic.

The following morning, the weather didn't look promising for any outdoor activities. It looked cloudy and cold with notable dark clouds suggesting a possible storm. Grandpa stood and sat repeatedly in his chair, watching the clouds passing by from the open porch with his peculiar coffee cup in his hands.

Grandma silently walked to her vegetable garden, where there was a large cultivated patch of tomatoes almost ready to harvest. But some were already fully ripened over the ground. Suddenly, it began to rain, and Grandma ran back inside the house, coming from the vegetable garden with some tomatoes in her hands. Shortly after, the dry floor of the patio became so wet. And the fertile land turned so muddy, sticky, and watery that they had to stay at home to avoid being wet out in the rainy day. Around noon, the rain intensified with violent winds, turning it into a windy storm. The wind blew so fiercely, moving the plants, bushes, and foliage from side to side and shaking savagely the leafy branches of tall trees while severe lightning flashed within the thunderstorm.

That day was the longest for them. They spent many hours inside the home until nightfall. The stormy day passed slowly until the dark of the night shadowed those hills entirely. The wind stopped its fury, and the peace of the night returned. The angry storm left broken branches lying on the ground and the short vegetation soaked in water.

Their return to the farm wasn't pleasant anymore. They spent most of the afternoons in silence, except when visits were around them. The absence of their sons was like an invitation to some friends and relatives to visit them; people kept coming from everywhere to Grandpa's farm to comfort them. But when they were alone in the house, they all were like strangers in their own home and unhappy for the unexpected loss. *Living in suffering, we will have difficulties and more than two or three worries to think about*, Grandpa thought and focused his attention on the main problem.

After the unexpected deaths of Grandpa's sons, they all changed. Grandpa, in particular, had changed significantly since then. He lost weight; his face was pale and puffy. He was on the edge of deep depression. His strength was not the same anymore; his countenance showed the absence of hope inside him.

As for Grandma, the loss of her sons was an unbearable pain. An incomparable emptiness filled her house every second from corner to corner for a very long time. She spent hours and hours in front of her sewing machine fixing her black shawl and humming the same tune over and over again. From time to time, she opened the door and freshened the air inside the kitchen. Sometimes the semi-dark room with the large window by the cooking area seemed to oppress her like a birdcage. But sometimes that room was her comfort. Inside their fragile thoughts was a world of obscurity, cold memories, a hopeless and dark ocean with a deep river of sorrows and pain running through their veins and consuming them day after day without knowing how to stop it.

One week had passed slowly. For Grandpa, it seemed like it was years. One night he was just about to lie down on his bed and get ready for sleep. He was placing his hat on the dresser and his leather sandals under the bed when he remembered the letter, Temo's note. He read the first line silently and slowly and word by word. He read it again and then one more time. As he read the entire note, he felt his heart beating faster, instantly increasing his blood pressure, while a strange desire of curiosity possessed him.

I'm profoundly sorry for your loss. If you'd like, we could arrange a brief chat about it next week. Look for me here in El Salitre, Lucy's place. Att: Temo, 'the judge.'

Grandpa was invited to talk in the drinking club.

Next morning, Grandma and Grandpa woke just before the sun came up over the farm. And half asleep or half awake, Grandpa dressed quickly and walked barefoot to the porch. He splashed cold water over his face from the clay pot located just outside the door. Then he gathered his huaraches and walked straight to the barn for his favorite mule. The formidable hybrid was black with a triangle white forelock, inspiring some respect among the farmers.

Grandma shivered from the morning's cold air and turned to her warm sweater before clipping firmly her uncombed hair against her head. "Have I missed something?" she kindly asked and gave him one of her charming smiles.

"No, no. I have to go and meet someone at El Salitre. I'll be back before sunset," he said to Grandma.

"Okay," she said slowly.

"I have to go there for some reasons. I'll explain it later. Please don't worry," he said and gave her a kiss on her cheek.

That morning, as soon as the sun gently kissed the face of the earth, Grandpa jumped on top of his mule and focused his thoughts on El Salitre, the village that hosted the eternal rest of his two young sons. "Okay, stay away from trouble, lovebug," Grandma said. She was standing at her open door. She liked to see him making his way slowly uphill on top of his mule.

After all, she said to herself, *he is a good horse rider, and I became a farmer woman with him, something that a modern woman might object to.*

Although the weather seemed perfect. The brightness of the dawn made her blink more than once. She had been standing at the door for more than forty minutes. Finally, she'd decided to give up and turned back inside the house. She went straight to the kitchen and began to prepare food to face the day. The kitchen was part of her daily routine, in which she cooked Grandpa's favorite meals. She spent a few minutes washing and cutting wild greens and red collards cultivated in her garden. Grandpa could never keep anything from Grandma. The truth would always be the truth, and she knew it.

After a short stop in the cemetery for a brief visit to his sons' graves and placing a bunch of colorful wildflowers on top of them, Grandpa rode straight to the village's edge, looking for Lucy's place, which was located on the outskirts of the village not far from the small plaza. He secured his mule outside the lonely bar. The place was virtually deserted and seemed like it was forgotten for a time.

And without any hesitation, he walked toward the entrance. The semi-dark room filled immediately with sunlight from outside when he opened the peeling door. He stopped for a few seconds while his pupils enlarged significantly, getting used to the dark inside the cozy place. His eyes surveyed the large room as fast as they could. The only sight of life in there, besides the beautiful bartender, was an old man drinking on the lonely table away from the attractive woman. The bartender was Lucy, the cantina's owner. She was dressed modestly but with a tremendous touch of sensuality from her wrinkled, thin blouse and an extremely short skirt, exposing a good portion of the natural beauty of her fleshy legs. Everything about Lucy was nice and could fill the pupil of anybody.

That place was so quiet. But Lucy made it interesting. And her beautiful presence made that place unique and tempting to open its doors more than once.

He could hear his own steps over the cracked concrete's floor as if a heavy dinosaur was walking into the place. "Hi. Good afternoon," he said.

"Good afternoon!" Lucy exclaimed with a sweet voice.

"So let me guess . . . this is the place where the cool people meet, right?" Grandpa asked while placing his hat over the bar's countertop and resting his elbows on it.

"Yes, sir, undoubtedly," she answered.

80

"Great!" he exclaimed.

"Well, it's good to see you around here," Lucy said, turned, and looked at him.

And with a few words while studying Lucy's splendid appearance, he said, "Good to see you too," he said, putting down and resting his weight over the bar's tall chair.

"You're one of my few customers today," Lucy said.

"Slow day, huh?" he said, looking around the empty place.

"Yes, it is," she agreed and paused. "How can I help you?"

"Please, a cola drink in a glass," he said.

"Um, I haven't tried it for a long time," Lucy said while she opened the cola bottle and poured it into a clear crystal glass.

"I've been so thirsty. Thanks," he said courteously.

"You're very welcome, dear," she said.

"Thanks again," he said.

"As far as I can see, I don't think you are from around here, are you?" Lucy immediately inquired.

"No. You are certainly right. I don't live here in the village but close by . . . Puerta Grande, the farm, to be precise," he responded.

"Oh!" Lucy softly exclaimed and paused. "Well, in this case, the honor is mine. And a glass of cold beer will be served on me." She served the cold drink to him.

"Thank you. I really appreciate it," Grandpa said politely. Suddenly, he noticed that whatever they said could surely be overheard by someone around them, even if the lonely old man who was drinking away from them seemed to be distracted and involved in his own stuff. Grandpa wasn't sure if someone else was somewhere inside the place.

Minutes later, the door opened. A strange bearded guy in his forties came and took one of the seats along the bar's narrow countertop, just right next to him. The intruder asked for a beer and started a conversation with Lucy, but he was doing most of the talking while she was just drying and hanging some beer mugs and nothing more than going with the flow with the barbón.

Hmm, this is the last thing that I need, more people inside here, Grandpa thought.

Then the stranger got up and walked away to the restroom. "I'll be back, pretty," he said to Lucy while walking.

"Just Lucy," she immediately said, protesting about the stranger's compliment, and quickly stopped brushing her long hair.

"Please, a cold beer . . . or one night with you in heaven, sweetheart," that intruder said while he was approaching the restroom's entrance.

"Hey. Hey, don't make me call the sheriff," Lucy said sharply.

"Are you sure, sweetheart?" that intruder asked with certain doubts and clenched his teeth.

"Don't try me!" she firmly exclaimed.

"Okay," he slowly said while opening the restroom door.

"Drunks," Lucy said, gritting her teeth with certain frustration. Then she looked and smiled to Grandpa.

"Alcohol makes men worse sometimes," Grandpa said with some sympathy for the beautiful woman.

"Or better, it depends on the case," Lucy said, looked at him, and showed a tempting smile with some air of harmless flirting.

"Sorry if I'm taking you away from your work. But I'm looking for Temo," Grandpa finally said in a very low voice.

"I guess you're in the right place. Just remain in your seat," she said and paused briefly. "We don't have to go nowhere to find him. Just wait here."

"Solution around the corner, ah!" Grandpa exclaimed.

"Well, this place is his second home," Lucy said and winked.

"Thank you," he said and smiled back to Lucy. While Grandpa thanked the woman, the stranger was coming back from the restroom and took the same spot where he was sitting before. This time, no words came out of his mouth.

Shortly after, the dark room lit again. There was a man by the entrance holding the door wide open with his right hand. A short time of silence with some air of fear and mystery filled the almost empty place. With cautious eyes, that man looked at all the faces around until he found the particular face that he was looking for. He placed his vivid eyes on Grandpa. "There!" Lucy happily exclaimed to Grandpa.

"Hmm . . . um," he muttered and fully turned his head toward the entrance.

Slowly, that man closed the door and walked into the place, approaching Grandpa, who remained on his seat, slurping his drink. "What on the earth are you doing here?" that man asked with a certain emotion and surprise.

Then Grandpa stood up from his seat and shook hands instantly with the stranger, who shook his hand with considerable degree of exaggeration but with sincere emotion. It would take him a minute or less to connect Grandpa's face with his name. "Mr. Odilon!" he exclaimed, looking at Grandpa's eyes.

"Temo?" Grandpa asked with some hesitation and stepped back from his seat slowly.

"Yes, sir, the same person you met days ago but with an ugly haircut this time," Temo said and laughed.

"It's good to see you," Grandpa said.

"Well, well, well, did I miss anything?" Temo happily asked.

"No, no, not much, well, except the beer," Grandpa said.

"Please," Temo said, opened his arms, and with a polite gesture invited Grandpa to sit.

"Chop, chop. Lucy, a drink for the gentleman and a large glass full of beer for me. Do we have a different brand? Preferably light beer," Temo demanded immediately but courteously.

"Nope!" Lucy exclaimed and shook her head. "I have dark beer."

"I'll take one," Temo accepted.

"I couldn't sleep enough to beat the hangover," Lucy said while serving them.

"Oops. Definitely. It gave me some kind of goose bumps to think about it," Temo responded with a rough smile. "Right, Mr. Odilon?" He focused his attention on Grandpa.

Finally, both men broke the ice and refreshed themselves with a couple of cold beers and some crazy laughs from Temo's good mood. "Oh, man," Temo said to Grandpa in a low voice. Then he paused, and looking around them, he turned his head toward Lucy, slid the zipper of his somehow new leather jacket, and took out his worn wallet. And from the money's compartment, he pulled out some bills and paid Lucy. Then he instructed Grandpa to follow him outside.

Grandpa got up from his seat and placed a few coins next to their empty beer mugs.

"Thanks, Lucy. I'll see you next time," Grandpa politely said to the beautiful woman, who was standing behind the bar's countertop.

"I'll see you guys," she responded with the same sweet voice and kindness, characteristics that were her very own.

"I'm sorry. But I don't like the smell of nosy people," Temo said in a low voice to Grandpa, referring to the strange bearded guy who quietly was next to them. Both men approached the exit, ready to leave.

Fresh air came to them from the bar's patio, which had a dirt and uneven floor where two lemon trees were planted among some bushes of pomegranates. They walked quickly into the shade of such green area. They spoke clearly and frankly while tasting some citrus. As Grandpa briefly explained what had happened on the cornfield, Temo carefully listened. He didn't talk much or anything; he just shook his head and softly bit his lips over and over again.

The conversation was simple and seemed to be free of suspicion and distrust. Both men spoke sincerely. "I don't want to raise your hopes, Mr. Odilon. It's a difficult task," Temo said and paused briefly, anticipating the facts very soon. "Now if you agree with me, I will recommend to meet with more people. I have some guys that look after me."

"I'm not planning to bring more people on it," Grandpa said without hesitation.

"Well, for some of the bastards, those who killed your sons, let's do the same. Let's pay them back in the same coin," Temo insisted.

"No, no, no, no, no. This is too much and absolutely unnecessary," Grandpa said and paused briefly. He shook his head slowly and with denial on his dubious face, and he turned to look fully at Temo's eyes. "I don't think that'd be a good idea."

"You know, you're a wise man. But if you're looking for justice, the authorities won't do much. You already know the way it goes. Come on, let's get square on it. Let's get even with those monsters. I know exactly what I'm telling you, Mister," Temo said, recovering some of his composure.

"God is great and sees everything!" Grandpa exclaimed.

"Sorry, I am definitely not talking about the Almighty or any source of unknown power. But if you're looking for divine justice, you are in the wrong place because you won't have none of it around here. We'll wait for it in heaven when the time comes," Temo said, nailing his eyes into Grandpa's face.

Grandpa didn't respond; his expression was doubtful and confused. For good or evil and without knowing it, he was already in the mouth of the wolf. And he would need more than one good reason to get out of the problem. Or simply, he would be like a true coward in front of the Judge's eyes. After a short moment of thinking, he just hummed softly three or four times.

"Come on, it's about your sons. How can you not be interested to whip out of this planet every single one of those cowards?" Temo asked insistently.

"Well, the boys are dead. And I—" Grandpa said firmly, leaving his sentence incomplete when Temo suddenly interrupted him.

"Why not?" Temo suddenly asked.

"I just want you to scare the evil around so they never get close to my family again," Grandpa said convincingly.

"Okay, that's understandable," Temo responded in a low voice with a questionable and frustrated gesture in his face. He paused and took a deep breath. "But I'm afraid that we started with the wrong thing. I don't scare people. I—you know it. So why not?" Temo insisted.

For Grandpa, that was part of his desperation to heal his thoughts with the unthinkable. He had gone too far, letting himself go with his frustration to fix the unrepairable. In fact, Temo wasn't wrong; to scare bad guys wasn't his favorite job. "Because I don't want to," Grandpa said with a firm voice and paused, looking straight deep into Temo's eyes for a brief moment. "And I expect that you understand it. It doesn't work this way for me."

"Then I suggest you bury your pains here, at home, but forever. Or just leave it to flourish where they are right now. You decide it, not me, no one else," Temo said. Even if he seemed disappointed, the Judge hid his objection in a show of kindness mixed with bits of confusion.

"Good advice, son!" Grandpa exclaimed.

"What do you want?" Temo asked and paused briefly. "Hmm, think and ask yourself what's going to be next for you or your family." He added it with great frustration.

"Let me tell you, son. What is done is already done. We can change the future sometimes but definitely not the past," Grandpa said and paused. "One of the reasons of my unexpected visit is what you've already heard. The other one is you. Yes, sir, you. I want to help you change your thoughts, stop smearing your hands with others' blood, and change your life for the better, for good."

"You can't be serious. I really appreciate your gesture, sir. But it really makes me laugh. Things can't be another way," Temo said and smiled.

"I understand. But please think about it," Grandpa responded and smiled as well.

"I'm like a friend, Mr. Odilon. I want you to know it. If one day you change your mind and decide to get even, to get square with those things, then you'll know where to find me," Temo said.

"That wouldn't be necessary. Sorry to bother you," Grandpa said.

Temo turned his head, walked away some steps, and slowly looked at him over his right shoulder. "I prefer to keep my life the way it is. But thanks for your sincerity," he said with emphasis, completely hiding his face from Grandpa's sight.

"My sons, I buried them over there," Grandpa said calmly, looking and pointing toward the elevated hill with a visible chapel. "See, no one wants to be over there yet. That's our cemetery. We are supposed to have been buried there but not yet."

"What do you mean?" Temo asked from a certain distance.

"I want to know if you can build up the courage to change, to stop your wrongs," Grandpa said.

"Thanks," Temo said and refused, moving his forefinger from side to side. "I definitely think you lost your sense of good humor, Mr. Odilon." He walked toward the bar.

"One single day can change the entire life of anybody, for bad or good, at any place. Remember it," Grandpa said while leaving the place.

"Thank you for coming this far. I appreciate it," Temo said, turned his face, and followed Grandpa's tracks with naked eyes from the cantina's entrance.

"Hey, don't worry, son. Hoping to see you soon!" Grandpa exclaimed distantly and paused.

"By the way, I'll leave my pains somewhere, where my pains are supposed to be. Meanwhile, my retribution for living this life is living it in the way it comes!" he shouted from far away while riding his mule.

There was only one way to explain why Grandpa didn't want to hire Temo, "the Judge," to strike the assassins and to get even with his loss as Temo suggested. Grandpa had a decent heart in him, and there can't be any other explanation. And as far his unchangeable decision, he wouldn't need someone pointing a gun on him to force him to do what he didn't want to do because he simply wouldn't do it.

One day I'd heard from Grandma that there was not a single day of his life that he ever stopped thinking about his dead sons. And no matter how many times he said that he buried his pains somewhere in the forest, it wasn't true. The reality was something else—Grandpa learned how to live with his pains somewhere within his heart.

In Puerta Grande, their farm, routine jumped back to life around the family. Two months had gone by. And they were doing great in their own way to forget things, what had happened back there in the cornfield.

Grandma still had the taste for cooking, even if she felt no desire to return to her kitchen. She continued preparing the dough for pastry and sweet bread that Grandpa used to bake in his mud brick oven. It seemed like a prehistoric times cavern from the outside but had accurate precision. At first glance, their living seemed normal. But something was missing; the main ingredient wasn't there. It would never be the same anymore.

Sometimes Grandma removed herself from few activities, isolated in her thoughts with nostalgic emptiness, asking God for peace in her isolation. One night my father saw his mother crying. The anger he felt for the suffering of his mom was immense. The desperation broke his heart while entering into the kitchen, where she was standing and praying in a very low voice. There was not much he could do at his age of fourteen but just hug his mother. He slowly leaned the right side of his head over his mother's chest; he could feel the beating of her heart on his cheek. And with a low voice, he asked her with some disappointment or resentment, "Mom, what's the point of praying to heaven?"

"My good boy, please don't say that," she said and paused for a brief moment. "It's just a matter of faith."

"Does heaven really listen to our request?" he asked.

"Yes, God always does. My good boy, we'll have to believe in the Almighty. He is everywhere," she said.

"Okay, Mom. Blessings will come from heaven. We'll wait for it," he said.

"Yes, son. You're such a good boy," she said, and she really meant it.

"Thanks, Mom. Do you need anything before I continue with my task outside?" he kindly asked while walking out of the kitchen.

"No, son. I should be fine," she responded. But no one knew the pain inside Grandma's heart, no one, nobody.

She caught herself crying from time to time most nights. "Who owns the right to punish me?" she yelled out angrily while sobbing. Then she wet her cracked lips with the tears from her eyes.

And she started praying, "Dear God, it's me once again with the same request. Please keep the soul of my boys next to you. They were killed, and they're with you now. They are good boys."

"There is no happiness without pain. We all suffer in one way or another. But we have to keep going all the way to the end in the best way we can," Grandpa said softly and courteously to Grandma.

"Everything seems so strange now," Grandma said, sobbing.

"See? God works very hard in a mysterious way. He will fix things. Leave things in his hands," Grandpa said, comforting Grandma.

"I know. It's good to pray to heaven. It makes me feel better," Grandma said.

"It's good to believe and to have a strong faith," Grandpa said.

"It's like Papa Simon used to say," Grandma said and paused for a few seconds. "Sometimes bad luck follows good people." She remembered her uncle's words. Papa Simon was like a second father to her, her elder sister, and her younger brother after their parents died.

"Hmm, and he was right!" Grandpa exclaimed, emphasizing how important it was to have faith.

"You know what?" she asked slowly and paused shortly. "Sometimes I wonder how it was still possible to have a life out here."

Then suddenly, she smiled. She imagined her son Narcizo in the garden. "You poor boy," she added. Grandma was remembering when Narcizo was a kid. And he used to help her pick tomatoes and green peppers from the vegetable garden.

"Life sometimes is too short. But it seems we live long enough to learn a little bit more about it. And with a little touch of good luck on our side, we'll see a thousand and one things, darling," Grandpa said.

"Well, life is not fair sometimes. My boys grew and became good men and got killed. How is it possible?" Grandma questioned herself.

"There is nothing we can do to bring them back to life. We have to think of the living. We have to think of ourselves," Grandpa said.

Grandma's face seemed tired, and there was not any motivation to bring her natural smile back. When the family sat around the kitchen table for dinner,

Grandma couldn't even stand next to Narcizo's and Guzman's empty chairs. Right away, sad thoughts ran inside her mind, and more tears wet her cheeks. Even if those tears were a particular relief for her soul, there was no remedy for her sadness yet.

She took Narcizo's favorite red currant tea out of the table and hid it inside her kitchen cabinet. *I will taste red currant tea when I feel better . . . later*, she thought.

As for Grandpa, he had made a little discipline of keeping his guilt out of his mind but always with both eyes on Grandma, helping her minimize her pain. "Sorry, darling, for your suffering," he said and paused. "I should have paid more attention in what you said that day."

"Don't forget to pray for them," Grandma told him.

"I won't," he just responded with a smile on his face.

Three months had passed—fast or slow? What was it if, by the end of the day, time seemed to be an eternity for Grandma? She entered the house and started walking slow toward a silent and empty room. Her eyes were scanning every single corner of the lonely bedroom where Narcizo used to sleep. She threw a look at Narcizo's closet; all his usual stuff was in there. His colorful cowboy shirts were hanging well organized inside the narrow room. He used to wear shirts of various colors, but blue was his favorite since he was little. And curiously, just black pants hung inside his closet. He was an open-faced brown-eyed man with gentle manners and humble appearance. And of course, he had a natural smile inherited from Grandpa.

Grandma stood in the middle of Narcizo's room, holding two empty cartoon boxes with her right hand. Two boxes would be enough to keep his clothes out of the closet. She walked slowly, approaching the quiet bedroom's closet, and discovered a secret compartment inside the small closet where assorted bottles of wine were hidden on the floor. Then from another secret compartment in the wall, she pulled out a small package of wrapping paper with a tiny black box; an engagement ring was in it. *Pilar* was the name engraved in the precious jewel.

Suddenly, the bedroom's door began to open slowly as if a ghost or an invisible entity was getting into the room. Cold sweat ran along Grandma's back. A strange feeling within her brain commanded her heart to pump faster while goosebumps spread all around her skin, erecting the tiny hairs on her arms. It was Xoloscuintle, their dog, which was sneaking inside the house while the door was ajar.

"Oh my god!" she exclaimed with relief. "What are you doing here? You almost killed me! Odilon! Odilon, please come over here!"

Grandpa was outside the house. But he was so absorbed in his thoughts that he didn't hear Grandma's voice calling him.

"Odilon, please come inside the room!" Grandma called him louder this time.

"Are you okay?" Grandpa asked, preoccupied. He got up from his chair and walked from fast to faster toward the room, following Grandma's voice.

"I'm fine. Come in. Come over here," she said calmly.

"What's the matter?" he asked while approaching the room.

"Please, honey, take the dog out of the room," she said as soon as Grandpa set foot inside the room.

"Are you okay?" Grandpa asked her while he was taking the dog out of Grandma's sight.

"Yes, I'm fine," she responded in a low voice.

"If they were alive, this farm would be different," she said louder with some resentment in her voice.

"Please forgive me. It was all my fault," Grandpa said, admitting his mistake within seconds.

There was not much rejoicing in the farm anymore. Anyone could sense the emptiness in those lands. The house was full of all kinds of memories during the day and night. Sometimes Grandpa tried to spark Grandma's motivation by doing unusual things in the house. It was out of the ordinary watching him cooking or sweeping the kitchen floor. But that particular morning was one of those days. He put down over the kitchen's pretíl a considerable number of eggs from a large palm basket that was hanging from the wall. He fried the eggs with some bacon. And with a huge touch of consideration, he gently placed a large plate with food over the dining table.

"Chitlacua chichiquini. Chitlacuátl chichiquini, cihuacuacualtzín." (The food is ready. Hurry up, beautiful woman.) He spoke words that he learned from Grandma's dialect.

"What? For the love of Coatlicue, I never thought that you would remember those words," she said and smiled.

"Your breakfast is served with tons of love," he said kindly, trying to bring Grandma's motivation back.

"Very well, sir," she said, giving him a lovely smile while taking a plate with some food on it.

"No, no, not that one, the other one, the one with bacon," he said to Grandma, pointing to the biggest breakfast plate.

"But this is too much food for me," she said, looking at the plate.

"Darling, you have to eat. You need more than a large breakfast and a good nap to recover," he said while he sipped his coffee out of the crafted clay cup.

"Eating by ourselves, huh?" she said, and a feeling of nostalgia filled her mind.

Grandpa took another sip of coffee and then put down his cup on the table, and he intended to comfort her.

That weekend, Sunday in the morning, that little face that Grandpa used to see smiling for many years turned thirty or forty years younger. And that hidden smile somewhere inside Grandma's mind came back to her naturally like magic. "I have to let them go forever. We can't bring the dead come to life," she said.

"Wise words, sweetheart!" Grandpa exclaimed.

Then Grandma removed a little homemade altar that she and Grandpa built on the patio in memory of their dead sons, just saving the old photograph of the boys when they were little kids. She just prayed to the infinite, to heaven, and looked at the photograph and softly kissed it for the last time. A gentle wind swirled the dry leaves and loose dirt over the slightly uneven floor of the patio as if an invisible entity was there, playing with the magic of the wind and raising their hopes of eternity in the afterlife.

CHAPTER EIGHT

EPIFANIO

After living for almost four weeks on Grandpa's farm, Epifanio and his two brothers landed in Oxtotitlan, a village near Teloloapan, Guerrero. They immediately rejoined an old buddy, Silvino, a man best known as El Pecas for the freckles that he had on his pale face. Even if Epifanio had a wide network of occasional friends who could help them, he decided to stay with his friend, his compadre.

Silvino, "El Pecas," Epifanio's compadre, was the elder son of a man named Genaro Balena, who was the ranch owner. El Pecas, an irresponsible party guy in his thirties, was a money-hungry man. If he ever had a chance, he would sell his own soul for money to maintain his drinking habit. The outlaws knew it very well, particularly Epifanio. But he ignored it; after all, El Pecas was his compadre and not just a friend.

In their desperation to run away from justice, Epifanio and his two younger brothers had fallen back once again to the temptation to shelter themselves in Silvino's house. They went back to the very beginning, to the place where they started their criminal activities in their early years, six years ago to be exact. A light rain was falling as the brothers from Pueblo Nuevo arrived happily into Silvino's house. Light or heavy rain, it didn't matter; even the dark of the night meant nothing to the bandits, no trouble at all. They already got used to and mastered bad weather conditions. With their abilities to open the doors of the corrales, they would find an opportune time to determine when to break down the gates of wealthy cattle farms. And quickly, they would make their way through the storm or darkness of the night to the front of the strong gate in the corral or stables; and with a great ability, they would force the cattle out of the corral. And after they accomplished the task, which was always so easy for them, they would move forward like beasts of burden, carrying as much cattle as their strength allowed them. So light rain, instead of being a trouble, was like a blessing for them.

The three men dismounted their horses and released them into the stable. Then they walked freely through the wet patio. The house was a small ranch-style place. Hanging from the porch were some pots of fresh mint that must have been transplanted at least two months earlier for its size. It was a beautiful house on Genaro's property that Silvino had inherited a short time ago from his father.

Seven months earlier, Epifanio and his brothers had come to the same place with some members of their gang. Then two days later, they all returned home with a large amount of paper cash from their last robberies. Even if they stayed for short time, El Pecas didn't like it. He was fine with the brothers, but he didn't want the brothers' companions in his house. And he expressed his displeasure to the strangers far from Epifanio's eyes.

But this time was different; the three brothers had returned alone. As they walked through the patio, the brothers remembered and almost wished for the old times when they carried large amounts of money in two wooden boxes placed on top of a mule. But those days were old times, when they weren't on the run, when their names were unknown for many people.

It was still early in the day, somewhere around noon. Obviously, Silvino was not aware of the brothers' arrival. Suddenly, he heard the voice of Epifanio coming from outside the kitchen. Silvino and his wife, sitting around the kitchen table, were eating with their kids. As the three brothers approached the kitchen door from outside, Epifanio cleared his throat and asked in a smooth tone, "Compadre? Compadre?"

"Come in. Come inside here," Silvino answered from the kitchen.

"Hey . . . hey, everyone. Sorry to disturb you. But as my old folks said, when you find a good shelter to stay, it doesn't matter how many times you go away. You'll come back someday to the same place over and over again. Let me tell you, it's like destiny is calling you. And that's for sure. It's been proved hundreds of times. So here we are again in this glorious place," Epifanio said, laughing enthusiastically and spreading his good sense of humor while his brothers shook hands with the family.

"Sit down and eat with us. Everyone is invited to our dining table," El Pecas said from his chair, which was placed at the end of the table, almost facing the entrance.

"Thanks," the three brothers responded almost simultaneously. They all sat down on the handmade wooden chairs; they kept their smile as they spoke.

"I wasn't expecting you, compadre," El Pecas said to Epifanio.

"Compadre, you know me. What else is new with me?" He paused. "I'm full of surprises," Epifanio said, smiling and shaking Silvino's hand.

"Well, good that you guys are back. Feel at home. You're at home," El Pecas said kindly, welcoming them.

"Thank you, all," Francisco said, looking at Silvino's family.

"How's it going, guys? Working hard?" El Pecas asked while eating.

"Oops. It's just too hot to work sometimes, compadre," Epifanio said, and then he shrugged and placed his elbows on the dinner table, holding his face with both hands in front of his succulent chicken soup bowl.

"That's all, compadre!" El Pecas exclaimed and wiped his mouth with a piece of cloth.

"Yeah!" Epifanio exclaimed while spooning his soup. He always considered Silvino to be a real friend. He enjoyed visiting him, and he trusted him. He just felt comfortable talking to him since El Pecas was friendly and seemed not to judge him for his lifestyle.

"What's the matter with you?" Silvino asked his young kid. "You don't like the food?" He realized that the kid hardly had touched the food on his plate.

The kid simply smiled and got up from the chair without any word, running slowly and happily laughing while looking over his shoulder at the guests around the dinner table with his left eye. "Spoiled brat!" Silvino exclaimed and softly laughed.

Even if Silvino knew about his friends' activities, that wasn't any of his business. He never involved himself in it. He only accepted their visits from short periods, providing them shelter and some kind of protection in his house as a friend and compadre for Epifanio. But what did he have to do with all that? Well, let's blame his ambition this time. He knew very well who was offering a reward for the brothers to be caught dead or alive. And this time would be different; even if he treated them kindly, his ambition was bigger than his own friendship with them. Silvino wanted the reward; he needed that money. And the check was in front of him; he just needed to turn it into cash. And Epifanio and his two brothers were right there all together. One thing was for sure—he wouldn't ask for permission to anybody to do that. This time, the three brothers' presence really called the attention of his ambition.

There was money at home, a potful of solid gold. Silvino silently said to himself, *All I need is to cash it.* That man was as happy as a snake in a hole full of mice and rabbits. And that reward was easy money, easier than working for a living all his entire life.

Silvino started to watch Epifanio's movements with a nonsuspicious eye. Francisco and Chon were of a different character; they never worried too much.

They knew that Epifanio always kept an eye on them, and they both shared his elder brother instinct's cares. So for Silvino, those two were flour from another sack; without Epifanio, alone, they would fall.

No one knew Silvino's evil intentions, not even his wife or his elder brother, except his brother-in-law, Tereso. Tereso was aware of everything; they both planned it for a long time. They were just waiting for the outlaws' arrival, and finally, they got it. Their plans were full of confidence and trust. They partnered for fifty-fifty of the reward.

"Compadre, between you and me, I have the gift of your friendship, and I am sure about it. I think you know it as much as I do. I can easily count with the fingers of my hand my real friends, and you are one of them. But I must know something from you," Epifanio said and then paused while he looked at Silvino face-to-face. "If for any reason I wouldn't stay longer in this arena, promise me that you'll keep an open eye on my children."

"Compadre, por favor!" Silvino exclaimed with a certain relief and paused. "Why do you say that?" He lowered his eyes to the ground. "Of course, you can always count on me. But before that, let's go for those ninety-three years that you were planning to live."

"Okay, that just came to my head," Epifanio said and smiled.

"So come on," Silvino said and smiled back to Epifanio.

"Anyways, whatever happens to me, just keep an eye on my two boys. My little girl will be always under her mother's fine care," Epifanio said nostalgically.

"Since you are here, I will invite you to my friend Antonio's wedding. We'll go to the party, and you'll forget your melancholy over there. How's that? That could work for you!" El Pecas exclaimed, awakening his compadre's taste for mole rojo.

"Sounds interesting," Epifanio responded curiously.

"The wedding is in two days in my friend's ranch three miles from here, just down the river crossing. He will barbecue two bulls for his party. Antonio already invited the whole town. He is a barbecue man. He barbecues here, there, and everywhere," Silvino said, motivating his compadre to be part of the party with the hidden intention of exposing him to his enemies.

"Umm, great spirit for cooking and love for food, I must say," Epifanio said, moving his head up and down.

"Awesome, eh?" Silvino said.

"Antonio . . . Antonio who?" Epifanio asked curiously.

"Antonio Abad," El Pecas answered.

"The name sounds to me like a name for a priest or saint," Epifanio said and smiled.

"I totally agree. And Antonio knows it. I told him about it. He just laughed," Silvino said.

"Antonio Abad, umm . . . I've heard about him. I've never met him. But certainly, I've heard about him," Epifanio said.

"He is the man around here. He owns a big part of the land and a large number of cattle," El Pecas said.

"I won't refuse the wedding invitation, compadre." Epifanio said and briefly paused. "I'll go."

"Great!" Silvino exclaimed.

"Well, when it comes to barbecues, count on me. I'll go, hoping that you won't find me dead next day after overeating," Epifanio said and laughed louder.

"Dead? What do you mean?" Silvino asked curiously.

"Yeah, dead for eating too much," Epifanio said, joking to Silvino.

"Compadre, I want you to know what's going on." Silvino paused for a few seconds. "Look, when you are in my house, when you are here in town, you don't have to worry about anything. You are part of my family, like a brother. No one will mess with you because they will mess with me. And when things come that way, very few people knows me," Silvino said, inspiring trust in Epifanio.

Silvino was nothing but a big piece of well-digested food. No, probably, that was not the right description but something closer. Well, whatever his description was, he was not too far from being an asshole to his own compadre. El Pecas was a liar, a hypocrite. And for some six years or so, Epifanio never caught him. Good for him because if Epifanio had, Silvino might have broken his yellowish teeth and eaten them piece by piece. But Epifanio never thought what Silvino was capable of.

The nights for Epifanio and his two brothers were peaceful and relaxing in Silvino's house. This was the third time that they hid themselves in the little cabin built right next to Silvino's house. This was more comfortable than last year, when they had to sleep on the ground over a thick lamb fur blanket with two or three holes in it. This time was a lot better. There were two beds with twin mattresses and soft pillows. And everything was paid with the money that Epifanio gave Silvino's wife the last time that the outlaws came by.

Deep in their sleep and far from any suspicion that could harm them, the three brothers rejoiced inside the comfortable wooden cabin located next to the main house. Not one of them imagined anything unusual happening that night. Not even in their dreams did they notice that Silvino left the house after midnight, at one o'clock sharp in the morning to be precise. He walked in the dark silently to Tereso's house, a two-room house sitting by the edge of the hill in the same land, just fifteen minutes away from El Pecas's home.

When El Pecas approached the wooden door, he stood by the entrance and looked all around to make sure that no one followed him. Everything was clear; just the moon witnessed from a long distance his cruel intentions. Minutes later, Silvino cautiously proceeded, and a gentle knock on the door was heard. He softly knocked on the door three times using his right knuckles while sharply whispering Tereso's name.

On the other side of the door, it was not difficult for Tereso to wake up. As an open-minded and stubborn gambler with empty pockets and with a pregnant wife at home, he wanted that moment. He liked challenges, and danger moved his adrenaline like a Russian roulette, where you win it all, or you lose it the same way. And he was waiting for that particular knock on his door for a long time.

Right away, Tereso recognized the voice outside the door. He quietly got up from the right side of the bed while looking at his wife, who was peacefully sleeping and snorting under her blankets. Finally, he set foot on the dirt floor and slowly walked toward the door while he was tightening his pajamas firmly. When he opened the door, Silvino was sitting down next to it. He was totally prepared to sell the life of Epifanio, his own compadre. And the reward needed to be paid in cash only as he'd require it.

"Hey!" Tereso exclaimed using a regular tone in his voice while he opened the door.

Silvino looked at him quietly and shushed him immediately. Then he crossed his forefinger over his lips as a sign for Tereso to speak in a low voice. "Guess who's got a friend in high places," Silvino whispered and paused for a couple of seconds. "Me and you, the great one."

"Tyson Becerra? El Comisario? What's about?" Tereso asked in a low voice with great curiosity.

"Shh, shh." Silvino said, placing his forefinger across his mouth. He paused for a few seconds and then spoke in a very low voice, almost whispering. "Si, señor. Yes, sir. Now listen carefully. I've made the decision. I already had come to a conclusion, and there is no stepping back. We'll need to continue on it. I want you to take this note." Silvino paused again while pulling out a well-folded paper out of his right pants pocket. "Take this note to our man and tell him that we might have what he wants, but we need an advance proof of the reward. Three fish, three nets." Silvino instructed his brother-in-law and placed a written note in Tereso's hands.

"When you said three nets, you mean three bags of money, right?" Tereso whispered, and then he smiled almost in silence.

"That's right!" Silvino exclaimed, and then he asked, "We got this straight, right?"

"Oh, you bet," Tereso answered.

"Thursday at one o'clock. Simple as that," El Pecas said, whispering close to Tereso's right ear.

"Wow, you really grew confidence in yourself. I do not know you anymore, brother-in-law," Tereso said in a sarcastic tone while joking a little bit in a low voice.

"Shh, shh. We'll all win," Silvino whispered and pressed his forefinger across his lips.

"Well, El cabrón Comisario, he may not believe me," Tereso said, hesitating for a few seconds. "What should I say to convince him, if necessary?"

"Trust me, he will believe you," Silvino whispered, full of confidence.

"Not too bad for starters like you, Silvino," Tereso said in a low voice in a goofy way.

"Thanks. What the commissary wants to know is written in there. Instructions are on it. The three bricks around the base of the lonely mesquite tree next to the river bridge, that will be the signal for the target passing by between 1:00 and 2:00 p.m. But 1:00 p.m. seemed most likely," Silvino explained in a low voice.

"Okay, listen, I don't want to pay for any mistake of yours," Tereso said, defiant.

"Look, you just leave all this on me. No worries. Take the note and explain to him the plan," El Pecas said, almost half-whispering.

"All right, we are fine then," Tereso said calmly.

"We can't continue being loyal and protecting them just like that while they keep doing the same bullsh—they are bandits, and sooner or later, they're going to bring trouble to me. Problems are the last thing that we want around here. Sometimes one pays for others' errors," Silvino said in a low voice.

"Okay. Keep it low. You stay with them in your place, no suspicion, no malice, but watch them closely," Tereso said, almost whispering. These two were a good mix, made out of the same clay on the day of Creation. Well said was the phrase "God makes them, and they alone come together."

So early the next day, just right after the sunshine bathed the top of the mountains on the left side of Oxtotitlan, Tereso went out of the village; he focused his steps straight to the municipality. But he was not alone; he was accompanied by a thousand and one words written on the note inside one of his jeans pockets.

Two hours later, Tereso arrived to the municipality's office. The door was half-wide open. He stopped a few feet away and cleaned his sweaty face with a cowboy neckerchief around his neck. Then he walked toward the entrance, holding his walk, before he gently knocked on the door. "May I come in?" Tereso asked, keeping a fresh tone in his voice before he walked into the office.

"Come in," a person answered from somewhere inside the office.

"Good day, Mr. Tyson," Tereso said, approaching the man who was alone behind his cherry desk. The light in the room was bright enough for the commissary to show up well behind his desk, which seemed almost filled by the big man behind it. He sat very still, dressed with his double-sized camisa guayabera and his white astilla hat, typical of the rural people in that region. El Comisario, like many people called him, was a double-sized man for his height and large belly. His eyes were extremely black and his gaze petrifyingly cold, black as obsidian beads embedded into the clear glass, and cold as the ice on the mountain. He turned toward the newcomer and rapidly surveyed him from toes to head while the stranger was approaching him.

From his desk position, the newcomer seemed to have a shaved head covered by a paisano hat and firmly resting on top of a skinny neck hidden under a cowboy neckerchief. "Tereso?" the curious commissary asked and immediately recognized the newcomer. "What a pleasure to see you around here!" He paused and got up from his chair while extending his hand in a gentleman's gesture to Tereso. "How you've been, my friend?"

Wow, mucha papa para un ranchero! (Lots of cream for the tacos!) Anyways, the commissary was a well-prepared man, educated, polite, and knowledgeable of his position. And after all, he was the commissary, the person in charge of the municipality. After they shook hands as a respectable salute, the lawman, still standing behind his desk, placed both of his hands with the palms firmly flat over his desk and pushed back his large body upright. Tereso stayed placidly in front of him. "I've been fine, Mr. Tyson. Thank you for asking," Tereso said respectfully. "How are you, sir?"

"Well, my friend, work is my name," the commissary answered, smiling and laughing softly, exercising his mouth that was a little bit wider this time, giving Tereso the chance to see his big teeth and his great smile.

"I won't question that," Tereso said and smiled.

"But please tell me, what brought you here? Any problem?" the Law man asked curiously.

"No, no, Mr. Tyson. I was sent to your office, bringing this note from my brother-in-law Silvino, 'El Pecas.' There is something that you might be interested in as we are. Please read it and let me know if you are interested in it," Tereso said, pulling out the note from his pocket and later placing it in the regidor's right hand.

The man unfolded and carefully read the mysterious note; there was a significant moment of intrigue and silence. Then he showed his superficial smile, which was a very particular thing of him. "Well, well, the best thing for you is to keep your distance from people like them, my friend," the Politician said with a thin smile. He paused, walked slowly toward his office's entrance, and closed the door.

"No worries, señor," Tereso said cautiously.

"I personally saw them a couple of times but only from a distance. That happened years ago. Epifanio and his two brothers were very young and quite suspicious by then. But I never thought that they would become what they are now," the commissary said.

"We never know about the future, Mr. Tyson," Tereso said.

"Of course, we are interested. But Pancho Patiño will perform the job. And about the money, not today, not tomorrow but one week after the hunting if we succeed. As you can see, everything is just a matter of time," the Politician spoke clearly. People such as Tyson Becerra, who was the commissary for many years in charge of the municipality, and Pancho Patiño, his friend, belonged to a class of a certain level and a privileged category with some personal sources of money. And of course, many people followed their instructions without questioning them.

"Oh!" Tereso exclaimed, and rapidly, El Comisario interrupted him.

"Let me tell you this, Tereso, you better give them the bridge to stay away from you and Silvino. You guys will make the way for them to be a clear target. Give them considerable distance. And then get the hell away from them," he said and paused.

"Run! Take off out of the place immediately. That's the best way to end up alive!" El Comisario exclaimed with intensity, referring to the three brothers' hunting.

"Okay," Tereso responded.

"And just like I told you, Patiño is righter than right. He knows when the door of hell opens and the precise time when Saint Peter closes the one for heaven as well," the commissary said slowly, trying to impress the little man.

For many years, Pancho Patiño had hated Epifanio and his two brothers. He accused them constantly of being thieves, and he'd kill them if he ever got a chance to put his hands over them. But certainly, Pancho was afraid of them most of the time. And when he wasn't scared, it was because he surrounded himself with fifteen, twenty, or more of his best friends with enough ammunition and guns on their hands.

So one day Pancho couldn't take that any longer. He was one of the first people who offered a reward for those bandits. And with his charm, he convinced the commissary to be on his side and to hunt the outlaws as well. After a time, Pancho and El Comisario had heard enough of the brothers. They both began to persuade most of the ranchers who owned cattle in that region and asked them for monetary contribution to give a reward to anyone who could help cure the disease in their community and surrounding places. It was as simple as that—killing them would be the solution for all of them. "When the dog is dead, the rabies is gone," they assured the villagers.

Tereso gestured toward the man like offering something and suggesting something at the same time. "Well, we'll need some motivation. We are putting ourselves in great danger," Tereso said, looking respectfully to the commissary's eyes.

The commissary displayed a slight hesitation before he spoke about any money to be paid for the deal. "It isn't going to be easy, Tereso. You should know it," that man said.

"I certainly know it, Commissary. But I want you to understand my point," Tereso insisted.

"Okay, no more words. You win. There is something here. It's not too much. But it will compensate for the information that you guys provide. And it will help us for you to be well motivated," the regidor said, and then he turned around his desk and struggled to unlock the desk drawer. Finally, after a few tries, he stopped and took a deep breath. "It's an old desk, but it's very safe." He tried one more time and immediately opened the old drawer, bringing up a paper envelope.

"Thank you, Mr. Tyson," Tereso said in a humble way.

"Well, this is worse than just carrying a large watermelon over your shoulder for the entire day," the Politician said, expressing some concern.

"I totally agree, Mr. Tyson," Tereso said and smiled softly.

"I know. It sounds cold and horrible, but let's bring them down. People got enough of it," the lawman said.

"And what is worse, those bandits haven't got enough of what they do," Tereso said with some touch of hypocrisy.

"I don't know. Personally, I'm not suffering from their actions. But I'm not content with it. And all I wanna do is to hunt those guys down," the commissary said.

"We'll do more than what you think to help you," Tereso said.

"Like always, it's good to preserve the peace around here and outside our municipality too," the commissary said.

"It's a fine thing, sir," Tereso said.

"Better for you to stay away from them," the Law man replied.

"Yes, sir," Tereso responded.

"Follow me," El Comisario said, and both men left the office. They walked across the narrow hallway.

That heavy man opened a door from a small room. "Please get inside," he told Tereso and followed him. "Sit down." That wasn't so strange. The commissary wasn't an honest politician. That was funny—an honest politician. But everyone already got used to hear all kind of stuff about him. Meanwhile, someone might have some doubts about it. And we better leave it with the benefit of the doubt.

For Tereso, that was the first time in his entire life he negotiated with one of them—and probably the last. He questioned himself, *Why are we inside this strange room?*

Finally, after the regidor got himself comfortable in one of the chairs, he placed the paper envelope on top of the small table that was in the center of the room. "Please open it. It's all yours. Count it," the commissary said, looking Tereso straight in his eyes. For Tereso, those words were a big relief after so much mystery.

"Okay," that man responded slowly and nervously but with some caution at the same time. He licked his teeth, moistening his dry mouth, and swallowed his saliva. He picked up the mysterious envelope and opened from one side to see with unique fascination the stash of money that was inside. Then he started counting the coveted bills one by one.

"Money . . . money, my friend. It goes hand in hand, doesn't it?" the commissary asked while watching the ambitious man.

"Si, señor," Tereso responded without looking at the commissary's face.

"Part of the money in advance for your information and cooperation, a great advance as a gesture of appreciation for your big help. But you should also be aware of what you guys are getting into. Here, there is no room for mistakes. Errors are paid at a high cost, and I want you to be aware of it," the commissary said, placing his black eyes steadily over the table, where Tereso was counting the money.

Then suddenly, he added with a clear tone in his voice, "You are responsible for this amount of money. Do you understand?"

"Yes, sir," Tereso said, and he gave a thumbs-up twice with his right hand. "All the instructions have been written in the note, so we will cooperate with every single detail. Just follow the instructions, and Silvino will take them to the target spot as we already agreed."

"Everyone gets what everyone deserves. And you deserve this money," the commissary said and paused while watching Tereso counting the money. "I wouldn't say that if I couldn't see the future from here or anything like that. But some people certainly do that, and you are one of them. You see the future as well as I do. Well, as you can see, I've been working for justice for years. And I'm proud of it. I use everything around me, all the tools that I have in my hands, for justice. Those bandits don't know what being decent is. They don't even know the meaning of a decent life, no, not even in the deepest corner of their brain, in their own conscience, or whatever they have inside their head."

"You're totally right, Mr. Tyson," Tereso agreed.

"But they will get what they really deserve someday, and that day is coming soon, dear Tereso," that politician said.

"Well, Mr. Tyson, the first step was already done," Tereso said and smiled. "Five thousand pesos!"

"Yes, five thousand pesos, exactly, all in high-denomination bills." The politician confirmed the amount of money from the paper envelope, and then he paused and ordered with an authoritarian voice, "I want you to hold the money. I have to take a picture of our deal for our safety. That's how it works." He prepared the camera to take a quick picture of Tereso, holding the stash of money with both hands and without saying a word.

"We won't mess up, Mr. Tyson," Tereso said.

"I know it. No tricks, Tereso. Tell Silvino the same," El Comisario said.

"No worries, Mr. Tyson," Tereso said, and then he left the politician's nest, waving his right hand as a sincere goodbye.

"Be careful," the commissary said, waving his hand and giving a thumbs-up two or three times from outside his office.

Silvino was just a regular guy with colorful ties with Epifanio's enemies. Of course, Epifanio didn't know that. He didn't know that his compadre was a knife with a sharp double blade, ready to cut. Epifanio never knew or even suspected that. The three brothers knew so many people. But this time, they backed on the wrong ones, at least this time.

That day, Epifanio had spent the morning with his two brothers in front of Silvino's house, helping them clean fresh corn. It was around ten thirty when he decided to go out for a haircut. He crossed the unpaved street and walked decidedly into the lonely barbershop. "Good morning," he said to the barber and sat on the only chair that was inside the place.

Then immediately, an old man came up to him and asked, "How would you like your hair, Mister?"

"Well, I'm going to a party, a wedding. And I would like to dress elegantly—I mean, respectable, with good clothes, shiny shoes, and of course a nice haircut," Epifanio said with a considerable touch of enthusiasm and paused. "First-class haircut, is it possible?" He winked with his right eye.

"I see. You're looking for high-quality service, Mister," that barber said while grabbing scissors that seemed new judging from its shiny metal.

"Well, sometimes the physical appearance blanketed with some good clothes and a nice haircut changes the monkey and represents a high degree of respect," Epifanio said and smiled.

"Undoubtedly, and that makes sense," the barber responded.

"Right!" Epifanio exclaimed and laughed out loud.

"Well, it's a nice, lovely day for a wedding," the barber said.

"Absolutely, it is," Epifanio said, smiling.

While Epifanio was in the barbershop, with the barber trying some miracles over his head, Silvino was at home, cutting some pumpkins to be cooked. By that time, Epifanio should know better than anyone else his compadre, but none of them noticed Silvino's dark intentions. They had seen too much of each other, good or bad, through the last six years, when every one of them partied frequently. But that was a long time ago. Even if they were not older than forty, they all seemed to be older than their real age.

On September 15, 1955, at around one in the afternoon, while the sun was still high up the sky, Silvino and Tereso were courteously leading the three brothers over the dirt trail through the bushes. Epifanio was the only one well dressed. He was wearing new shoes and clothes for the wedding—black pants and a light blue fine silk shirt with long sleeves. His automatic pistol rested hidden somewhere around his waist and eight loaded cartridges inside his pants pockets. None of the brothers had the remotest idea how that day would end for them. At the request of Silvino, they left their guns and plenty of ammunitions at home. Only Epifanio took his inseparable pistol with him against Silvino's request. El Pecas strongly suggested that morning not to bring weapons to his friend's event. The wedding was the occasion, and they wanted to have some fun. They left everything in Silvino's hands. They even left him a little behind from time to time.

At some point, Epifanio noticed that Tereso was kind of nervous and kept looking back as if someone was following them and anxiously looking toward the river's bridge constantly. But Epifanio never thought or suspected something unusual. And knowing that Tereso had a birdhouse look by nature, he thought nothing of it. After all, this wasn't the first time that they walked together.

"You've become quite elegant, Epifanio!" Tereso exclaimed nervously.

"You look like a lawyer, compadre," Silvino said while looking at Epifanio's shoes.

"Totally exotic and elegant, big brother," Chon said, teasing him.

"Thanks. Thank you for realizing the good," Epifanio told them while straightening his shirt's collar and walking with some style, smiling calmly.

"Especially your haircut, almost bald, brother. How much did the barber pay you for that tremendous disaster?" Chon said and laughed out loud.

"Don't get too excited. It's nothing new for me, especially if I can afford it. Why not?" Epifanio responded. His new hairstyle, trimmed and cut low almost to his scarred scalp, was enough to know that he looked different, although he couldn't claim to look better that day.

"Yeah, yeah, blah, blah, blah!" Chon exclaimed while laughing.

"Stop it, bunch of losers," Epifanio said, laughing.

"What? Losers?" Chon dramatically complained and paused. "Winners, you might say, don't you?" He teased his elder brother.

"I have one for you, my dear brother. If you don't go for a haircut, I'll cut your hair while sleeping," Epifanio said to Chon while all of them were laughing.

"That's a good one, brother. I like the idea. But it's not that simple. You definitively might need some help!" Chon happily exclaimed while joking.

"I guess not. But I could try, little brother," Epifanio said and laughed.

"Hey, no worries. I'll give you that job, comrade Epifanio," Chon said, teasing his elder brother.

As they neared the bridge close to the riverbank, El Pecas and Tereso unexplainably leaned out of the narrow trail. The first false step was on. The three brothers walked toward their destiny, facing a trip to hell with a good passport on it. *Surrender*, it was the wrong word for them.

Even if it was around one ten, darkness was approaching them, coming in silence to straighten up their fate with punishment as an adjustment of debts for their wrong actions. The three brothers didn't know what was inside Silvino's brain. But Silvino allied with Tereso, the commissary with Pancho Patiño, and twenty others. And they wanted to quiet them down forever.

Quite certainly, the brothers were in the proper place for them to be a clear target. The killers set up their own waiting area early in the morning out the sight of passersby. That place was semi-deserted, and Pancho with twenty men were ready to hunt. Tyson Becerra, who was the commissary, never even intended to catch them alive or to place the three brothers behind bars. He had already prepared everything in his mind to get rid of them forever. El Comisario had also decided to quit his job after bringing an end to the brothers. And his future, along with the solution, was in Patiño's hands.

But who really was there? They set up the ambush early that day. And twenty men were assigned for that task, all under the orders of Pancho Patiño. They were hidden and waiting in silence like lions around gazelles in the savanna. The chubby commissary, master of the plan, was sitting in his office and waiting for the results.

The day was bright—blue sky with few clouds. Soft wind was scraping and gently brushing the top of the tall vegetation over those hills. Epifanio, Francisco, and Chon were happily joking and walking on the narrow dirt trail into the leafy bushes over the edge of the main valley near the small bridge that crossed the river. Just right on that spot, they heard a soft clicking sound, but they ignored it; even if they noticed a significant part of the dense vegetation flatted down, they continued on their way to the small bridge without any concern.

Tereso and Silvino discreetly slowed down their walking before they approached the hot spot where the ambush would be. By then, the assassins had mapped out the area and chosen a perfect position to attack from behind the bushes with the strong instinct to kill the brothers. And they knew who the main target was—Epifanio. There was no doubt it.

A short time later, the hidden killers sensed and heard the three brothers approaching the hot spot. Pancho Patiño looked around from the leafy bushes and immediately recognized them. "The bandits are here," he whispered to his men, seeing that Silvino and Tereso were leading them toward the ambush but walking slowly and far away behind the brothers, exposing them in front of the enemy for first time but from a certain distance.

"I've been waiting long for this opportunity, and I won't waste it. All this needed to be done. You should know the reason why. However, we can't fail the commissary," Pancho Patiño said in a very low voice, almost whispering to his men. The assassins' conversation was held entirely in whispers. If anyone else was around, trying to overhear, they simply wouldn't be able to hear anything. They all knew and fully believed that Epifanio was the main target. And he was a tough cookie, a hard nut to crack. So one mistake would be awful for the assassins; one mistake could ruin the plan.

Finally, and for first time, the three brothers had fallen in an ambush. For a moment, Epifanio felt a strange presence around him and then took his gun out and slowly lowered it after he cautiously surveyed part of the vegetation. But to start his bad luck that day, he looked on the opposite side where the enemy was. A few minutes later, Tereso and El Pecas disappeared out of the brothers' eyes, leaving the brothers in the hands of their enemies for the first big strike. They were not allowed to cross the other side of the river. Suddenly, the three brothers were a clear target. And an avalanche of bullets was allowed to come over them.

Epifanio was confused for a moment. The attack was unexpected, but he was determined to defend his life and his brothers at any cost. He cursed in a very loud voice. "An ambush! Get down on the ground! Get down on the ground! Don't run! Get down on the ground!" he shouted while trying to locate the enemy's position. Suddenly, he jumped up. His pistol, glued to his right hand, was aimed straight up. There was a burst of fire around him, and the loud noise of his pistol broke the silence for a few seconds.

The frightened men responded by aiming their rifles over the side of the bridge, looking desperately to put a bullet into that man. There was something Epifanio did not understand, and he was sure that no one of his brothers either. They were caught by surprise. *Who is behind it?* he thought.

Within a few minutes, his trouble was bigger than the enemy's shooting. His real trouble was another; he was alone. There was no sign of his brothers; maybe they ran and escaped, or they were killed.

Life for the brothers was full of all types of adventures. Their poor childhood was followed by years of partnership and loyalty. Whatever experiences they had had, they were always together. Since they were children, they became extremely close to one another. All for one and one for all. But now they left him alone. This time, it seemed like his two brothers forgot everything about him. And his compadre El Pecas and Tereso left him on his own. They ran, they left, they escaped. But this time, there was something he learned about his friends; he never knew them. He cursed his luck, blaming his hunger when he was young. He felt useless once again; only his pistol was his inseparable companion.

"Come on, show up! Show me your face like a man!" he shouted desperately at the top of his lungs, standing half-covered behind a leafy bush and extending his arms open from side to side with his pistol in his right hand.

"You're not one of us, cabrón! And you'll die today!" someone yelled from the bushes.

"Cowards!" Epifanio screamed.

"And believe it or not, the devil is going to die here . . . today," someone said sarcastically from a considerable distance but behind the bushes.

Suddenly, two bullets struck him, breaking the bones of his right hand. Epifanio went backward and lay stretched on the ground after the impact, forcing him to see his pistol flying away out of his broken and bloody hand. Luckily, the gun fell only a few feet away from him. He struggled to stretch himself over the ground to reach his pistol, but he grabbed it using his left hand. Epifanio remained quiet on the ground for some time. He was petrified when he looked at his right hand. It was practically tearing apart, hanging from his arm, soaked in blood. Full of pain, he got the courage to grip his own hand and tighten it using the sleeve of his fine shirt. Dragging himself, partially crawling, twisting and turning his body with quiet and sudden movements on the ground, he finally reached the trunk of a tall tree, where he began to cover himself as much as he could from the rain of bullets.

He wasn't even sure if his body, now with two bullets in his right hand, could take all the punishment for all his crimes. This time, he was convinced that everything was about to be over. He was done; death was inevitable. "Anyways, this way could be the best," he sadly whispered to himself. But at the same time, there was something strange, a rare relief, some weird excitement mixed with a kind of good hope inside his thoughts. He messed up, but he might survive. He simply comforted himself for his mistakes.

Somewhere in the tall vegetation not far from him, the shooting stopped for a few minutes; but those moments of silence turned into great desperation, an infinite time of suspense, anxiety, and torment in his mind. Whatever little chance for him to escape would probably be at night. But to survive seven hours behind the tree trunk, that would be difficult. His legs began to cramp in less than one hour. And on top of that, he was completely sure that his ammunition would be insufficient to afford six or seven hours of trying to defend his life. He closed his watery eyes for a brief moment and pushed himself up to lean his back against the tree trunk, feeling the burning sun roasting his sweaty face while his dehydrated body remained sitting on the ground.

He was there, trapped, nowhere to run this time. There was no sign of his two younger brothers; they could be dead or alive. He wasn't sure about it. He was left alone to face his enemy, his demons, his fears—everything at once. Then he suddenly remembered something. A few years ago, someone had warned him, "Always keep watching around you, over the top of your shoulders, from side to side. Watch your back, Epifanio, more than anything else, my dear son." He thought about the words of his mother. Then he wiped his mouth on his shirt's sleeve and smiled, blowing a silent kiss to the air.

Finally, he understood that he signed his own death by returning to his compadre's house. And what was worse, he trusted in him. Indeed, Epifanio didn't have not even one hair of foolishness on top of his head. But now he was there on the edge of nowhere, with the horrors of death yet to be discovered. There was nothing else he could do, too late now. *Anyways, it's a good lesson to learn, and I will go all the way to the end*, he thought and smiled in silence.

Then his vision fell and focused on a certain spot. There was a leafy bush near him where he counted five or six of his enemies. Those men were waiting for him to make a mistake and move out of the mesquite tree, where he was hidden. The thick trunk of the tree obstructed their bullets from hitting the target. Certainly, Epifanio's enemies were afraid, and that impeded them from killing him. They knew that man could be hurt, but they were not sure at all, completely ignoring the severity of his injuries and letting out the great opportunity to finish him.

For first time in his life, Epifanio wasn't able to use both hands to place a loaded cartridge into his pistol. He had lost his right hand completely in the first burst of bullets that he faced. But his desperation to defend his life pushed him to load his gun, grabbing the pistol with his teeth, cocking and placing a loaded cartridge into the pistol using his left hand, squeezing his mouth against the tube of his pistol, pressing it with his left arm. The struggle to load his pistol wasn't bigger than his desire to survive, keeping his life inside him. And his pain was just a pain, nothing else.

The whistle of a noisy shot passed by, brushing the spiky stems of the grass and lifting some debris out of the ground just a few inches where he was. "Bastards!" he screamed. Then he wiped his dry mouth using his left hand while placing his pistol on the ground for a few seconds.

"Your brothers are not coming back," Patiño's soft voice gave him a hint of threat.

"How do you know that?" Epifanio asked.

"Because . . . they are dead," Patiño answered with cold and calculating words.

"Do you want to know what happened to them?" someone asked from behind the bushes.

"They're gone, Pifas. You are alone, and you won't make it. Right now, you are about to fall. Your hind end is the one that's hanging over the edge of the cliff. So give up," Patiño said calmly, highlighting a friendly alias for Epifanio's name, and sarcastically encouraged him to drop the towel.

Epifanio had begun to count his ammunition; nineteen bullets were all he had left while 75 percent of his body was embracing his life. "Stop the fire. I'm getting out," Epifanio said, trying to trick and confuse them. But there was no response.

"I wish I had more bullets. But one thing was for sure—I won't die miserably," he whispered in a very low voice to himself. Epifanio promised himself that he wouldn't ever give up. *No way, José. But words are just words. Life is life, and it doesn't come back.*

The sun broke through the clouds for a few minutes above the spot where he was abandoned to his own luck. The firing had stopped, and silence remained for a little while. But the enemy was somewhere there camouflaged with the vegetation, just waiting for the right moment or for him to make a mistake.

For Epifanio, there was a price to be paid, and he was ready to pay or everything at once. Then he crossed the fingers of his left hand, the thumb over his forefinger, forming a small cross as a sign of blessing and kissing it slowly while he looked at the sky. His full attention returned to the bush near him, where he suspected that more than five guys were hidden, hunting him, and ready to kill him. He threw down a small stone, seeking his enemies' reaction to the unexpected noise. And right away, a movement was detected behind the bush. Epifanio slowly raised his pistol with his left hand and aimed the gun straight to the bottom of the bush. His hopes of escaping alive were revived once again after he shot them. An angry burst of seven bullets from his pistol ended the life of at least three of his enemies, leaving the right leg of one of them completely broken by the bullet's impact into the femur bone. Others jumped out of the bush with minor scratches on their flesh.

Epifanio felt a lot better. There was a little hope for him. *After all, hope dies last and I with it*, he thought. But the enemy was a large group of twenty, now only seventeen, with one of them with a broken leg. And he was standing by himself with his soul in his heart and his life depending on his own left hand, his pistol, and twelve bullets left.

Epifanio wet his lips with his tongue and passed his saliva through his throat. He sat back down and cautiously covered himself behind the tree trunk. He combed his short hair constantly, running the bloody fingers of his left hand over the scalp of his almost shaved head. And again, he loaded his gun with the same difficulty that he had the previous time.

He had a sour expression on his pale face because it was daylight and because of the nature of the valley in which the enemy was. His motivation and hopes crumbled once again when he realized that, after killing some of his enemies, the opportunity to escape alive was not greater than zero. So he stayed behind the tree and waited impatiently for them to leave or the night to come, making the darkness his best ally to escape. On the other hand, the hope of his brothers' return was a vivid flame that was still lit in his heart. But minute after minute, his face was reflecting some sort of pain and disillusion until the physical pain, the doubts, the sorrows, and remorse began to dance in his mind, overwhelming his own willpower.

Meanwhile, on the other side of the mesquite, the enemy moved closer to the tree's location to have a better view of him. Two men crawled over the grass and approached him from the back side. They moved closer, keeping their bellies flat against the ground while carefully helping themselves, alternating their elbows in coordination with the knees over the green vegetation. They reached a perfect spot in front of him. Now the bandit was a clear target; they never had a better opportunity to finish him. They attacked him by surprise. Pancho Patiño was the one who shot him last, placing a bullet right into Epifanio's heart, killing him instantly.

Epifanio fell perfectly flat, lying on his back on the ground with both of his arms to the side of his dead body. His pistol was barely out of his left hand and his eyes open as if he was watching the sky with joy. The delivering of his soul to the Almighty had given him the peaceful look that we would find a few times on the face of dead people, those who died far from pain while enjoying a moment of pleasure or happiness and having a happy death or, better said, a happy end.

Finally, someone succeeded in killing Epifanio. Pancho Patiño came toward him, walking slowly, full of pride, with his eyes on Epifanio's face. He calmly shot him once again, discharging his anger on the lifeless body as the outlaw lay dead on the ground. The bullet hit Epifanio's body above his left groin. Then he approached the dead man and took his pistol away. "This is more for the living. I need this more than you will in hell, my friend," Pancho said with a semi-broken voice but in a sarcastic way while he read the pistol's engraved inscription—EC as in Epifanio Cuevash.

Here that came, the strangest thing. After Pancho saw his rival's dead body, there was a slight tremble in his hands, and his voice wasn't clear. He whistled an old song to disguise his notorious fear and ran a hand over his sweaty forehead. Then he caught his breath more than once and exhaled deeply, attempting to recover the normal sound of his voice in front of Epifanio's body. "Uta madre! Today is my lucky day," he said to the others, lowering his voice, while placing Epifanio's pistol in his chubby waist.

"Let's get out of here. He is dead. He's gone," someone said to Pancho.

"Okay," Pancho accepted, and then he smiled and winked to one of his men.

Pancho Patiño and twenty men ambushed the brothers, and shortly after, eighteen disappeared into the landscape, taking back home three dead men with them and leaving Epifanio in the same spot where he was killed. That hill was silent with death around. The life of a fugitive ended. Just like that, along the edge of a lonely valley near Teloloapan, Guerrero, on September 15, 1955, Epifanio Cuevash was assassinated at one thirty in the afternoon.

Epifanio and his two brothers knew it; they would never live another day as freemen by going the wrong way. They totally knew it; going that way, they would never last long enough to see their children grow up. They would end up being gunned down or jailed for the rest of their life. Or even worse, they could end up hanging from the branch of a tree with a rough rope around their neck. Epifanio had analyzed part of his life before his death, and he had seen the horrors of his demise coming faster to close the circle of his destiny. But he never realized that Silvino was a traitor, a person well connected with his worst enemy.

Epifanio's death was a singular accomplishment for his enemies, particularly for Pancho Patiño. The others were flour from a different sack, especially Tyson Becerra, "El Comisario," who was wealthy and powerful. And of course, he never overpaid for things, having the great Patiño at his disposal.

For Silvino, the trick was to gain full confidence from Epifanio and his brothers. For Epifanio, he was totally captured by the attention that Silvino offered them. Looking at how the ambitious man was loading their minds with wonders of trust, they never realized the false words and hypocrisy.

But was Silvino really involved in Epifanio's death? No doubt about it. His involvement was confirmed by the fact that he and Tereso pretty much disappeared when people started asking them about Epifanio. "I absolutely have no idea about what you ask," they both frequently replied as a typical answer for the curious villagers.

The promised reward for Epifanio's death never was paid in full. Tereso and Silvino didn't get all the money. But it wasn't much either compared with the deaths and damages that their foolish ambition caused. Soon after Epifanio's death, El Pecas and Tereso's involvement was clear. And it didn't matter how many times both men claimed that not one of them had anything to do with that. They got to the point where nobody believed them at all. And the families of El Pecas and Tereso, with the help of their wives, vanished overnight from town, leaving no trace behind them.

Tyson Becerra, the commissary, got himself killed in a car crash after celebrating Epifanio's death, just two days after the outlaw's demise.

CHAPTER NINE

THE LEGEND

By sunset and after the bad news got into people's ears, some relatives and a few of his friends convinced the local priest, and all volunteered to identify and recover Epifanio's body. From a certain distance, they all surveyed the area. There wasn't any evidence of life in Epifanio. The dead man seemed to be glued to the ground judging from his body's position.

The priest started walking around the body and looked closely at some of the footprints over the smashed vegetation. He carefully examined the body, and nervously poking his right ear, he raised his voice to be heard. "Yes, Epifanio is here!" Then he bent forward and touched the dead man with his hands. "Yeah, that's him," he finally said.

Epifanio's dead body apparently turned heavy, and his legs must have stretched out because people said that he seemed taller than how he was. Just after sunset, his body was taken to a small funeral home located next to the church. His body at the funeral home's display room was recognizable. Some people stood around him; his head was uncovered inside the cloth-covered coffin. His face was free of scratches from any type of harm; his expression was peaceful inside the smooth casket. He seemed happily asleep, but he was dead.

The next day, some people from the church went out to see what could be done about arrangements for the burial. Many of them were trying to comfort the fallen man's family inside the cemetery's chapel; others placed his coffin at the center of a small wooden platform that was set up earlier that day. Innumerable flowers around the coffin were visible from a certain distance through the cemetery's entrance.

The multitude outside the cemetery cheered with Epifanio's name. "Epifanio! Epifanio! Viva Epifanio!" some people cheered from loud to louder constantly. He was no doubt a man with a dark reputation but with tremendous charisma, an enigma with great doubts even after his death. It became a habit to most of the villagers to hear all sorts of things about him. In the end, Epifanio's character seemed to grow and get attention from a large number of curious acquaintances and strangers, everything about his dark world that had never satisfied him since he was a little boy in Pueblo Nuevo, where he was born. Suddenly, that world began to shine with his demise. Not once since those days when he hadn't yet learned to steal someone else's little things or from one's home and pretending nothing had happened, simply playing a fool, or just playing funny and whistling a happy tune while looking in the opposite direction every time that he was doing something wrong and caught by his mother, feeling like a spoiled brat—not once since then did his world become so interesting. Inexplicably, that dark world began to shine precisely one day after his death. What irony—to die to be able to shine, to be forgiven, or seem to be loved. *That's totally ironic*, Epifanio would say that if he were alive.

When he was a teenager, he was always complimenting Chon more than Francisco or Heriberto. That was because Chon was the youngest, and he also understood how helpful and remarkable Chon was. Francisco was fine, and Heriberto was out of the question, totally away from his brothers' activities.

A great multitude came to say goodbye to a man who soon would become a legend for most of his friends and a monster for all his enemies. And in the end, Epifanio—the outlaw, the bandit, the man from a small village—had the luck to find himself surrounded by all sorts of people cheering his name in front of his coffin, some with considerable sympathy, some with hidden hypocrisy, but the noise was the same.

That seemed incredible; a big proportion of the surrounding population was in the crowd. Everyone had the enormous curiosity to see for last time the dead body of a man who disturbed the peace around the region. But their curiosity seemed to dominate the anger of many of them who were against him just a few days before his demise. And now they were sympathizing and accepting the fact that we all make mistakes through our life all the way to our last breath. But every day is a chance to become better human beings and to clean up the mistakes from yesterday with today's good actions, to learn from the mistakes of others, and to confront the past without being too late or afraid of what we are.

A vast multitude continued cheering, singing, and repeating his name over and over again with fraternal enthusiasm outside the cemetery's metallic fence. Besides the unexpected multitude, the fence was another important part of the cemetery that day. It was adorned on three sides, mainly by the entrance, with fresh wildflowers. "Epifanio! Epifanio! Viva Epifanio!" People outside the cemetery cheered and sang his name louder and louder intermittently. Besides his wrongdoings, Epifanio always kept good impressions of well-defined humanity with most of the needy people around him, especially when his pockets were full of cash.

Chon, Epifanio's younger brother, was alive, and he was there. He and Francisco escaped unharmed, without a scratch from the violent attack where Epifanio was killed the day before. Chon was walking slowly into the multitude, approaching his brother's coffin. He disguised himself as an old woman to participate in his brother's burial without being detected by their enemies, who for sure were somewhere there, sneaking in silence into the crowd.

Chon applied some makeup over his face after shaving his thin mustache and fixed a ridiculous but real-looking wig with gray hair over his head, looking so like an old woman that no one even cared who she was. He was smart enough to work his way to around to be close to his dead brother. Looking like an old woman with that disguise and with the granny appearance, not even Epifanio would recognize him at first sight. Chon had come around near the wooden platform where his dead brother's coffin was placed. He picked up a flower from a bucket next to the casket and placed it over Epifanio's coffin. He sobbed softly, almost crying; caught his breath; and walked away from the small platform after praying in silence for several minutes.

Chon passed a young woman who stared at him unconsciously. But the woman was looking at him a little too much. She stared at him with attention, trying to read something in his sad wet eyes. The beating of his heart increased quickly. He couldn't imagine what he looked like to others with that uncomfortable disguise. Some curious person could discover him, and it could be a catastrophic moment for him because his safety was on it. That was the moment when he totally realized that his presence in the crowd wasn't yet under his control. Although the sun was shining over the place, it wasn't hot to be sweating. But his sweat kept running from his neck, wetting his back, while he easily could hear the beating of his pulse. *Anyways, here I am*, he thought, walking and keeping his concentration as an old woman. The feeling that he would never see his brother again, that Epifanio was truly dead, came fully to his mind. But no matter what, he found a way to feel safe, to be close to the burial site at the cemetery.

A brief silence fell over the noisy crowd. A man of average height wearing a black soutane approached and stepped up the wooden platform to begin the religious ceremony as soon as the platform was empty and ready for him to climb up the stage. Some mourners felt the tension in the funeral as they waited for the religious man to deliver his comforting message. However well prepared the priest was to share his speech, he seemed nervous when he approached the podium, but he was able to recover his posture. Soon he was the center of the crowd's attention. Finally, the priest stood at the back of the coffin, placing his right hand on top of the smooth silver casket for a couple of minutes and praying in a low voice as if he was talking to the dead man. Then he took a step back and started blessing the coffin, spreading holy water on it.

The religious man just couldn't understand it and called the demise of the unfortunate man an act of sin and shame for the community. "It's a sacrilege," he said to the mourners once he got up in front of the audience.

While the priest was speaking, Chon silently stayed at the back of the crowd. He watched the holy man talk on the upper site of the small platform, just behind the coffin. From there, he was sure the priest could see every face in the crowd. Meanwhile, Chon could hear sniffs and sobs coming from some of his relatives, unaware that he was there, feeling the same pain and watching them under a colorful disguise for his own safety.

Most of the people were standing on the ground, facing the coffin during the religious ceremony. Then just at the end of the service, the Priest called everybody to pray. "Brothers and sisters, today we are here together, praying for the soul of our brother Epifanio, and we all prayed humbly and confidently to God. So, brothers and sisters, once again, mercy for all those souls that suffer the insults of our faults," the Priest said with a clear voice, and then he paused for a moment and looked slowly at most of the people in front of him. He cleared his throat more than two times, and then he intensified the tone of his voice and continued his religious speech. "I know, you know . . . we all know it. Someone is out there, somewhere here, somewhere else. I want each of you to place your hand on top of your sincere heart, to stand up. One by one, stare first at the holy cross next to me and then look me in the eyes and say to yourself, 'I'm not the one who inflicts pain on others. I'm not the one who murdered Epifanio.'" The priest concluded his speech; slowly placed his fingers against his lips, forming a cross with his thumb and forefinger; and kissed the cross.

A good number of people were standing around the empty grave, praying to God for his eternity. Then a few minutes later, relatives and friends placed the coffin on top of the hollow grave and slowly descended it into the blessed earth for Epifanio's eternal rest. "Amen," the Priest finally said after blessing the grave.

An old man walked slowly and softly grabbed the arm of a woman to lead her to the pit where the body of her dead husband was put to rest. The widow approaching the grave had a tormented cry and was loudly screaming for her loss. She knelt next to her husband's grave and prayed the Lord's Prayer as last rites for him.

Francisco watched the burial from a distance, away from the noisy crowd. Through the trees near the cemetery, he could see the coffin descending into the empty grave. Suddenly, he focused all his attention in the crowd, and then his eyes opened wider. Apparently, he wasn't wrong. The whole area was watched by some of their rivals, moving quietly from side to side into the crowd.

After the burial, people began to leave slowly and carefully spread out in different directions. Minute after minute, everything was turning away in silence until no one was there. A little tombstone engraved with FOR OUR BELOVED BROTHER EPIFANIO CUEVASH. GOD BE WITH YOU was proudly placed over his grave in the cemetery.

After Epifanio's death, Francisco and Chon felt vulnerable; they both feared the inevitable—the end. However, the survival instinct was always ahead of fears and doubts, smoothing the rough texture of their thoughts. Epifanio was everything for them. But now he was gone.

Having been born in Pueblo Nuevo, Epifanio—the eldest of five children— had died at the age of thirty-six, leaving three children without a father and a young widow sunk in pain with a tormented, lost mind. She died just two months after him, leaving their children on their own. Ironically, some of the worst malefactors you could ever imagine became legends, immortalizing their crooked way and turning themselves infamous but famous.

CHAPTER TEN

FRANCISCO AND CHON

After Epifanio's death, life for Francisco and Chon was completely different. They spent most of the time at home with their family. They both had children, and for the kids, it was a miracle to have them around. They were filled with delight having their fathers at home.

One month passed by without any sign of possible trouble. Besides their fears, they both enjoyed the time together with their own family. Frequently, they were talking and planning an escape to the city, but Chon was taking too long to come up with a final decision.

The blood inside Chon demanded him to be connected to the fancy life, to be around the cattle's stables. Even after Epifanio's death, everything they touched turned upside down. It wasn't easy for him to move in the right direction. And he redoubled his thoughts before he decided to talk with his brother Francisco about moving to the city. *The city, what's that about?* he always thought.

"We're still safe, bro," Chon suddenly said and paused. "What do you think?"

"Not sure. Are we?" Francisco responded with certain doubts.

"Of course, we are!" Chon exclaimed, giving him a big smile.

"Don't you care about your safety anymore?" Francisco asked and paused. "You should leave for your own safety. You're totally behind enemy lines with your thoughts."

"I don't need you to tell me how I should live my own life. You're already starting to sound annoyed about it," Chon said with an involuntary gesture of rejection.

"What the hell do you think this is?" Francisco asked and paused. "Those bastards will never leave us alone. And you're acting as if nothing had happened."

Francisco paused longer this time while looking into Chon's eyes. "You have your entire life ahead of you." He gave him a friendly slap on the back.

"C'mon, Francisco, you don't let this whole thing eat your mind and soul for the rest of your life. It's been over a month and not a sign of trouble," Chon said and jammed his hands in his pants pockets.

"Let's face it, Chon. There's no future for us in this place. I'm taking my wife and kids with me and moving to Mexico City," Francisco said.

"The city . . . the city again. There are issues that people like us can't handle over there," Chon said.

"We need new beginnings, brother," Francisco said, trying to convince his stubborn brother.

"Don't worry, I'll take care of this," Chon said.

"If there's something that will keep us away out of this thing, it's our own family but not here in Pueblo Nuevo, not in this place," Francisco said.

"Well, you fix your own problems. How about it?" Chon asked defiantly.

"Chon!" Francisco exclaimed.

"I can take care of myself," Chon responded.

"We started this thing, and I'll never forget you, bro. But I need to think about my family," Francisco said.

"And what do you want me to do?" Chon asked and paused for a brief moment. "Give me a chance to think about it. Give me time!"

"Time?" Francisco asked and shook his head.

"I have to think about it," Chon answered.

"Don't let me down, Chon," Francisco said with considerable concern.

"Whatever you say," Chon said.

"I've never been that close to anybody, brother. Don't let me down, Chon. Did you hear me?" Francisco asked while looking into his brother's eyes.

"Whatever," Chon answered and walked away without looking back.

By the end of October, Francisco decided to travel to the city, thinking of finding a house for him and his wife to raise their children away from the farm. He thought that once he established his wife and children in the city, Chon would follow him without thinking twice. And he took his chances and immediately migrated to the city.

Some years later, in the summer of 1962, Francisco and his family went back to Don Chon's farm for a short visit to his parents. But he found the most terrible news that made him shake his head and his entire body tremble. Some teenagers playing soccer on the edge of the grassy valley just a few feet away from Don Chon's backyard suddenly interrupted their game; two of the boys had seen them and immediately recognized the visitors. The local teenagers looked at them

120

with scary eyes, and without any word, they silently pointed toward his father's house. Francisco felt cold sweat running through his back, and then he turned his attention and looked toward his parents' house, scared as he had always felt after Epifanio's demise.

Francisco and his family started to walk toward the lonely house. Soon after, a young kid approached him and whispered something close to his right ear. A chilling sensation ran over his back and then over his entire body. His shaky toes were already numbed, approaching that little house where he and his brothers grew. "Great god! No, please!" he exclaimed, horrified, and paused. "That's not how I figured it." He cleared his throat.

His wife attempted to make conversation to calm down his desperation. "Hey," she protested.

"My brother Chon has been killed. They attacked my dad's house this morning."

"Oh!" she exclaimed and placed her right hand over her mouth.

"You sons of the holy mother won't catch me here!" Francisco shouted angrily.

Chon was the youngest of the five brothers; besides the name, he took after his dad a little bit more than the other four. Rebellious, stubborn, disorganized, ambitious, and a little crazy were characteristics well defined in Chon Sr., Don Chon. But Francisco, the middle son, was something else. His oval face with some scars dotted here and there over his natural tanned skin made him look older and about four or five times angrier than how he really was. It was one of the ninety-nine reasons why people walked off when he was pissed off. His uncontrollable temper made him act against the gravity of his cautious instincts, losing his head almost immediately.

He picked a glass and poured some water out of the old pitcher on the table. His face turned red while he was walking from side to side inside the house, holding the glass of water with his right hand. Suddenly, with an uncontrollable impulse, he threw his glass full of water against the ground, violently shattering it into a thousand and one pieces all over the dirt floor.

The situation went from bad to rotten when a knock was heard at the front door. Someone gently knocked at the back side of the door. And he rapidly grabbed his dad's rifle while carefully looking through the old window, which was dusty and partially full of spiderweb with some remains of dead bugs resting behind the old rag that was placed as a curtain over the window frame. "It's me, Matilda," a female voice gently sounded, coming from outside. There was an old lady outside the house, standing right behind the door. He opened the wooden door, and she entered as quietly as she could and slightly closed the noisy door behind her.

"What is it? What had happened here?" he rapidly asked, holding the rifle with his hands.

"They took your father alive. I saw him. He was hurt, very badly hurt. He was shot at least one time," that old lady said firmly.

"Bloody hell!" he desperately screamed.

"By the way, Chon is dead. He confronted them and got shot. His body is in my place. Your mom ran to my house, but she is fine. No worries. She will be safe in there. People are comforting her, including my family. I just came to let you know because I saw you coming into the house. Now I'll go back there. You guys can come with me, if you want to," Matilda said.

"Thanks. Please comfort my mother's pain from me," Francisco said and paused for a few seconds. "Don't worry about me." Then he raised his right eyebrow and thankfully gestured to the lady. "Thank you, Matilda."

Without going around, life for Francisco and Chon was a total decline, a chaos, something far from what it had been when Epifanio was with them. They were doing good, but after Epifanio's death, things turned into a disaster. As the old song said, "Everyone has what everyone deserves. And for them, that was time to pay their wrongdoings. That was just a matter of time."

A remote thought from childhood crossed Francisco's mind like a quick flash. When they were children, his parents tolerated and accepted most of the stolen things that they brought home. Everything started with their neighbors' toys. Then through the brothers' growing years, they were bringing home more and more valuable things, including chickens, goats, and more livestock. They never heard anything from their parents. And later, their father had felt the necessity to cover up their wrong activities. Instead of saying something, he had become an accomplice with his silence. *It is already too late to correct them*, he thought.

"Are you really going to do this thing by yourself?" Francisco's wife asked him, concerned for the situation.

"Hey, no worries. I got a bunch of friends everywhere. They'll look after me. You just keep a good eye on the kids and the other on yourself," Francisco said and blinked his right eye once.

"I'd like that," she said while nervously partially braiding her long hair and wrapping it around her head sadly, placing her eyes on her children, who were around their father.

"I'll bring my old man home! Tell Mom!" Francisco exclaimed and walked toward his wife.

"Be careful," she said and looked straight into his eyes, which were as unreadable as an ancient language.

"Be good with Mama," Francisco said while he kissed his children.

"Stay with Matilda," he said to his wife. She responded with a slight expression, enlarging the corners of her mouth, evidently nervous, with a silenced but lovely smile. Her brown eyes stared deeply into his face.

Then he walked away, taking his pain and the thirst for revenge inside him, with a loaded rifle hanging from his right shoulder. He walked downhill toward the sandy riverbed and followed the possible tracks of his father's captors and his brother's killers, humming his brother Chon's favorite song, "Cielito Lindo." He was moving fast, walking as rapidly as he could over the rough terrain.

After two hours of nonstop walking, the sunset scarcely shadowed the forested hill. Francisco slowed down his frenzied walk over the semi-dark pathway until he finally reached an abandoned, empty stable. A lonely tiny shack with some holes through the wooden walls was built like a small old-time barn. The unpainted and cracked wooden door was semi-attached to the shack's frame with two hinges, one of which was broken, leaving a considerable space to sneak into the half-destroyed cabin. He tightened the door with some handmade ropes and walked inside, where he tried to get a few hours of sleep and rest, waiting for the dawn's light, allowing him to continue his search for his father.

The breeze of the night was cold, not common for a hot region. The abandoned place was located close to the forest and near a huge cascade. The waterfall seemed to carry the water of two or three rivers for its noisy and uninterrupted sound. But who cared about the weather or how cold or hot it might be when you carried a heavy load on your shoulders? He needed only solid and sharp thoughts in his mind to continue. At the moment, there was no room, no time, and no space for weather preferences or scary cascades.

At that point in his life, Francisco could easily define his life in a few words. He could define and frame it as a sad sunset, as a bitter awakening, or simply as the tragic life of Pancho Pelotas. Any of those titles could frame his life perfectly, he thought.

At sunrise, Francisco got up quickly and walked to the forest; he stayed in silence. Then he brushed the moist and dry leaves with his boot repeatedly and scratched a wide spot on the forest floor. And with the help of a long wood stick, he dug a small hole on the ground and threw some pieces of dry leaves thrown on the ground into the firepit. The man picked up a great deal of dry leaves from the ground, piled them up over the firewood, and then lit a small fire to warm himself and boil fresh water out of his drinking container. He finally sat around the fire to taste the bitter coffee that he always carried with him. The burning firepit crackled over the ground, and the smell of firewood filled the air as he quietly watched the sparks leaving trails of smog in the air.

As Francisco proceeded with his forced and unplanned camping trip that morning, he didn't notice that someone followed him. They spied the cloudy spirals of smoke from the burned firewood, and going toward it, they silently reached the place where he was sipping the bitter and relaxing beverage. His enemies were greatly pleased to see him. That was what they had been looking for.

Suddenly, Francisco heard some whispers. And the sound of dry leaves crunching on the ground under someone's feet had reached his ears as the intruders made their way through the forest floor. He alerted himself, taking his rifle, and stayed in silence behind a tall tree. Quietly, he spat away the salty pumpkin seeds from his mouth and cautiously surveyed with his eyes the area around him. He was trying to hear where the noise was coming from, but it was difficult. That sound simply dissolved into thin air, mixed with the natural murmur of the forest.

Francisco, at his age, was tough but not tough enough to take everything at once. And every minute, he felt the adrenaline running through his blood from head to toe. And his heart pumped faster and scared, revealing all his hidden fears at once. *Come on, man. Feel the life, the fresh air. Take in the life as long as you can. Breathe deeply. Hold the air as long as you can, more and more. Then let it go. Exhale it slowly. Come on, just do it*, he said to himself silently in his mind.

After a little while, everything turned silent. There was no noise at all. Even the chirping of the birds had disappeared for a moment, leaving that place plunged into a mysterious silence. And aiming his rifle at some directions, Francisco carefully moved and inspected once again with open eyes every single thing around him, and there wasn't any sign of intruders in the area. *Might be some deer hunters passing by*, he thought. Then he lowered his rifle, placed it against the tree trunk next to him, and continued drinking his still warm coffee while he was planning his next move.

"Don't move! Stay still! Don't move!" someone shouted from a short distance right in front of him.

A spine-chilling sensation ran through his back. A spark went through his mind, interrupting his thoughts, while his disoriented eyes increased their size to survey around him. He immediately realized his mistake, but it was already too late. They had probably spotted him before he even woke up in that stable. How could that be possible? The hunter became the hunted. Undoubtedly, the oversights and overconfidence, most of the time, would take you straight to the wolf's mouth. Francisco should have imagined all that, surely in that precise instant.

He intentionally dropped his clay coffee cup and tried to reach his rifle. But he abruptly stopped the effort to pick his weapon; he couldn't. A single shot struck the tree, not far from where he was. "Stay still! Remain in place! Or we'll kill you if you move!" someone else shouted from his right side.

Suddenly, three men emerged from a ditch right in front of where he was. They simultaneously walked roughly through the uneven floor, breaking the silence of the forest and aiming their guns toward the outlaw. They stood in front of him and faced him within seconds. He was sitting on the ground with his hands clenched tight at his sides and his gaze hidden behind his fury. One of the strangers pointed his rifle at him, gesturing with the head for him to stand up; and with an authoritarian voice, he instructed the prisoner to get up but not to come closer. "Put your hands behind your head," the stranger commanded.

There was no answer. But Francisco lifted his arms and placed his hands behind his head. One of the strangers carefully walked toward him and tightened his hands together over his back. That man was standing so close that Francisco could smell the bad breath coming out of his visibly rotten teeth.

Uta madre, este guey no se lava la trompa, Chon would have said if he were alive. (Damn, this dude doesn't wash his mouth.) Francisco remembered his recently deceased young brother.

They finally caught Francisco, accusing him of stealing cattle. He was cursing constantly and spitting on the ground the whole time. Six men exchanged ideas how to get rid of him in one of the cruelest ways. The strangers grabbed him and punched him on the face, the upper side of the stomach, and then his face again, cutting his lips and the skin around his cheekbones, causing him to bleed and vomit blood. Francisco had blood all around his face and clothes, mainly over his chest.

The aggressors finally stopped the brutal attack and left him on the ground momentarily. Then after he recovered, they pulled him up from the ground. A tall man grabbed him by the throat, strangling and tightening him up standing against a tree trunk. Francisco was coughing and cursing them; he was too lonely to defend himself against them. Only Epifanio and Chon could pull him out of this mess, but it was already too late. They were already dead.

"And what can you do now?" one of the aggressors asked just a few inches near his face and paused. "Very little, almost nothing, just wait to die." He laughed with sarcasm.

"For you . . . it would be like killing something, wouldn't it? So glorify yourself now that you have the chance, coward . . . because if you don't . . . I will flip the tortilla," Francisco said defiantly.

"What?" the same guy questioned him, confused about Francisco's words.

"I guess this makes you feel a complete man . . . little bastard," Francisco said, spewing blood on his enemy's face.

"Ah, you think you are a big macho cabrón. Well, let's see what you have," that man who seemed to be the leader said while cleaning his face with the lower part of his shirt. He was the tallest of the group, hitting over six feet but not less than that. His large face showed some wrinkle lines in the forehead and not a sign of beard under his pale skin besides the ten or twenty whiskers as a catfish mustache.

"I'm just a man," Francisco responded.

"So now what?" his aggressor asked and paused. "What do you have for me?" He challenged him with a soft tone.

"I hope you all burn in hell!" Francisco raised his voice.

"Oops. I'm sure we will. But you won't be too far from us," his aggressor replied sarcastically.

"The snakes can digest their own poison, but you can't digest your own anger and cowardice," Francisco said slowly.

The next thing he knew, the aggressor had pulled out a gun in less than five seconds. "I'll blow your brain out of the head," that man said, aiming the gun toward Francisco's forehead.

"Do it! Do it. Go ahead!" Francisco shouted defiantly.

"Imbecile . . . idiot," his aggressor said angrily while pressing the gun against Francisco's head.

"Coward. Just go ahead and kill me now! Just pull the damn trigger!" Francisco screamed desperately.

"From a distance, you look as tough as your father. But in front of me, you mean nothing. What do you think of it?" his aggressor said and paused. "By the way, your old man is down there in total silence, if you would like to know about it." He took the gun away from Francisco's head.

"Burn in hell . . . you piece of man!" Francisco shouted angrily.

For a brief moment, the six men stood there, silently staring at him. Francisco watched them through half-closed eyes. He dropped his head and waited for them to kill him and then partially turned his head slowly and spat some coagulated blood out of his mouth. He had been humiliated without any chance of fighting back, of standing up for himself.

Minutes later, the buzzing sound in his ears turned into whispers and voices coming from his attackers, talking while approaching him. He was lost in his thoughts, but he certainly knew that everything was over, that he was done. "What the hell are you doing?" he asked, panicking when one of his aggressors attempted to tear his pants, followed by a painful groan and a devastating huh. After the aggressors cut his private parts and partially placed it into his mouth, they fixed a noose around his neck and hanged him from the branch of an old tree.

Four men pulled him up and held the rough rope steadily while life was escaping out of his body. Unconscious from the outrageous torture, Francisco immediately lost his breath, falling into a suffocating agony. Then some bloody fluids mixed with saliva were dripping out of his mouth and slipping over his chin until he slowly died.

The next day, his family and some of his cousins found his body. They carefully placed him on the ground and removed the rope's noose. He had rope burns all around his neck, and a pair of religious scapulars were hanging from his broken neck, somehow wanting the Creator in his side and begging him for forgiveness.

Chon Senior died after being shot in his arm and taken into captivity. His family found his body just downhill, a few hundred feet away from Francisco's body. Their enemies plotted to kill them, and they finally succeeded.

Years before, the three brothers ran away from home. They could have done something good with their life, but they didn't. The three young men embarked on an adventure that brought them nothing but misery. They wanted to be wealthy, so they left home to find fortune. But they looked at the opposite direction, and they found the wrong way. And in the end, they only found their own death, taking their father's life with them.

CHAPTER ELEVEN

OUT OF THE FARM

Life out there was difficult, particularly in Grandpa's farm—the farm my father grew up in, where Grandpa and Grandma had lived and raised a large family. It wasn't the same anymore. There was a strong sense of fear always around them. It seemed a strange place to stay safe, a rare and unknown world in those rolling hills near a small town known as Apaxtla in Guerrero.

The significant impression that they were constantly on the watch was sufficient reason for them to feel uncomfortable. Grandpa's mortification increased when Xoloscuintle's behavior become completely strange, especially in the day. The dog was barking unceasingly while looking with steady eyes in the surrounding hills in a weird manner. Even the roosters and hens crowed profoundly unusually and scared like something or someone evil was hidden and watching them from the forest. Periodically, there were sounds coming from the woods, and anyone could hear the scared crows and flocks of birds flying out of the vast vegetation, but everything else was unknown. Everything seemed out of the ordinary as if the devil had stepped on those remote lands or as if their imagination wanted to take them to another world between good and evil.

One good day Grandpa was digging a water well in his land. *Un pozito*, he would have said. He looked up to the sky, and the sunlight warmed his forehead intensely as his motivation renewed the spark to continue with the farm. He felt the smooth touch of the wind spreading the heat of the sun over his face like a silent blessing from beyond. Nobody was there; nobody was around him. But he felt the presence of someone close to him.

Next morning, he found an old guy digging deeper next to his water well. "Plenty water here!" the stranger exclaimed while placing Grandpa's digging utensils slowly on the ground. Grandpa looked around, trying to understand who that person was. And before he could have a chance to ask any question, the stranger was out of his sight. Besides the tiny vegetation and the small bushes nearby, there was not much of a place for the stranger to hide. None of the others in the farm saw the strange man digging or leaving either. But days later, Antonio—Grandpa's eldest son, drinking water at the well—told him that he noticed something passing by around noon, something like a ghostly person dragging chains, but he didn't pay much attention on it.

Grandpa knew definitely that someone was out there, someone evil with bad intentions. That place where they had lived for many years and raised a large family lost its magic and safety. It wasn't the same anymore, and a wise decision should be taken.

One afternoon while Grandma was placing her belongings into a cardboard box, she found a picture from old times; it was Guzman's picture when he was barely seven years old. She ran her fingers around the edge of the wooden frame. "Wonderful smile . . . my little boy," she said and exhaled deeply.

Grandpa hummed from a considerable distance. "Come here!" Grandma exclaimed.

"I missed them," Grandpa said after he carefully scanned the old photograph with his watery eyes.

"I still have a few of his toys and some of his old baby clothes," Grandma said and paused for a brief moment.

"It's a lot easier to forget the pain, thinking about the happy moments," she sadly added. Talking about them brought back tears in her eyes. Grandpa approached her, sat on the edge of the bed, and embraced her kindly. She cried softly and then, with a deep exhale, placed her arms around him.

"It's late. You should get some rest," he said.

"I'm just tired. Anyway, I can't sleep," she responded.

"You should lie down," he insisted.

"Okay, darling," she agreed and stretched her neck over the pillow. "I'm tired, that's all." She sniffed and blew her nose more than two times.

"I care about you too much, honey," he said.

"I know you do. And I never allow myself to doubt that even for a moment, my darling," she responded.

Silence fell again, a short time of silence this time. Although she appeared calm at the moment, the conversation continued like some other times in the past, sometimes filled with some happiness or sometimes reflecting some melancholy and nostalgia. Then Grandma was finally feeling sleepy and, with a voice more asleep than awake, said, "Good night, darling." She laid her head back over the soft pillow again. The cold breeze that came up from the forest had become unpleasant but tolerable under the blankets. She was quiet again next to Grandpa.

One night Grandpa and Grandma sat on their chairs outside the house on the cozy patio. They were drinking a cup of coffee. That evening was the least cloudy one in weeks. The moonlight fully illuminated their cozy path on the patio, glowing through the trees and on the tender leaves of some branches. A strange bird had swooped into the leafy tree, some twenty-five feet over their heads. Grandpa lifted his face and looked up to the stars. His view of the sky was perfectly framed by thick branches from the tall tree. The branches were full of leaves, embracing the top of tall trees on the patio and exposing a rounded nest built on the restless branches of the tree. They both watched the lonely nest for a few minutes.

"Really, what is it?" Grandma whispered, pointing up with curiosity.

"Not sure, but whatever it is, it's up to something," Grandpa answered in a low voice.

"What kind of bird do we have here?" she asked curiously.

"I don't know. I sincerely don't know," Grandpa responded.

"Poor little thing," Grandma said.

"I'll find it out tomorrow," he said.

"That's better!" she exclaimed.

"All right, sweetheart," Grandpa said, looking around, conscious that someone could be watching them, hidden in the obscured shadows of the trees around the house. Finally, they sat back on their chairs, marveling gratefully at Mother Nature.

He turned his head toward Grandma and said, "I think it's better to move out of this farm. We'll find a new place somewhere else."

She hesitated at first, got up from her chair, and walked between twenty-five and thirty feet away from her seat, silently facing the obscure forest at night, not convinced at all. That suggestion seemed excessively foolish, and for the moment, the idea was doubtful. She clearly didn't like Grandpa's suggestion at all. "Without a place like this, what do we have?" she asked.

"How long do we have to live like this, under these strange circumstances?" he asked.

"What strange circumstances? Darling, there is nothing wrong," she said.

"Someone can make a serious attempt to hurt us," Grandpa said.

"What do you know that I don't know, darling?" she asked with extreme curiosity.

"Look, we don't know anything. But something bad might be out there," he said, pointing with his head toward the forest.

"It feels like we're running away or trying to hide somewhere," she said.

"Running away? No, we're not," he said.

"We should not leave from here. Those bastards might think that we are running away from them, like scared chickens," Grandma said while looking on the opposite side of Grandpa's chair. Meanwhile, Grandpa continued sitting still on his chair without any word to say. Then Grandma slowly retraced her steps, reached her chair, and sat in full silence next to him. She was clearly upset, but she didn't let it get to her too much.

"Do you really intend to sell the farm?" she asked doubtfully. "Darling, selling this land after all these years, how does it work?"

"I totally understand the way you feel. It's our home. This land has been in the family for years. But I can put part of the property up for sale, and we'll keep the rest of the land. I know it sounds sentimental, but there's nothing wrong with being sentimental," he said, leaned back in his chair, and took a position he favored for talking.

"Want more coffee?" she asked with a pleasant tone in her voice.

"No, no. Thank you, honey. I appreciate it," he responded quickly but politely.

There was a brief moment of silence during which both of them studied each other with mutual understanding. Then the quiet air of the night was suddenly broken. The dog started barking desperately, pointing its attention toward the narrow walking trail that connected the forest with the farm's main entrance. While the dog's barking echoed through the entire area around them, the loyal animal was running closer to the farm's entrance, bravely barking from loud to louder.

For a few minutes, they looked at each other without saying a word. While the moonlight was reflecting on the ground their misshapen silhouettes, he gently grabbed Grandma's hand. "What's that?" she asked, talking about the dog's behavior.

"I don't know. But Xoloscuintle perceives something that we don't know," he responded.

"Do you think someone might be out there?" she asked with some concern.

"Yeah. But we don't really know," Grandpa said and paused. "You understand?" He looked straight in her eyes.

"But—" she said, but he suddenly interrupted her.

"Look, sometimes there is something some people can't handle even if the person is capable of doing it," he said.

"Sometimes?" she questioned and paused. "Well, you might be right. We never learn something until it's too late." Grandma apparently made up her mind, approving of the idea to leave the farm.

"Did you talk to our sons?" she asked.

"Yes, they work with the idea," he answered.

"Then okay," she said, giving the green light for him to take the next step on the matter.

"If we don't walk away, we'll have to fight back, and revenge is out of my mind," Grandpa said.

"No, we can't to do that. Anyhow, they already robbed a precious part of my soul. And whatever is done is already done," Grandma said.

"I have some good friends that we could wholly rely on," Grandpa said.

"Okay, find a safe and interesting place to live," Grandma said.

"That's understandable and reasonable. See, if we don't push ourselves to have good dreams, then what's the reason for living?" Grandpa said after he had persuaded Grandma to leave the farm since they'd heard a distant gunfire a week before their last conversation about it.

As time was passing by, he realized he needed to become a protector of his family's future. He wasn't afraid; he was afraid of the possible consequences that his decisions would bring to his family. For him, there was more than one reason to walk away, to leave the farm. A few days before he moved his family out of those lands, his fears turned into curiosity, wanting to find out what was in the forest. And he decided to inspect some spots in the woods. He found traces of intruders on the area, like small firepits for provisional cooking, remains of cigarettes on the ground, even a bed made of palm fiber and some raw potatoes in a clay pot. Unmistakably, someone was hiding and missing no opportunity to watch them from a certain distance and with unknown motives for them.

CHAPTER TWELVE

GRANDPA'S NEW LIFE

By the end of 1955, just days before Christmas, Grandpa bought a new land; this time, the size of the property was smaller compared with the farm that he owned in the past. His advantage was that the land was six or seven miles away from Highway 51, the interstate that connected Guerrero and Michoacán on the south side of the country. It was an area named La Tierra Caliente (the Hot Land) because of its warm climate. Certainly, Grandpa's land was located right on the limits of the tropical weather, but the climate was phenomenal, hot in daytime and pleasant at night.

He established a small new farm and started from scratch over again. Grandpa had the ability and experience anyone needed to survive in the mountainous region, and he worked his land with his heart, hope, hard work, and whatever was available to move forward. Once again, his perspective was unique—a land where his family would grow older and flourish basically through daily work.

At some point, it was hard for them to start again from the beginning. They built two houses, one as a kitchen with comfortable cooking space and large dining area and the other as a sleeping building with four separated rooms. A shallow ditch divided the surface of the ground outside the construction along the back wall to lead the run of water in rainy days and drain it toward the lane that flushed the bathroom, which was a small shack not far from the sleeping building. Every wall of the house was made out of homemade mud bricks. The asbestos sheets were firmly attached with large screws to the wood on the roof.

The stable was totally unfinished, made out of wood and without any type of roof on it. A large tree, almost in the middle of the wooden corral, adorned that place. And it was the perfect spot for some horses and a few calves to relax under its shade. A small cabin was built next to the stable. That was the nesting place for poultry, in which they had a considerable number of red hens, breeding them for their brown-colored eggs.

Somehow they had survived the unexpected change in their life. After all, Grandpa was a fine maker of Cincho cheese on those lands. He had the experience and the proper touch for dairy. "Cheese . . . cheese, queso de Cincho," he said while he held out a tempting piece of it on his hand.

After five months in the farm, he started planting fruit trees on some parts of the property—mangoes, plums, guavas, and white zapotes, a type of persimmon that was soft and sweet when ripe. Through the years, some of those fruit trees would greatly grow in size, providing not much fruit but enough for the family. The rainy season was from mid-May to end of August. During this time, the backyard was a small version of the jungle; vegetation appeared to grow like magic from the ground. A line of washed clothes hanging from a long tight rope firmly attached from a small tree to the kitchen roof extended all the way through the grassy area just behind the house to dry under the warm kiss of the sun almost every week. May was the perfect time to grow corn, beans, pumpkins, and many of the typical seeds that they used to harvest. That was when the vegetation flourished open wide on those hills. In 1963, my mom with the help of my grandfather and my dad planted two trees of ciruela cuernavaqueña, a very unique type of plum that was bright red and intense yellow when fully ripe with a large wooden pit inside the juicy fruit. The plum trees grew and flourished on the right wing of the patio, scraping the barn's roof with their large branches a few years later.

As result of rainy days, a narrow stream was formed along and between the lower junction of the hills, just half a mile away from Grandpa's house, the place where I would see the light of this wonderful world for the first time in 1965. And apparently, it was the same distance between the stream and my parents' little house, built years later in 1971. The seasonal stream was carrying the water toward the lower part of the hill, spreading a small part of the precious liquid into the lowest and wider area of the main hill, giving birth year after year to a round-shaped lagoon. That lagoon flourished in rainy months and dried off completely in the dry season, leaving behind a cracked and deserted soil without any drop of water or any sign of vegetation on its eroded floor, except the bushes surrounding that masterpiece carved by the excess water close to the trunk of an umbrella-shaped old oak tree in the striking landscape. The round and strange lagoon would be named La Poza Airienta (the Haunting Lagoon).

In the dry season, they all had problems with fresh water. The property depended mostly on the lonely freshwater spring located one mile away from Grandpa's house. The dry season forced domestic and wild animals to share the liquid around the water well surrounded for the gigantic shade of a tall willow. Soon after Grandpa set foot on his new land, he named his farm with a peculiar name—El Barrancon—for its location over the narrow steep-sided valley.

The summer was long gone. Grandma established her own patch garden to keep herself occupied. While she stayed in the house, Grandpa and the boys dealt with livestock every day, mainly in the mornings when they had to milk the cows. One good day somewhere in mid-January, the heat of the sun was low. Even if the sun looked bigger and brighter, its rays were just enough to warm the ground; its heat couldn't have been more comfortable that day. Grandpa walked into the kitchen; that room was long but narrow, enough space for them. The hot food was impeccably cooked and placed over the dining table, delightfully served by his younger daughter under Grandma's supervision. "Yummy!" he exclaimed.

"Sit down." Grandma anticipated Grandpa's words.

"I can't wait. I'm starving," he said. He poured a spoonful of fried rice and steamed vegetables on one of the plates. Then he carefully lifted the omelet's edge out of the frying pan and placed it on the plate. When he finished his maneuver, he put the plate on Grandma's side of the dining table and tried to start a conversation while eating.

"Isn't the omelet delicious?" she asked him while she began cutting the edge of the tender omelet.

"Yum!" he exclaimed while pouring some soup into a bowl.

"So do you still have some concerns about our safety?" Grandma asked kindly.

"Not here, sweetheart," he answered.

"I'm glad to hear it from you, my darling," she said.

"It's not easy. It's difficult to move on when you don't know how things work," he said while taking almost an erect posture on one of the chairs around the dining table.

"But we do, darling," she said.

"See, sweetheart, I can't disagree with you on it. You should know that sometimes life is like running water, a meticulous journey with some ups and downs into the river," he said while persistently chewing some bits of food into his mouth.

"You know, that saying reminds me of some words, something that I learned from Papa Simon when I first met you," she said and paused pensively, thinking deeply before she continued, "I'm glad we moved here, darling. It's just that I had never thought that life here would be amazing." She placed her right hand casually on the back of Grandpa's chair.

"Yep. Here we are, sweetheart," he said and smiled.

"Yes, sir," she said and returned that pleasant smile.

In the case of Grandpa, it was clear he hadn't left his old farm voluntarily. But he knew that was the best decision to be taken to save the rest of his family. Ironically, no one even thought that he or Grandma would never return to their cozy old farm in the middle of the wild terrain.

CHAPTER THIRTEEN

GRANDPA'S JOURNEY

By the first week of July 1969, Grandpa was getting so tired that the man lost his appetite. And the taste for most of the foods that he used to enjoy was gone. He naturally thought that he might have anemia or something alike. He lost weight, lots of weight; and with that, his physical strength fell, slowing the ability to think clearly and help himself or even accept the help from Grandma and others. Maybe it was a little bit because of his own ego or because he just did not want Grandma to worry.

"There is a doctor who must see you immediately," Grandma said, confronting him.

"Doctor?" he asked and paused. "Physicians and those medical clinics scare me more than death." He smiled.

"Well, we'll go tomorrow early in the morning," Grandma said firmly.

"I'm fine, darling," he said, got up from his chair, lifted his hat out of his head, and hung it inside the porch.

"I'm totally concerned for your health. We all need you, and I care for your health," she said slowly and calmly.

"Oh god!" Grandpa exclaimed, and then he took a deep breath and paused for few seconds. "I appreciate it, but I'm fine. I'm just a little weak, but I'll be all right soon."

"Please . . . I beg you to listen this time. It's for the good of all of us," Grandma said, gasped, and exhaled quickly while carefully looking into his eyes.

"Okay, we'll go then . . . just to please you, woman," he finally agreed and walked back straight to his chair while surveying everything around him with a sour gesture in his pale face. His voice was polite, but his expression wasn't. It was physical pain hidden somewhere inside his body. It would be his second time in a medical clinic for the last ten years. The first one was when he had strong pain in his right groin, high blood pressure, cold, and high fever. He got over the pain in his groin, cold, and fever. But his high blood pressure persisted, even if he never smoked; that was a condition that followed him for years.

The next day, they left the house at first light in the morning, and they would return at night. Grandpa, with his unshaven beard, almost white with lots of grays in it, was seated on top of his mule and dressed in white clothes; he was saying goodbye. Grandma approached him with a loving look and, standing next to him, holding her old-fashioned purse in her hands, smiled at me. I was standing on one foot, with the other against the dry trunk of a zapote tree, watching them from a short distance.

I remembered my grandpa with his grown beard, his hazel eyes, his dark brown hair already mixed with tons of grays, and his polite words. He was a handsome man and probably athletic many years ago as a young person. Well, except for the sensitivity of his health and the gray color of his beard and hair that was reflecting his age, his physical features were well defined. Meanwhile, my grandma was heavyset with native features and long thick, straight hair. I was three and half years old when Grandpa left El Barrancon and traveled to Mexico City for a doctor's visit in 1969.

Then he silently left the house in the company of Grandma and Clarita, one of their daughters, and turned around the slope of the main valley out of my vision. Suddenly, he turned back and came into the patio again while Grandma and his daughter waited for him somewhere down the slope. He smiled and slowly dismounted the mule. Then he walked toward me and touched the upper side of my head. "I had left my hat in the kitchen," he said and crossed the patio slowly toward the room. I clearly saw a couple of tears escaping from his hazel eyes.

As he started to mount back the noble animal, he stayed for a few minutes standing up on his feet next to the waiting mule. Then he stared at me for a short while as if he was thinking or wanting me to know and understand something. Slowly, he walked toward me, carefully bent forward, and pressed his cheek lovingly against mine.

"Lonche, hurry up! It's getting late!" Grandma, who was waiting for him, shouted from a considerable distance, interrupting the silence. She called him using a friendly alias for Odilon.

"I'll be there in a minute," he replied, trying to hide his broken voice and wiping his eyes with his hand. Then Grandpa mounted the patient hybrid, and he was gone out of my sight in a matter of seconds.

Soon the golden rays of the sun dried off the morning's haze over the landscape, and the glittering dewdrops on the grass vanished like magic. Rapidly, the air turned thick with moisture while the gentle wind spread hot humidity over the valley, making me sweat in my old clothes. Far away, the crowded city was even worse. The sun rose with heat again over the extended smoky lane of vehicles along the smoggy highway, reflecting against the paved areas with visible energy of steamlike spirals that dissolved into thin air, leaving behind an unpleasant smell of burnt rubber and oil penetrating into the walls of the pedestrians' nasal cavity.

They had finally arrived to the city's bus station, Taxqueña to be precise. The common odor of fresh asphalt filled their nose immediately while the deafening noise vibrated in their ears, reducing the ability to orient themselves to the big city. The bus station located on the south side of Mexico City was something else. Strange voices announcing the arrivals and departures to cities nearby were heard loudly through the speakers placed in four different points inside the station, increasing the annoyance and noise. The building was crowded with people wearing colorful clothes, others with weird haircuts and rushing to work, some running to catch a taxi.

It was a hot day. Grandpa was lucky to stop a taxi in less than forty minutes. The bright sun glared off the taxi's windshield fiercely while the driver got close to them. The colorful taxi advertised a wonderful product to clean teeth using a few images of happy faces and shiny smiles printed on the exterior of its doors to persuade people to buy the useful toothpaste. A pleasant scent of vanilla air freshener drifted out and mixed with the air around them as soon as the driver opened the taxi's door. As the family took a seat into the buggy-shaped car, the driver loaded his passengers' belongings inside the taxi's trunk.

"To 500- W. Chapultepec Av, por favor," Grandpa told the taxi driver in a gentle way. Soon the driver took El Periferico, the busy highway that would take them to the clinic.

Grandma sat by the taxi's window. "Sit here and feel the wind blow," she said to Aunt Clarita, allowing her to sit on her spot.

"Grrr! I'm starving. I'm hungry," Grandpa said.

"We are hungry too," Grandma responded.

"When will we have a nice meal?" Grandpa asked.

"After the doctor's appointment, I guess," Grandma answered.

"I definitely can hear the rumbling of my intestines in my belly," Grandpa said and smiled.

"I'll get a snack for all of us," Grandma said.

"How about a vanilla ice cream cone?" Grandpa asked and suggested the tasty dessert.

The colorful taxi, slowed down by heavy traffic, arrived at the doctor's office later than what they expected. Finally, they were in front of a white building with the number 500- engraved right on top of the main entrance. Grandpa was the last person to get inside the clinic. "Is there a health problem here?" the Doctor asked gently and walked toward the family.

Grandpa was feeling well and motivated to talk while the doctor chatted and diagnosed him. "Doctor, I'm awfully sore. I'm more sore than sick," Grandpa answered, showing signs of good mood.

"You are healthy . . . healthy enough to jump up on top of your horse and compete in any derby tournament," the Doctor said, looked at Grandpa, and made a small gesture, lengthening his mouth and letting out a slight smile toward him.

"Well, Doctor," Grandpa said slowly and paused, "when I was a young man, my father had a bunch of wild horses. And my dad and I used to ride all of them. None of those horses got away from feeling my spurs."

"See? What this big guy needs is rest, relax, and eat good food. He's such a strong man," the Doctor said to Grandma.

"Well, I'm surprised," she said pensively. "He was pale, and I don't think he is fine."

"It's the high blood pressure. I'll give him some tablets to control it," the Doctor said.

Since Grandma didn't respond, there was a brief silence inside the consultation room. "You need a good meal and rest. It's the best medicine for you. But I'll prescribe some supplements as well. You'll be fine soon," the Doctor addressed Grandpa.

"That's perfect, Doctor!" Grandpa exclaimed.

"What about your knees? How's your arthritis?" the Doctor asked while writing on a blank note over his desk.

"I have pain. But I have no arthritis," Grandpa objected immediately.

"My fault. I thought you have arthritis," the Doctor said as he continued writing.

"Not that I know of, Doctor," Grandpa responded and smiled.

Brief silence remained inside the room while the doctor continued signing the prescription and providing the right instructions to follow the high blood pressure treatment. "You people go home. He is just tired and stressed. He will recuperate at home. You just make sure that he doesn't forget to take these medications for his high blood pressure. And he will be fine in two or three days." The doctor spoke calmly to Grandma. Then he looked toward Grandpa and smiled.

"Thank you, Doctor," Grandpa said, opened his wallet, and pulled out some wrinkled bills. He counted the old bills and gave it to the doctor, which he put into his pocket for Grandpa's consultation.

"A short daily walk would help you regularize your blood pressure," the Doctor said, advising him.

Certainly, besides his high blood pressure and the minor pain in the upper side of his right groin, Grandpa didn't look truly ill. According to his own understanding, there was no reason for him to travel all the way to the city for a consultation.

Back at home, his work activities would be the same—same routine. And since he was an excellent horse rider, he would ride with Grandma near him at least two times a week for a couple of hours, looking over the glittery stream from the top of the hills. All that would help him stay active and improve his high blood pressure significantly.

Four and a half hours of sitting on the totally uncomfortable bus sounded difficult, like a true road trip for him. Above all that, the way back home would take a little more effort for them. At least one hour of walking on their own foot was waiting for them after getting off the bus. Even if Grandpa felt better, that could definitely be a tremendous workout for a sixty-nine-year old. But no one realized that.

Grandpa straightened his legs as best as he could and tried to enjoy the uncomfortable ride in the crowded bus. "It's cold," he suddenly said to Grandma. "It's very cold, sweetheart."

"How could you be cold?" she asked him and touched his forehead with the back of her right hand. "The weather is hot, and it's hotter inside here." She didn't give importance to the matter.

Grandpa didn't say much. He just smiled softly and snuggled quietly over his torn seat.

"I can't wait until we get to the farm," Grandma said while wiping sweat from her face with a piece of rag.

Grandpa seemed exhausted; he turned and looked back at Grandma. His thoughts filled his entire mind once again with a spark of motivation to get home. But his low energy quickly diminished his strength. And without a word, he tightened his shirt's collar and pulled it up closer to the lower side of his chin. Then he closed his eyes and pulled down his wide hat over his nose, comforting himself. Exhausted, Grandpa slumped against the seat's cushion and fell asleep in the bus.

Grandma looked carefully at him sleeping peacefully, a usual characteristic of his good sleep. She moved the hat, which by then covered his entire face. And Grandma almost fainted when she touched the skin of his face. Grandpa was dead;

she rested her cheek over his lifeless chest for a few minutes and tried no to cry. But the tears flowed thinly down her cheeks, making a lump in her throat and wetting the collar of her blouse.

And so my grandfather finished his journey in 1969. Somewhere between Ciudad de Mexico and Teloloapan on Highway 51. In that simple way, Grandpa closed his circle of life, leaving behind the unforgettable traces of his existence among family and friends.

He told me more than once that death is the final rest, the eternal sleep that we all have ahead of us, the only thing that no one can escape from, Grandma said in silence to herself. She never thought that day would come so soon. *Death is something that nobody wants to be prepared for. And it's logical. It means the end of everything around here.*

Grandma covered his face with her shawl. His expression was kind and peaceful; it looked like he was deeply asleep. The man who married her for fifty-one years was gone; he was truly dead, although she wanted to think that everything was just a nightmare, a bad dream. *After all the things he had endured through his entire life, to die like that—no, it's not fair,* she thought.

There was loneliness, thoughts, and more thoughts inside her head. Without even knowing what to do, thousands of thoughts crossed her mind, but none could make her understand reality until an angry blast of cold wind was howling and sweeping the wild and green foliage lined over the side of the road, blowing some fresh air inside the bus through some of the half-open windows near the driver.

Grandma sniffed and wiped her tears from her face silently. Then she stretched her arms toward the bus window and slid to the left the metal frame around the glass to open it with her shaky hands. A cold but comfortable wind from outside blew through her hair and face, feeling the fresh air passing by her well-moist nostrils. Grandpa's body remained lifeless in the seat next to the bus window.

As he always said, "There is no place to hide or run from death. The bony lady will always find you because she is the eternal companion for everyone."

"Papa is dead," Grandma whispered to her daughter, whom they had sat in the back seat.

"What?" Clarita surprisingly asked in a low voice.

"He just died," Grandma said, almost whispering.

"Mom, I knew it. He wasn't well. His face was so pale in the clinic. I should have said something to the doctor, or better yet, we should have done something else to keep him in the hospital this morning. I should not have been such a chicken and left things in the doctor's hands just because we were exhausted. It's all someone's fault, Mom," Clarita said in a low voice, almost whispering.

Grandma sniffed and took a shaky breath, and then she half-turned her neck from the seat and raised her face to look at her daughter. Tears ran down her cheeks immediately. "Mom?" Clarita whispered and pressed her lips together to hold back her tears. She reached over Grandpa's seat and touched his face. The young girl touched her father's face again and asked for forgiveness. Grandma nervously hummed as she struggled to control her anguish.

At La Parada, the bus station in the village or, rather, the bus stop in Villa de Ayala, Guerrero, where they had to get off the bus, it seemed as if the entire village was waiting to help them. Grandma's voice almost faded as she made her way out of the bus. Her husband was dead, and she was on her own. "I'm sorry for crying like this and disturbing your trip," Grandma said with a trembling voice and paused briefly. Then she looked at most of the faces inside the bus while she stopped near the driver's seat. "Who wants to help me with my husband's body?"

"One step at a time, Mom," Clarita told Grandma while going down the two or three steps of the bus.

Some passengers stood up immediately. It seemed as if that group of people was willing to help and share the same pain. And with the help of the driver, they lifted the body to get it off the bus. A few minutes later, the back side of a pickup truck was loaded. Grandpa's body should be taken to Reyna's house, his eldest daughter, located in between Villa de Ayala and Buenavista del Aire, where the cemetery was.

The next day, the burial procession to the cemetery was quiet and without much noise. Seventy or maybe eighty people walked, carrying Grandpa's body to his last resting place, exchanging memories, and paying their respects to the great old man that he was. Grandma stood always next to his humble coffin. She was quiet, silent, sad.

At the cemetery, Grandpa's coffin was open for a short time, giving everybody a chance to see him for last time. Grandma took a shaky breath and lovingly rubbed Grandpa's cold hands. Then she looked straight at the face of the man who loved her so much for many years. She gently ran her fingertips over his face, and then she bent forward to kiss his forehead. "Thank you, sweetheart. Thank you for everything. God bless you always, darling," Grandma said while looking at the pale blue sky that afternoon. Her face was sweating, her tears were running over her cheeks, and her heart was totally broken. For Grandma, that was the end of happiness and one more mark of pain in her shattered heart. Those were her own words years later.

Some gentlemen lifted Grandpa's body and prepared to fill the empty, open grave with his corpse inside the casket. Soon they placed the coffin down on the bottom of the open grave. Minutes later, the Catholic priest started blessing the

145

grave and sprinkling holy water on top of the coffin. "God bless you forever," he said with consolation and a gentle expression before he began his lecture.

Soon the coordinated rhythm of the shovels cutting and biting into the ground came into Grandma's ears, and the grave was finally full with dirt and Grandpa's lifeless body, making deeper the pain in her heart and suffocating her mind. A whisper of wind passed by. It lifted the black veil around Grandma's head, and then she used the palm of her left hand to hold it. While the wind blew the fine dust out of the mount of dry soil on top of the grave, she sneezed and looked at the dust over the grave site. She rubbed her eyes and tried to stop sneezing, holding her nose for a moment, while the wind lifted the veil off from her face again.

Little by little, the people walked in silence, leaving the burial site empty. Grandma blew a kiss to the sky in memory of Grandpa and walked away from the grave site too. She left for first the time her beloved husband alone at the cemetery's grave somewhere in Buenavista del Aire, Guerrero, Mexico.

CHAPTER FOURTEEN

THE FAMILY YEARS LATER

D espite events that slowed down their life with tears, worries, and pain, sometimes the struggle to have some minimal chances of survival was real. But no matter how difficult things were around them, they never gave up and continued to kick under any types of circumstances. Almost everyone in the family understood that life was something unique, something beautiful, and not just a wonderful word with good meaning written somewhere in a page of the dictionary. Everything related to the family was defined in a few words— Grandma's job. But in reality, there were many things far from her hand and wisdom, like dreams and thoughts for successful things for each of her children.

Personal success is an individual achievement; it's something waiting far away from us most of the time. And of course, every human being makes the effort to achieve their desired goal, sometimes against their parents' wisdom. Although we often confused the real essence of life with miscalculated hopes of progress and economic well-being, for my grandmother, that seemed not very clear at all. According to my grandmother's ideals, things within the family should be done as a group for a stronger attempt to focus on what they pursued, what they wanted, without neglecting the true essence of life. That was my Grandma's philosophy at the end of the day.

Contrary to my grandmother's desire to preserve family unity, all her children took separate and very different paths. My father and the youngest of his sisters were the only ones who settled permanently outside their home country. The rest of the brothers would take different routes within their country.

Grandma, during her life in El Barrancon, always missed most of the things that they used to have back in those years in Puerta Grande. She grew older and never stopped missing Grandpa and their two elder sons whom they buried years ago in El Salitre, a rural village close to Apaxtla in Guerrero.

In 1972, many years had already passed. Slowly or fast, there was no difference in her mind. Grandma was seventy-two years old when she decided to buy a small land just one mile away from Highway 51, Mexico City–Altamirano. There was a natural spring surrounded by leafy bushes in the lower part of the amazing hill. The mountain was called El Cerro, located near the edge of a small village named El Aguacate. The place was awesome, fantastic. Two white buildings were visible from a distance about a mile away from my house. That construction was the elementary school Alvaro Obregon, a rural school in Villa de Ayala or La Parada (the Stop). That village had everything: five grocery stores, elementary school, post office, cars, and Doña Santos's Fonda, a little restaurant for passersby located at the first bus stop going south over the S-shaped Highway 51, the restaurant where I used to sell homemade cheese and sour cream every weekend when I was a kid. An open flea market every Saturday was the cherry on the cake for the mini-city, bringing merchants with their products from all around the small village.

By the beginning of 1975, almost a dozen rural homes had been built into Grandma's amazing property. Two of those houses would be my home for the next three years till 1978. Grandma's home was the closest house to mine and the one that had the most magnificent 270-degree view, built almost on top of the beautiful hill.

During my life in that place, I caught Grandma many times sitting quietly on her rocking chair and pointing her eyes toward the east. And probably, her thoughts were in El Salitre, the place where she lived happily for a while a long time ago. "Sons, daughters, and their offspring should know the origin of their parents. They must know where they come from," Grandma told me in one of those occasions.

"Don't worry, Grandma, one day I'll say to my family that your ancestors came from Chicomostoc and that you belonged to the last tribe of the seven caves," I said with a certain touch of affection and in the most innocent way.

"You are already halfway to being a big boy. And I know you will. I certainly know it," Grandma said, and she exhaled deeply.

"I will, Grandma. You bet. I'll promise it," I said and smiled.

"My little Hummingbird," she responded while she ran her fingers through my dusty hair.

For Grandma, it was a time of relief, even if she lived alone in her house. She never felt alone; she was surrounded with her grandchildren most of the time, bringing back her smile one more time after many years. Now she could visit her daughters Reyna and Rafaela, whose houses were half a mile away. She could also visit Grandpa's grave, which was two or three miles from her home in Buenavista del Aire's cemetery.

In 1980, Grandma was moved to Mexico City. I would say that it was against her will. I saw her every day from 1980 to 1982 because I also moved to the same place for school. And I ended up living with them in Uncle Antonio's house, who was my grandmother's eldest son. That would be a blessing for me to see her every day, mainly in the evenings. I used to help Grandma with her little activities in the house. During those years, I probably became her favorite grandson. She never said it, but that was the way she made feel.

The kitchen was a big deal and a super interesting room when Grandma was in it. The smell, the delicious aroma from the cozy kitchen, was really remarkable before we even started eating. She never used measuring spoons of any sort. Grandma seemed to know precisely how much spice to add to any dish she prepared. Being born in the farm and raised in Mexico City, I had the chance to live many years close to my grandmother and the opportunity to learn a small part of her cooking secrets.

Somewhere in 1982, I asked Grandma about her origins and more details about her ancestors. She spoke to me for first time in her original language. I was totally surprised after I had heard her with my own ears. She fully dominated her original language. And then she tried to teach me Nahuatl or, as she called it, Mexicano.

Most of the words were utterly strange and some kind of familiar except for the accent; that was totally unfamiliar to me. And of course, the meaning of those words was completely not understandable for my brain's microchips. But she spoke the ancient Aztec dialect. I heard my grandma, on many occasions after, saying some words in Nahuatl during our conversations, like she wanted me to learn her language. And I learned just a little and remembered to this day only a few words of her dialect as well as being alert with certain people.

I knew since childhood, I'd always known, that my family had no sympathy or trust for the Morales clan or the Patiños. The strangest part about all this was that one of my nieces fell in love with one of the Moraleses, a direct descendant of the clan frowned on by my family. "The ironies of life to frame the episode," I definitely would say.

In those days, getting along with the enemy wasn't the easiest thing, at least not from the farm people in my town. The introduction of the young man was going well until my uncle Antonio asked him about his origin. "Morales?" Uncle Antonio asked doubtfully after the young man shook his hand respectfully.

"Yes, sir, Morales," he answered.

"Where were you born?" Uncle Antonio asked him with curiosity.

"El Salitre, Guerrero," that young man responded.

"I don't care how good he is or how good he might be. He is a Morales descendant. And that's enough for me." Uncle Antonio said to Bella with a rude tone and paused briefly. He exhaled deeply, took a breath, and looked at every single face around him. "His parents or his grandparents were some of the assassins of my brothers."

"That was a long time ago, Grandfather. I wasn't even born yet," Bella interrupted immediately.

"Don't you know the boy? He's got some Morales blood on his father's side, and that's not acceptable to me," Uncle Antonio said firmly while he looked straight to his granddaughter's eyes.

"No, it doesn't make no sense. It's a primitive thought, and that's not his fault," Bella said loudly.

"I want you to stay away from him," he said firmly.

"What? That's not possible, Grandfather," Bella complained while she walked a few steps away.

"Bella, you listen to me!" Uncle Antonio exclaimed. Then he got up from his chair and approached his granddaughter slowly. "I swear on the divine holy cross, I'll punch his face next time that you invite him into this house." It seemed like he really meant it.

"Sorry, Grandfather . . . but this isn't going to work," Bella said defiantly.

Uncle Antonio would hear none of any good reasons. And with a perfectly straight face, he stood in front of Bella. "Of course not," he challenged her. "Bella, this is not going to work for me . . . and for you too. I don't want my family's enemies inside my house. I don't want anybody of them to find out where we live or what we do. Did you hear me? No one. Do you understand?"

"Yeah, I totally understand your point. But he doesn't have anything to do with this or whatever you are thinking. Do you understand it?" Bella asked.

"Sweetheart, you are eighteen years old. You can surely find someone else but not my enemy's descendant. Come on. Do you understand my point?" Uncle Antonio said.

"I didn't know that. I didn't know that he is one of your enemies. No, I didn't. But I don't care. If you don't want him here in your house, then I won't visit you no more. I love him," Bella said and squeezed her narrow eyes to hold her tears. Uncle Antonio coughed involuntary, pulled a chair, and sat in silence while the bitter taste of discussion went over his head.

When I was young, I met some members of the Morales clan and Pancho Patiño's nephews as well. We were not friends, but occasionally, we met through other friends in Mexico City. There was nothing really special about it; those coincidences were only occasional encounters with some conversation about the past after a few drinks. But it turned out that we had two or three things in common. Well, everyone knew the same thing that I'd known since childhood or heard something similar like what I had heard as a child: "Watch what you say. Think before you speak. Don't ever get along with any of them. They're evil. They're traitors. Stay away from them. They're enemies." Can you imagine that type of advice for a kid?

Now as an adult and, of course, with other perspectives, I see that those days were a different world. In the end, I was still trying to understand their thoughts combined with my personal point of view to describe in my own words this whole thing in the most colorful way. But for sure, whether a Morales or a Patiño descendant, no one of us could forget a little something or a little too much of what had been said, whether right or wrong. No one.

In 1983, twenty-eight years had passed after Guzman and Narcizo's demise. Uncle Antonio returned to a place where he didn't belong any longer. It wasn't a happy return. Despite the earliest memories that sparked into his mind, he seemed out of place. The real reason for his long trip from Mexico City was the sale of the land property in Puerta Grande, Grandpa's old farm. He already had a client interested in the land. They would meet there in the old farm. It was part of the agreement.

Uncle Antonio first arrived to El Salitre and chose to proceed on foot rather than riding a horse. He passed by, walking in silence, unnoticed; nobody recognized him. He started his journey with mixed emotions and unexplainable fears. However, his emotions increased as soon as he remembered the land where he was born and played as a child.

There was a place he had to stop by, the cemetery. On the way there, he picked some wildflowers and walked straight to the abandoned place. He couldn't waste the opportunity to visit his brothers' graves after so many years. *Anyway, where else could they go? They wouldn't go nowhere*, he said to himself.

The graves seemed strange, out of place in the cemetery. A long time had passed, and everything seemed to be not on the same spot. He took a while to recognize the right burial site. There was not even one single gravestone or any other sign with their names on it. Some of the other graves were marked with broken, crooked, or fallen crosses with some written names on it, like hieroglyphics inked on the wall of an ancient cave. It seemed as if the years had taken care of punishing that almost forgotten place. And only a few of the graves had fresh flowers on it with readable last names and other words.

Finally, after removing some grass on the ground. He was able to read Calixto's name in a small flat stone, and then he guided himself to his brothers' grave. He carefully removed his cowboy hat and held it softly against his chest with the right hand. He stood quietly next to his brothers' burial site and placed some flowers on it while a few clouds passing by were shading the sun's rays intermittently and witnessing the lonely scene. Many years had passed between laughs and sorrows, and Uncle Antonio visited that place where the earth preserved the eternal asleep of his two brothers. And maybe he would never return to those valleys, to those mountains, again.

From the cemetery, he turned back to continue his journey in haste. Another place, stretched out far downhill, was waiting for him—Puerta Grande. He proceeded toward the farm and finally made it down to the dense forest after passing the great plain valley. He walked faster until he arrived at the end of his journey, expecting to find the prominent buyer. His arrival to the old farm was quiet; nobody was there. Only several crows cawed desperately from the branches of tall trees, watching him intensely, like complaining about the unexpected human presence within their domains. The intruder was studying the lonely place and turned his attention to the congested grapevine near the forested patio, ignoring the noisy and stunning complaints as his reception. He sat for a few minutes under the shade of the wild grapevine. Bunches of ashy purple grapes hung heavily through the leafy vine, enhancing the desire to put those berries into his mouth. He rested his feet while enjoying the sweet nectar of the exquisite fruit.

That place was silent, only interrupted by the characteristic chirping and peculiar dance of wall-jumping birds around the abandoned farm. There was an abundance of small reptiles and fire ants on the ground. And different types of insects were buzzing disorderly around him. He felt strange in front of this ivy-shrouded building. But he was there, right there, right in front of his parents' house, where he grew up and lived happily for many years. He could have described every corner of that place day by day from stories told to him in his childhood by his parents and Don Chucho, a good friend close to them.

Lost in his thoughts, Uncle Antonio noticed the twisted barbed wire from the old fence lying rusted on the bushy ground and almost covered by grass and short vegetation. Then a sudden flash of memories blasted into his mind. For a moment, he had a vision of the walls from the house where he was born and lived his entire youth, until he married his wife in 1939.

"Diantres. Yes, time had passed in a blink of an eye!" he exclaimed softly while inhaling fresh air and exhaling it repeatedly.

The house's foundation and walls got damaged through the years. The heavy rain and extreme weather conditions chewed the house as if millions of moles had worked together over the homemade mud bricks. There was a triangular pile of broken mud bricks at the right side of the patio, where the kitchen was. And he saw a mound of scooped-out, fresh dirt at the edge of a rounded hole. Apparently, a smart rodent's nest was active, located almost by the kitchen entrance right there in the same spot where Grandma liked to stand. There were narrow alleys that led to the edge of the forest under the roof of tall bushes and hanging branches of leafy trees, like tunnels or long caves made by wild animals, at the right side of the corral. Most of the connecting trails were narrow just to allow the wild creatures to touch one side of the forest, slipping out under the canopy of the vast vegetation.

A thousand and one years appeared to have gone since he left the land. However, that opportunity offered him a look back, a direct passage to his old life and to all the moments lived in that distant place.

The old farm, with the most fertile lands in the region, was wild and deserted like he had never seen it but far away from being devastated. The land's vegetation and fauna flourished through those years and seemed to be part of the wild forest in front of him. Even the lazy stream that twisted through the entire length of the valley like a shiny snake decorated different parts of the main hill with pools of glittering water, surrounded by thick vegetation and weeds completely visible from a certain distance.

The soft breeze breaking through the dry air refreshed his saggy skin and recomforted his mind. Then his thoughts were suddenly interrupted when the buyer approached him from the opposite direction. "Hey! Hello!" a lonely voice exclaimed and recited a couple of words in a smooth tone from a considerable distance but not too far from him. Then Uncle Antonio adjusted his thoughts and his clothes to enhance part of his refinement as a city person. He turned his head and followed the smooth sound of the voice while his eyes looked toward the short and stocky man who was coming closer to the patio. He waved to the newcomer and kept his full attention on the shoulder-length hair that flew with the wind out of the narrow hat that undoubtedly adorned that chubby man's head. The man walked slowly with zigzag movements, kicking up some fragile vegetation with his old boots and whistling a happy tune, something similar to "La Mula Bronca."

"Hello, friend," Uncle Antonio said amiably while waving. He felt much better; at least someone was there. Finally, he talked to someone because it seemed as if the forest had him wrapped in its magic or in some kind of enchantment.

He and the newcomer had about the same age, somewhere between sixty and sixty-three. He had some visible wrinkles on the face and grayish sideburns but a well-defined shape over the visible signs of beard at the top of their cheeks. "Why did you tell me to come all the way here?" that buyer asked funnily from a certain distance.

"Diantres. Too involved in my thoughts, I almost forgot about you," Antonio responded, smiled, and paused. "Well, the only thing remaining to be done is around here. I've decided to sell the remains of the land as you can see it."

"You don't have to be specific in the details. I already know these lands. It's a wonderful place. Anyways, I couldn't decline the invitation to meet you down here. This is paradise," the buyer said and paused. "How do you do, my friend?" He extended his hand toward Antonio.

"I'm totally fine. It's a pleasure, Mr. Marciano," Antonio said while they shook hands and greeted each other with affection.

"I love the outdoors, the farm life!" the buyer exclaimed.

"Mmm, I can see it," Uncle Antonio said simply.

"How long have you been waiting for me?" the buyer asked while removing some plant thorns in his pants.

"Not too long. But it seemed a thousand and one years," Antonio responded and smiled.

"Well, let's go, cowboy. I'm ready to take over!" the buyer exclaimed with an emotional gesture on his face.

"How do you like it over here?" Antonio asked seriously.

"Antonio, I have to expand, and I need more land. I'm buying it. I've been near livestock for many years, and lately, my numbers increased. I have a big piece of cattle, and these lands are what I need," the buyer said enthusiastically.

"Land being a necessity of living, right?" Antonio asked.

"Space, yes. We need space," the buyer answered and agreed.

"Well, here, you will have space and the entire forest. But you will definitely trim the vegetation at the sides of the old trail," Antonio said.

"Yeah, that's not a problem. I'll make sure to remove unwanted plants and some debris over the path before I move my livestock to these lands," the buyer said.

"Lots of work to do," Antonio responded.

"Cowboy, that's what I call success—to seek better opportunities, work hard. You gotta do what others can't, what others don't want to do. And of course, have some sense of humor in it and do what is right. Never forget that," Mr. Marciano said and smiled.

"You're correct, I guess," Antonio agreed.

"This land waited many years for someone's return—your return, Antonio. This is a glorious land, and I'll keep it," the buyer said firmly.

"Well, the better the fields, the worse my family got," Antonio said ironically.

"That was almost impossible to believe," the buyer said, referring to Antonio's brothers killed on the cornfield in 1955.

154

THE LAST RED SUNSET

"Well, for many people, death is the quick solution to punish others," Antonio said.

"Umm, totally wrong!" the buyer exclaimed.

"Yeah. And until this day, I have to be careful about certain things. You know what I mean?" Antonio said.

"I understand," the buyer responded.

"Besides whatever thing and as my father used to say, I'll go to my grave with one belief—I'll leave the judging to God," Antonio said with resignation.

"I'll try to work and to better these lands. Anyways, you'll be very welcome at any time. This is still your home, Antonio," the buyer said politely.

"Thank you, Mr. Marciano. It's a fine thing of you, and I appreciate it," Antonio said.

"I will bring the money two weeks from now to Mexico City," the buyer said after the two men reached an agreement for the land's total price.

"Fifty thousand pesos, Mr. Marciano," Antonio said firmly.

"I totally agree on it," the buyer responded.

"I think it is better to go into town. I need a bath and some sleep," Antonio said.

"That's awesome, cowboy. I agree with you. Thank you for coming all this way," the buyer said.

"Well, thank you too. I know you'll do something great out of it," Antonio said.

"Oh, you bet, cowboy!" the buyer happily exclaimed.

"Good luck," Antonio said and smiled while shaking hands with the buyer. The deal was done. Uncle Antonio successfully closed the deal; the land was sold for fifty thousand pesos. And a lifetime of efforts and dreams would end behind those words, but another story would begin in that remote land, giving chances to the hopes of a new dreamer.

In 1983, after twenty-eight years without human activity in Puerta Grande, Grandpa's old farm on the outskirts of El Salitre was an extreme ghost farm, a forested place full of memories from the past. Uncle Antonio was entitled to dispose of those lands and divide the money among his brothers and sisters. And with that, he closed the final chapter of the past.

My father escaped death when he witnessed the killing of his elder brothers in 1955 and survived in those lands for a while. He left the farm when he was a kid and never returned to El Salitre. He was moved to El Barrancon at the age of fourteen, where he grew up and married mom in 1963. The rest of the story wasn't history; it was just a little drama, a perfect description of a unique experience learned from a mountain of mistakes through the journey of my family in this world.

My niece Bella and her Morales Latin lover married a few months after she confronted Uncle Antonio, just some days after Bella's graduation from high school in 1983. She and Morales were still happily married to this day.

Uncle Antonio died of a heart attack in September 2004 in Mexico City. At the end of his life, he had only one thing to do—to agree with his granddaughter's decision and to accept Morales as part of the family. Ironically, he remarked once again the old saying "Have your friends close but your enemies closer."

CHAPTER FIFTEEN

BACK TO THE CORNFIELD

On the way back to my dad's cornfield in El Limon, Fernando was singing, and I cheerfully followed his tune, humming the catchy melody with inspired disdain and mocking the kid to piss him off. But that didn't work, and I gave up before he called me lucass, slang for "loco." Taking a more serious posture and far from jokes, we both walked toward the small lagoon; and about a couple of hundred feet before approaching La Poza Airienta, something stopped my walking, freezing my legs, and immediately stopped my happy mood.

Suddenly, my eyes doubled or tripled in size and opened wider, carefully surveying the glittering water in the small lagoon. What I saw over the pond's water was something without any explanation. I slowly turned my head to the right side and silently looked over my shoulder. Fernando's face was frozen. His expression was cold and scared. His face wasn't tan anymore. It was totally pale, and with a hissing sound, he made clear that we had to remain silent. He was looking exactly at what I was watching over the pond's clear water.

And we both looked at the shore of the pond, where the ground was swelling with fresh water, gradually crumbling some of the forest fragments into small pieces and washing it away after a few turns in the water but leaving some remains in the lowest part at the right side of the lagoon. The floor of the pond had a fine-grained sediment forming an impermeable layer of clay mud over the rotten soil, smoothly and fiercely broken by the incessant current of water. Some pieces of fallen plants and debris moved almost in a circle because of the water's movement in the pond.

Certainly, at my young age, I had seen a tornado rising like a large dark funnel high in the air. I had seen mountains of corn and piles of colorful pumpkins on the farm's patio. I had seen a baby bull born with two heads over his shaky body, a double-yolk chicken egg on my dinner plate, a dead raccoon with a swollen belly about to pop out. I had seen owls, hawks, rattlesnakes, foxes, skunks, and wild goats but never something close to what I saw that day in the lagoon.

Fernando and I stood in complete silence and looked at our mysterious find. The pupils of our eyes were fixed on the angelic creatures or some kinds of spirits here on the earth, alive just like us. There was a group of three little children at the center of the lagoon playing in and splashing the clear water with their hands. The glittering waterdrops were slowly falling through the air like diamonds in slow motion, returning and quickly disappearing into the precious lagoon.

I could picture that scene in my mind so perfectly to these days. Those three children were totally naked. The color of their skin was radiant, literally white and soft pink, milky smooth, full of life. We couldn't see their feet. A small portion of their legs, ankles, and toes was in the water. I could certainly say they were seven or ten inches deep into the pond's surface. I must mention that the lagoon's water right at the center was at least five feet deep, and there was no doubt about it, because I measured it years later. It was absolutely too deep for three- or four-year-old children. And it wasn't deep enough to hold the weight of those fleshy and playful unknown creatures in the form of little kids.

There was not even one couple with children of that age in or around the farm. And no one let little kids swim or play in the wild by themselves, let alone in a five-foot-deep lagoon in the middle of nowhere. All options seemed to be far from logic, from reality. Simply, odds were out of the matter. Something was wrong, and those beings had probably escaped for a moment from their world.

We scanned our surroundings, looking uphill and downhill, but nobody was there. Uphill, the stream was noisy, surrounded by short vegetation and a few tall trees along the right side. Downhill, the stream disappeared under large trees and tall vegetation, which formed a natural canopy, shadowing a big part of the shallow waters of the stream. It was a perfect area where the trees and wild vegetation grew taller than anywhere else in the wild valley.

While those three mysterious creatures in the shape of human beings played and splashed glittering water on the pond, Fernando and I sat on the ground, and we both curiously observed them in silence. We stared at them and watched the splendor of their mysterious apparition. Whatever it was, that thing was right there, right in front of us.

Shortly after, those unknown creatures noticed our presence. They simultaneously turned their face toward us, and we were able to see their full face for the first time. It was far away from what you could imagine. They seemed harmless and friendly; physically, there was nothing strange about them. They had

158

nose, ears, eyes, hair, lips, mouth, and belly button just like us, like any human being, like you and me.

But there was something weird, and it didn't take me too long to notice the absence of sound in their mouth. They were mute, I first assumed. And I was right. They moved their lips and mouth slowly, like saying something in slow motion, but we couldn't hear words or any sound coming from them. There was no doubt those creatures were mute. And they probably didn't belong to our world. Or even worse, they were probably from some unknown and hidden dimension. But they were right there, just in front of us inexplicably. We couldn't believe all that was real, but that was totally real like the moon or like the sun. And that was happening to Fernando and me.

Then suddenly, they started waving their hands, calling us with silent hand signals and muted movements of their thin lips. Naturally, we did not understand any of what they tried to say, but it was clear that they were calling us to approach them. Even if we didn't understand what was in the front of us, we certainly sensed that something was wrong. We were not hypnotized or mesmerized by those strange entities; we were totally aware about the conscious world around us. I clearly was able to hear the chirping of birds, the buzzing of insects, Fernando's voice, and the noisy stream along with the typical sounds in the valley. Fernando and I got up and ran away immediately like bullets, without even looking back.

Minutes later, we returned to my house's front door. "What is it?" my mom asked curiously.

"Those children back there!" Fernando exclaimed, pointing with his forefinger straight to the lagoon's location.

"Yes, Mom. There's something there. Children," I said, trying to catch my breath.

"Los duendes, the goblins," she said while she explained a little about those magical creatures.

My mom rubbed tobacco and some rubbing alcohol all over our neck, face, and head as protection from evil or bad spirits. "Good stuff against bad spirits," she said and paused. "All right, let's go. I'll walk you guys back there." She showed no fear.

We walked all together, and Fernando and I saw the spooky lagoon again. And those children, angels, alien creatures, or whatever that was disguised as human beings had disappeared and vanished somewhere there. But nobody was there when we returned to the cornfield. Or maybe they became invisible to our eyes.

Who knew exactly? What was the meaning of those children's unexpected manifestation? The opinions could be numerous, but the real answer I would never know.

I couldn't say that it was a bad dream while we walked, much less an abduction from an advanced super intelligent being. I would fall short to think like that. Possibly, they were unexplainable signs of lost spirits from a forgotten primitive civilization of an ancient world in those desolated lands. It could be wiser to say. But everything seemed like another puzzle or mystery to understand possible hidden messages from beyond.

Many people believe spirits have some sources of powers and that they are messengers between human beings and some divine deities. My bag is already full of questions when the case of the matter comes to this point. Unfortunately, each question has a thousand answers, making it more difficult to find the truth. And ironically, I probably won't ever know the truth about those creatures' apparition. And that's weird, but at the same time, it is not because until today various people have alarming encounters with the unknown, with the unexplainable. If you have not seen unusual events like this one, surely, someone already has had the honor somewhere else.

Soon after, I stared at a blue dragonfly flying over a sharp and pointed rock partly buried just below the water's surface. The colorful insect was circling and hovering constantly, remaining in one spot in the air less than ten inches over the water, and descending rapidly around that particular rock, searching for food or a warm spot to land. I picked up a small stone from the ground and strongly threw it, trying to hit the defenseless insect. But I missed it. Then my mom disapproved of my action, and I apologized for it.

"Where are you going?" My mom looked at me and asked with authority.

"Over there, Mom," I responded and pointed to the other side of the stream, where the greenish stain of water gave away its color to the permanently exposed gray rocks and sandy stones. The crossing of the shallow stream was low, absurdly low. Anyone could cross the stream very easily, walking on tiptoe over the pointed stones from one side to the other.

Finally, we reached the other side of the shallow waterway. We were pleased at my mom for her help, and rapidly, Fernando and I changed our mood and went back to the kids' world. Then she walked back home after making sure that Fernando and I were safe. And she stood briefly, waved at us from a certain distance, and returned home.

"Come on!" I exclaimed, and I leaped up on top of a rock next to Fernando.

"Mm-hmm, okay," Fernando said.

"So let's go, man!" I shouted, and I let him lead our return journey to my father's cornfield.

"What did you say?" he asked and turned his head toward the lagoon.

"I said nothing. What the hell are you scared of?" I asked and paused briefly. "Are you turning into a chicken-chicken or something?" I laughed out loud, imitating a chicken's winging. "Cua, cua."

"Whatever," he responded and smiled.

"Come on, Fernando, don't start with your fears. Kick your paranoia away," I said sarcastically.

There was a brief silence; he was lost in his thoughts. Then finally, he broke the silence. "I remember the first time that I went to the church," Fernando said and paused while he turned his face and looked at me seriously. "I went to see God with my mom." His voice said that he really meant it.

"And . . . you saw him?" I asked curiously.

"Of course, he was there!" he exclaimed with a soft voice.

"I'll take a trip to the church with you guys next time," I said.

"Deal," he responded.

Then I followed him downhill into a narrow dirt path thick with tall grass, weeds with some yellow flowers, and some tropical bushes crazily trimmed over its sides. Fernando was an obedient, good boy. I never heard him complaining. And he didn't understand any of what we both had seen that day in the lagoon.

In my case, I still couldn't understand those strange events. Whoever lived and ran those lands in the past long before my grandpa bought that farm left no record or any type of clue about what types of activities people had practiced there. Yet my new experience with those angelic creatures playing on the lagoon's water filled me with some kinds of strange and inexplicable experiences. But it was just the beginning of a number of strange episodes that brought questions to my life about the unknown.

I grew up never free of questions. What exactly was that? Was there more than one dimension in this world? And only heaven knew how difficult it was to live with it. Many times, I'd tried to avoid thinking about it. But I never had enough strength to erase that out of my mind.

I thought often about those angelic creatures that so long ago opened up a world of questions for me. And in one way or another, probably without even realizing it, they changed my life that quiet and peaceful summer's afternoon in my grandpa's farm. And to this day, some people would just smile when I asked what it could be. So I guess it was just one more secret of the mystery hidden somewhere in those desolated lands.

"There is a reason for everything. Simply remember it," my grandma used to tell me.

"You'll grow up. You will be a wise man. You'll understand it one day," Grandma told me the first time that I spoke about it when I was a kid.

Through the years, I came across more stuff like this that were simply unexplainable. But I would never forget all the courage that Grandma always tried to pass on to me with her words, with her wisdom, with her dedication besides the mountain of mistakes. And as a child, I was lucky to be guided by her good advice, a miracle of her wisdom as an older person. Although we always lived around or near her house, it was my grandparents' house on my father's side that held my earliest memories, my earliest fears and questions.

Finally, Fernando and I reached my dad's cornfield in El Limon. My father was waiting for us, sitting next to Uncle Lupe. Fernando extended his right arm toward my father and delivered a small package in a bag. I just placed a small bag on my father's hands while he kindly thanked us.

Minutes later, he bravely walked downhill with a loaded gun in his pocket. And in less than five minutes, he was face-to-face with his noisy neighbor. My father walked in front of the man and faced him. He abruptly stopped walking and placed his eyes right in front of his neighbor, who was standing up in silence, with his hands clenched tight at his sides. The angry man avoided eye contact with my father and appeared to be nervous, looking around constantly. "We don't want to fight, macho man, okay?" my father said firmly.

"Hmm." The noisy neighbor shrugged.

My father stepped to the side and shook his head in slow motion from side to side. "We don't want to fight," he said louder this time, trying to keep his angry neighbor on his hook.

"Hmm." The angry man spat on the ground.

"Looks like you don't have nothing else to say," my father said firmly to his crazy neighbor.

"Hmm." The angry neighbor mumbled something in a very low voice.

"I've heard a few times that you enjoy to prey on those who are humble. Is that true?" my father asked and paused. "I will give you another chance, even if you don't deserve it."

The neighbor started humming an old tune.

"If you don't stop your crap, I'll break your legs," my father said and made it clear that it was the end of the foolish argument.

"Was it all?" that neighbor asked, and some words came out slowly and weakly out of his mouth. "I'm profoundly sorry. You are right. I'm wrong." The neighbor made an effort to control his broken voice and buried his face on the ground with embarrassment.

"Next time, watch your tongue, dear neighbor. I couldn't afford to hold a lifetime grudge for your insults," my father said, smiled, and walked away from his regretful neighbor.

"To remain calm, in control of yourself, it's not always an easy task," my father said to Uncle Lupe.

Even if in the old days, an apology was a confession of weakness; it was the most proper thing to hear when you felt insulted. My father just pretended that nothing happened. He continued talking and saying hello to his neighbor but always kept the distance a little wider than usual.

But that wasn't the reason that my father left the farm and never returned during his life to those crop fields. He was a strong believer that he would be successful far away from his town. And he did it. He accomplished his dreams and his own beliefs. "A single little step will take you to another later on," he told me more than once.

CHAPTER SIXTEEN

BECOMING AN IMMIGRANT

March 1973, El Barrancon, Guerrero, Mexico

Early in the morning, I saw my father talking with two of his friends, Catalino Arroyo and Alberto . . . Alberto something—I could not remember his last name. Absolutely, I never knew his last name. The three men were in the patio. They moved some wooden chairs close to the persimmon tree and sat under its cool shade, waiting for my mom to serve breakfast. The sun was warming up and dissolving the haze of the dawn with its gentle touch.

Alberto had a shiny, loose-fitting silver watch around his skinny wrist. Suddenly, I noticed that he was checking the time in his watch constantly during the strange conversation between them. I invented one thousand and one excuses to be around them, pretending not to hear their low and secret dialogue. Alberto was very kind and playful. He was the one who mostly talked with me every time that I approached their cozy spot.

And for my young age, I clearly saw the concern, the worries, in my father's brown eyes. He was dressed in dark clothes, wearing black leather shoes, and had a nice haircut. Constantly, my father got up from his chair and walked around the patio, tapping me on my fragile shoulders from time to time and smiling to me frequently with some degree of mystery and love at the same time. "Hey . . . Papa," my father said softly while he looked straight into my eyes.

I walked fast, almost running close where he was, under the pretext of getting my marbles from the ground. But in reality, I wanted to be next to my pops and feel untouchable at home, safe and unbeatable as a superhero. That moment was the last of my childhood near my father because the necessity to find a better future far away from home had stolen my father's love forever. "He is good and kind. He is a loving son," my father said while looking at his friends.

"I got an idea!" Alberto exclaimed; approaching my father, he whispered something in his ears.

"Hmm . . . okay. Just wait a little more," my father responded. His voice remained low and even, his arms crossed with a tense and nervous posture.

"Let's get out of here. It's getting late," Catalino said abruptly. Then they looked at each other as if they were up to something—something with a certain mystery, I would say.

My father became determined to migrate to the United States, Chicago particularly. It was about three months since my father had left home when we first received his first letter. That was the first time that we heard about him in three months; that was a good relief for all of us, especially my mom. At least my father was alive and safe, and he was about to start a new job. There was great hope for us.

My mother, on the other hand, never wanted to leave our country. She was afraid that something bad might happen during the risky trip. But finally, she did it to be with Dad. So she ended up taking the risk to bring my little brothers in one piece to the Windy City.

Because of the tragedy that took place during my father's childhood when he lost his two elder brothers, he turned himself into immigrant in 1973. After that, he set foot in our country only four times—1976, 1984, 1995, and 2004. That was a total of no more than three months in Mexico during his four visits.

MY FATHER'S JOURNEY

"Dad!" I cried out in desperation. "Help!" I ran to my father's side. He was in the right corner of his house's backyard. He firmly stood on the snow between five and six feet away from his garage door, facing his building. My dad was bleeding in the mouth and nose; his blood totally soaked his mustache, chin, part of his jacket, and clothes all over his chest. I ran to my car to pick up my cell phone, and quickly, I dialed 911. I returned to him immediately, and I started talking with the 911 representative while I was almost running, approaching my father. He stood still, standing firmly on his feet with some four or five-foot-tall pile of snow between him and his building.

The evening was cold and partly dark. But it wasn't for me or for him. I held him in my arms. I clearly saw his face. His eyes were steady, open, and lifeless. His face quickly turned pale.

I had heard my daughter coming from inside the building, asking him for something. "Hi, Grandpa, do you want me to leave the door open?" she asked him without knowing what was happening around us.

There was no answer; my father was dying. And I was there, in one way or another just keeping him company in his last moment in life. "Here, daughter, hold the phone and keep talking with 911. Grandpa is bleeding to death. Tell them to please come quick. He is dying," I said to my daughter. She was little confused but quickly understood what was happening.

A few minutes later, the paramedics arrived, and they tried everything to save my dad's life. But everything was in vain. He was gone. There is a humble gravestone with his name on it and the two memorable dates of his journey in this world—5/6/1942–12/19/2008—somewhere in Elmwood Park Cemetery.

In my defined reality and personal life, when it comes to culture, traditions, language, nationality, and more, I have to face and deal with two different things most of the time. It's difficult to walk in the middle of the road without being hit. Living between two cultures, it is not easy to look to the side of one in particular. Many people could say, "Hell yeah, it's easy." But it's not easy, at least for me. It depends on the depth with which everyone wants to address the issue. The traditions of my native culture follow me daily in life as the traditions of the culture where I live and walk in. It is difficult to incline the scale, looking in one way only, thinking whether to select a cultural identity or cultural continuity. But I think it is the challenges that make us stronger as human beings.

For ethnicity's sake and as a natural instinct, I have integrated myself into the immigrant society to follow and preserve my origin and probably to endure my cultural identity, traditions, language, and foods. Naturally, it's not easy to stand in the middle of the road, knowing that you have to deal with both ways.

Like my parents and many others, drastically, I have found myself being part of the modern era of immigrants, chasing day by day the American dream, looking for different opportunities and better ways of living. In my case, wanting or not, I've decided to live away from the place where I have been born. And I am part of the large group of immigrants in this promised land.

Today, thirty-five years after my departure from my hometown, when strangers ask me where I am from or my nationality, I can't respond with one word. But it doesn't matter where I find myself, here or there. I belong everywhere, to the world, to the same human species. And being an immigrant, it's just a matter of words. It is part of the game.

And at the end, I would say we all have a destiny, sort of. We have one way to follow, a little something to say, a little story behind us to tell. Let's get the words and ideas out into the world. These are mine. Where have yours begun?

I'm here. But I was there.

THE END

ACKNOWLEDGMENTS

S pecial thanks to Bianca Leoni Almazán, my daughter, for always being there. A heart full of love and hugs to her children, Manny Jr. and Stacey Yaneli.

Thank you, daughter.

GLOSSARY

adobe. Mud bricks

barbón. Bearded man

batos. Dudes

calmíl. Small plantation near a farm yard

camisa guayabera. Shirt distinguished by two embroidered vertical rows

candíl. Rudimentary kerosene lamp

cantina. Bar

coño carajo… no me chingues. Don't mess with me

fogón. Woodburning pit made of brick or stones

huaraches. Sandals

jumiles. Kind of insect that people can eat

meclapítl. Enlarged rod of porous stone to grind against the metate's surface

memelas. Enlarged corn tortillas but somehow fatter

mestizo. Spanish and indigenous descent

metate. Three- or four-legged stone with an inclined and curved surface to grind food

molcajete. Three-legged carved stone to grind mainly salsas

nixtamál. Semi-cooked corn kernels to make the dough for tortillas

pileta. Small pool to store water

pozito. Water well

sorchis-polis. Slang for soldiers, police

totolonche. Wild berries similar to blueberries

uta madre. Damn it

Better Way Health
SR

Bosmere

Dandelion Root
Tree

Amazon
Powered
Extract

Attra

Made in the USA
Monee, IL
29 June 2020